Llyfrgelloedd Libraries

×2/24

Please return/renew this item by the last date below
Dychwelwch/adnewyddwch erbyn y dyddiad olaf y nodir yma

MAESTEG
01656 754835
21 JUN 2024

awen-libraries.com

INKUBATOR
BOOKS

FOREWORD

'For every man there is a limit of humiliation, degradation, shame or mental cruelty. If pushed beyond this plateau, he will either disintegrate into dust or unleash a vision of hell.'

-Anonymous, 1652

PROLOGUE

10.00 pm, 2 May 1981
Hermitage Street, Carlton, Nottingham

The small child stirred in his bed.
There was that noise again. A crackling sound, like someone flicking paper. What was that smell? A sharp acrid stench that assaulted his nose and made him feel sick. His eyes were stinging and watering now.

He sat up in bed and looked around his squalid bedroom. Dirty clothes were strewn all over the threadbare carpet, which barely covered the wooden floorboards.

There was the usual white glow from the streetlight outside the window of his bedroom. The house was identical to the one next door and the one next door to that. All of them just little boxes. Seen as a temporary answer to the housing crisis partly caused by the German Luftwaffe, this was post-war prefab housing erected to provide homes for returning servicemen after the Second World War. Shameful that they were still occupied by poor families over three decades later.

As well as the dull white light battling through the dirty net curtains, there was another glow. This was a muted orange colour that was creeping in below his bedroom door. As he stared at the flickering orange light, he saw wisps of smoke seeping under the door.

A rising sense of panic made the boy throw back the filthy blanket he was sleeping under. He stepped over to the door and touched the handle. With a yelp of pain, he quickly withdrew his hand. The handle was red hot and had badly burned his hand. Starting to cry, he looked down and saw an angry red blister starting to form on the palm of his hand.

He shouted, 'Mum! Dad! What's going on?'

Three times he repeated this cry for help. The silence from within the house was deafening.

The smoke was getting thicker. For the first time, the small child saw an orange flame lick under the door and try to take hold of the rotting carpet.

The terrified boy now realised exactly what was happening. The house he was in was on fire. He dashed the few steps over to the window and yanked down the net curtains. From the first-floor window, he looked down onto the narrow street. There were people standing outside, watching his house. He could see them clearly, as the flames from the burning house illuminated their worried faces. They began pointing up at the window, where he was standing in his pyjama bottoms. He had never had the top to match the bottoms. They were so old that they were now almost up to his knees. He was seven years old and could not ever remember wearing anything else to bed.

He balled his tiny fists and began banging on the glass, screaming for the people below to help him. He could see people running about, milling up and down, pointing this way and that. He watched a man make a run towards the front door of his house. He got to within a yard before he was beaten back by the heat being generated from the blazing house.

Suddenly, he heard a sharp crack behind him. Choking against the smoke that was now filling his small bedroom, he wheeled round and saw a large split in the bedroom door. It ran from top to bottom, and flames were already flicking through the fissure, like a serpent's tongue. The boy stared at the fractured door, fascinated by the dancing flames. Those same flames suddenly dashed across the carpet and began to devour the bed that he had been sleeping in minutes earlier.

The heat was now unbearable. He felt light-headed from breathing in the thick smoke. Just before he collapsed, he could hear sirens outside getting louder and louder. The boy thought the rising sound only existed inside his head.

Like an angry animal, the flames suddenly leapt from the bed and landed on the boy, greedily consuming the bare flesh on his back. He tried to move to avoid the worst of the flames, but had no energy left to scream against the pain. The acrid smoke had, by now, robbed him of his capacity to shout for help. He opened his mouth and let out a silent, agonised scream.

The last thing he saw before blacking out completely was the intermittent flash of blue lights reflecting on the glass of his bedroom window.

Outside the blazing house, the first of two fire engines screeched to a halt.

Seeing the burning building for the first time, Sub-Officer Gareth Hayes spoke calmly into the radio: 'Control. Make pumps four. This dwelling is well alight. Possibly persons trapped inside.'

He then turned to the two men donning their BA equipment behind him and shouted, 'Quick as you can, lads!'

Gareth Hayes then leapt from the front seat of the cab as the two firefighters quickly donned their BA masks. The driver of the engine was already running out hose reels, ready for his colleagues to attempt entry into the inferno.

One of the neighbours, the man who had earlier been beaten back by the heat, approached Sub-Officer Hayes and shouted, 'There's a kid inside! Front bedroom, upstairs!'

Hayes turned to the BA crew and shouted, 'Persons reported, front bedroom! Get inside, quick as you can!'

Leading Fireman Mark Matthews and Fireman Wayne Hodges handed their BA tallies to Fireman Mike Wilson, the driver of the appliance, who was now running the Initial Entry Control Board.

Mark Matthews used his axe to force entry into the locked front door, and, backed up by Wayne Hodges, made his way into the blazing premises.

Using water from the hose reel, the two men courageously forced their way into the property, extinguishing the flames that were covering the staircase in front of them.

Mark turned to Wayne and shouted, 'We can't mess about, Hodgo! We need to get upstairs and in that bedroom!'

Wayne Hodges nodded. The two men began to move fast, scaling the weakened staircase.

Mark made his way to the door of the bedroom, which was by now irreparably damaged by the flames. Using the hose reel, he extinguished the flames surrounding the door and forced his way into the small bedroom. Stumbling through the thick black smoke towards the window, he almost trod on the severely burned, unconscious child before he saw him.

The flames in the room were now out, but it was still full of thick, acrid smoke. Ignoring the horrific burns on the child's back, Mark swept him up into his arms. Wayne had grabbed the hose reel from Mark before he lifted the child, and now the two men began to retrace their steps through the smoke-filled building.

The stairs were once again ablaze as the two firemen reached the landing. Ignoring the heat and the danger, Wayne pushed on towards the flames, clearing a path with bursts of water from the hose reel as he moved forward. As the two men made their way back down to the ground floor, the stairs below them creaked and moaned against their weight. The structure was now severely weakened following the onslaught from the deadly flames.

Reaching the ground floor, the two firemen ignored the flames in the hallway and pushed towards the front door. As they stepped out of the building, there was an enormous crash behind them as the staircase partially collapsed in a shower of fresh sparks. A second two-man BA crew entered the burning building as they stepped outside.

Ambulance personnel were already on standby, waiting to take the injured child from Mark's arms, as he and Wayne emerged from the blazing house.

Having handed over the boy, Mark sat down heavily on the pavement edge. He suddenly felt overwhelmed and exhausted by his efforts. Ripping away the breathing apparatus from his soot-blackened face, he greedily sucked in the cold night air. His protective clothing was still smouldering. Wayne sat down next to him and took off his own mask. The two men looked at each other and nodded, an unspoken acknowledgement of each man's courage and support.

Sub-Officer Hayes approached them and said, 'Good work, you two. The kid's got bad burns all over his back, but he's got a chance. The ambulance crew are giving him oxygen, but he isn't breathing unaided yet. It's going to be touch-and-go, lads.'

The last few words from the sub-officer were drowned out by the noise of the sirens as the ambulance sped the injured boy away in a life-or-death dash to the hospital.

Mark Matthews punched the ground in a silent rage and growled, 'What kind of evil bastard leaves a young kid locked in a house, on their own, at this time of night?'

Gareth Hayes said, 'That's beyond me, Mark. We need to let the police deal with that one, mate. They're already getting chapter and verse about the useless bloody parents, and which pub they'll be in, from the neighbours. You can both start getting your gear off now. The other crews have almost got the fire under control now, so you won't need to go back inside. Good job tonight; well done.'

Mark said quietly, 'What's the kid's name? Do you think he's going to make it, Sub?'

'You never know. The burns were bad, so we'll just have to wait and see. At the very least, you and Hodgo have given him a fighting chance. I've just been speaking to one of the neighbours. She thinks the kid's name was Billy.'

The sub-officer held out his hand toward the exhausted fireman.

With a resigned air, Mark Matthews took his boss's hand and pulled himself up before walking slowly towards the fire engine.

1

6.00 pm, 3 June 1987
Rock City, Talbot Street, Nottingham

The queue into the popular live music venue was steadily increasing.

Stephen Meadows and his girlfriend Suzy Flowers had arrived early and were standing with a group of friends near the front of the queue. The friends were all in a state of high excitement. They laughed, joked, and smoked cigarettes as they waited patiently in the light drizzle for the doors of Rock City to be opened.

There had been a growing sense of anticipation among them as the date for the concert had drawn closer. Everyone who loved this style of music agreed that Hammer of Thor were destined to be the next big thing in the heavy rock music scene.

The people in the growing queue were all serious fans of the music genre, and their attire reflected that devotion. The studded black leather jackets, torn dirty jeans, long hair and numerous tattoos all fitted the stereotypical heavy rock fan.

Stephen Meadows was no different.

Now in his late twenties, he had enjoyed heavy rock music ever since his school days. His long, jet-black hair was tied back in a ponytail, and his swarthy complexion gave him the look of a seventeenth-century pirate. Both of his arms and hands were heavily tattooed, and he sported a straggly beard and moustache. He wore a black leather motorcycle jacket over a plain mustard T-shirt and ripped black denim jeans. Heavy boots and a pair of John Lennon-style sunglasses, which masked his dark brown eyes, completed the look.

Normally, his appearance and the clothes he wore made him different from the crowd. He stood out as non-uniform and was happy to do so. Tonight, he was just another heavy rock devotee surrounded by long-standing friends, who all shared his passion.

The young woman standing alongside Stephen in the queue was still a relative newcomer to his group of friends.

After finally plucking up the courage to ask her out at a previous concert, Stephen had been dating the outrageous Suzy Flowers for a couple of months now. Suzy was from out of town and had only recently moved to the city. She was eccentric, with an effervescent personality. Loud and brash, but very sexy. His male friends had quickly taken to her, his female friends a little less accepting of the newcomer. Their clique of friends was one of many small groups within the wider heavy rock fraternity based in and around the city of Nottingham.

Surrounded by his friends from the rock music scene he adored was the one place Stephen felt really at ease. Although quite tall, very stocky and naturally strong, Stephen was extremely mild mannered. He lacked any real confidence, especially around the opposite sex.

Suzy was the complete opposite, and the epitome of the wild, rock chick.

Still in her early twenties, she had a shock of peroxide blonde hair that she had chopped into a short style herself. A born-and-bred Mancunian, she was studying fashion at Nottingham University. Her outrageous wardrobe was very much self-styled.

Suzy would buy cheap clothes from charity shops and use her expertise for design and colour to make the most outlandish outfits. She had made a special effort for tonight's concert. She was wearing a noticeably short leather miniskirt, deliberately holed and laddered fishnet stockings and biker boots. Beneath her elaborately studded, dark blue leather jacket, she wore a sheer black blouse and no bra.

Her outfit had caused some consternation for Stephen. He didn't really appreciate the admiring looks his girlfriend was now getting from most of his close friends. Suzy was quite a heavyset girl, with an ample bosom that now strained against the clinging blouse. Much to Stephen's embarrassment, Suzy's large nipples could clearly be seen through the translucent material of her blouse.

Although his feelings were crushed when some of his so-called 'friends' began leering at his new girlfriend and making suggestive comments, it never entered his head to take any of them to task over it.

It just wasn't in his nature to be aggressive; he was a gentle giant in every sense of the word.

Trying to avoid seeing the leering looks, and ignoring the raucous comments being made, he turned to his best friend, Darren Cox, and said, 'I hope the s-s-sound s-s-system is rigged well t-t-tonight. I've heard the b-b-bass player is throbbing. The levels need to be s-s-set exactly right though, or it will fuzz.'

Ignoring the devastating stutter of his friend, Darren just nodded.

Overhearing the comment made by Stephen, Suzy scoffed, 'You've always got to be the sound expert, haven't you, Stevie boy?'

Stephen replied, 'It's one thing I d-d-do know about. I was a s-s-sound engineer at Castle S-s-sounds for ten years.'

Again, Suzy sneered, ' "Was" being the operative word, Stevie. You got the sack, remember. God, you're so bloody boring! It's always "sound this" and "sound that". You go on and on about sound, and you c-c-c-can't even s-s-s-speak right.'

Ignoring her spiteful mocking of his speech impediment, he replied, 'I d-d-didn't get the s-s-sack, I resigned. In any m-m-music, the s-s-sound is the most important thing, s-s-sweetheart.'

'Well, it's certainly the most important thing in your pathetic little life – and don't I know it!'

Stephen was shocked by the venom in her voice. He said quietly, 'What do you m-m-mean?'

In an overloud voice, ensuring all their mutual friends heard her comment, she said, 'Well, it's obviously far more important to you than sex! You haven't got the first clue about that, have you, darling?'

Stephen heard the sniggers behind him. He could feel himself colouring up as his cheeks flushed bright red.

Suzy continued, 'I really don't know why I bothered. All your friends warned me, you were a boring bastard. They certainly got that right.'

Stephen could feel his friends staring at him. The one place he had felt comfortable and accepted was now being ripped apart by this evil woman's barbed comments.

He turned to her and said in a whisper, 'Why are you b-bbeing like this? Here of all p-p-places, in front of all my f-f-friends?'

She put her face close to his and shouted back mockingly, 'Because, sweetheart, somebody needs to tell you just how boring and sad you really are. You're pathetic in bed; you've got the most ridiculously small prick I've ever seen, and to make matters worse, you have absolutely no idea what to do with it!'

Her voice grew louder as she finished her sentence. For the first time, Stephen noticed the sickly sweet smell of sherry on her breath. Suzy had been drinking heavily, and was now drunk. The fact that she was heavily under the influence of alcohol made no difference to Stephen's distress. The entire queue waiting outside Rock City were all guffawing loudly and pointing at him.

Once again, Stephen felt totally embarrassed and humiliated.

It was a feeling he knew only too well. He had spent his entire life being scorned and bullied, ridiculed over his speech impediment from an early age. His only salvation had been his love of music. In particular, the throbbing beat of rock guitars and drums that wiped out any chance of other people picking on him.

Now, that final refuge was also being stolen away from him. By the poisonous, peroxide bitch now laughing loudly in his face.

As the people in the queue continued to laugh, Stephen Meadows reacted in the only way he knew how.

He ran away.

As he raced down Talbot Street towards the city centre, he could still hear the laughter of his so-called 'friends' ringing in his ears behind him.

Two hundred yards away from the spiteful sniggers and

ridicule, he stopped and skulked into a doorway. Standing in the dark shadows, breathing hard from his sudden exertion, he felt a change washing over him. It was a physical feeling, manifesting itself as a tingling sensation that started in his very fingertips and moved along his arms before burning its way deep into his brain.

It was the unjustness of it all that he hated the most. It was this mixture of unfairness and rage that drove the sensation he was now experiencing.

He had only ever treated people with respect and kindness. It had always been thrown back in his face by people eager to mock and humiliate him.

His short life flashed before his eyes. He was suddenly confronted by images of every person who had ever ridiculed, mocked and bullied him.

In that singular, lightning-bolt moment, he suddenly came to the realisation that enough was enough. He was not going to accept any more of life's shit being thrown at him.

Having come to that momentous decision, he stood in the darkness of the doorway and began to formulate his response.

After careful consideration, he decided that he would wait for the concert to finish and then meet Suzy as she walked down Talbot Street, to the taxi rank on the Old Market Square. He would offer her a lift home, to save her the cost of taxi fare. He knew she would accept the offer of a free ride home; she would do anything to save cash, the cheap tart.

As his planned response to her vicious mocking began to formulate in his mind, he wondered just what he had ever seen in the poisonous bitch. Although vivacious and very sexy, there was something extremely nasty about Suzy Flowers. He could see that clearly now.

Once she was safely in his van and away from prying eyes and ears, he would ask her why she had ridiculed him. Her answer would be an irrelevance. It didn't really matter to him what her reasons were; he had already made up his mind what he was going to do.

It was time for Stephen Meadows to strike back against a world that had mocked and ridiculed him all his life.

2

6.15 pm, 3 June 1987
MCIU Offices, Mansfield, Nottinghamshire

It had been another long day for Danny Flint.
    Finally, the jury at Leicester Crown Court had returned a verdict at the trial of Brandon Temple. The disgraced geology professor had been found guilty of the manslaughter of Detective Inspector Brian Hopkirk and the abduction of the fourteen-year-old schoolgirl Emily Whitchurch.

During the lengthy trial, there had been some doubt whether the manslaughter charge would achieve a guilty verdict. The doubts had been raised by a sustained argument from Temple's defence counsel, that the death of the police officer was merely an accident. A tragic event caused by the sudden roof fall in the caves below Nottingham. The jury had rejected this argument and followed the reasoning offered by the prosecution: that the death was a direct result of the actions of Brandon Temple. It had been those premeditated actions that had left the police officer with no choice other than to attempt the fatal rescue of the young girl. The jury had recognised the fact that had the officer not made that brave decision, then the young schoolgirl would almost certainly have died a wretched death, alone and abandoned in the caves.

The judge had sentenced Brandon Temple to twenty-six years imprisonment. A lengthy custodial sentence that highlighted the seriousness and evil intent of his crimes.

Now quietly reflecting in his office, Danny realised that the length of the sentence was an irrelevance. His friend and colleague would remain dead. No amount of punishment for Brandon Temple would change that. It all seemed so senseless and such a waste of life. Brian Hopkirk was a good man, one of the absolute best. The reason he had died was his overwhelming sense of duty, his desire to always put the safety and well-being of others before himself.

Feeling a dark melancholy descending over him, Danny picked up the note that had been left on his desk. Having read it, he screwed the note up and hurled it into the wastepaper basket. He let out a resigned sigh and sat down heavily in his chair.

The note had been from Detective Chief Superintendent Adrian Potter. It instructed Danny to attend a meeting with him at force headquarters at ten o'clock on the tenth of June, to discuss the long-awaited replacement for his deceased colleague.

Danny found it difficult to comprehend the unfeeling attitude of his senior officer. Today of all days, he had sent a note requesting his attendance to discuss Brian's replacement. It made Danny feel as though Brian Hopkirk had never existed. Danny recognised the rage building within him and fought hard to suppress his feelings.

He heard movement in the office next door and stood up to investigate. Opening his office door, he saw Detective Inspector Rob Buxton at his desk.

Danny said, 'I thought you would've been home by now?'

'I just need to file this report before I go off duty. I heard the verdict and sentence from Leicester. What do you think of the outcome?'

'I'm pleased the jury saw through the defence counsel's argument. The sentence doesn't really matter to me – it's not going to bring Brian back, is it? It's justice for his death, and that's all.'

Rob nodded. 'That's exactly how I see it, boss. Throughout all the interviews I had with him, that evil shit Temple never once showed any remorse for Brian's death. I hope he never gets out.'

Danny said, 'I've had a note sent through from Potter today. I've got to meet him to discuss Brian's replacement, next week.'

Rob looked incredulous. 'He sent that today? Knowing the verdict had just come in?'

Danny nodded. 'Yeah. He says he wants to talk to me about Detective Inspector Cartwright, a candidate from an accelerated promotion course at Bramshill. Apparently, she has three and a half years' service and is incredibly well respected by all her peers. Potter thinks she'll be a perfect fit on the Major Crime Investigation Unit.'

'What do you think? Has she even done a CID course?'

'I don't know about the CID course; I think you already know my thoughts on Bramshill and the accelerated promotion scheme. In my book, there's no substitute for experience. That's what Brian had in abundance. He was a career detective, through and through.'

'Do you know anything else about her?'

'No. I'll find out everything next week. Apparently, she's going to be at my meeting with Potter.'

Rob grimaced. 'That doesn't sound much like a discussion. That sounds like, "Here's your new detective inspector; get on with it."'

'My thoughts exactly. I do need to try to put my personal feelings to one side, though, Rob. I still need to give this woman, whoever she is, a chance. It would be totally unfair if I didn't. I just hope she knows the reason for her appointment, that's all. Knowing Adrian Potter, he's crass enough not to have mentioned Brian's death to her.'

Rob nodded and said, 'That would be typical of the man. When are you going to speak to Andy?'

Danny cursed inwardly. He had totally forgotten about Detective Sergeant Andy Wills, who had undertaken the role of temporary detective inspector since the death of Brian Hopkirk. He had also been interviewed as a possible candidate to be promoted into the role permanently.

'I'll phone Andy when I get home this evening. I was hoping he'd be promoted and continue the job he's been doing.'

'I think he was hoping for that outcome as well. He's been so good in the role; I don't envy you that phone call.'

Danny said, 'I'm not worried about making the call. Andy's a solid professional. He'll accept it and carry on working to the best of his ability. His promotion will come soon enough. It's only a matter of when, not if, with Andy. I'm more worried about the continuity of the Major Crime Investigation Unit. The last thing we all need is a new broom sweeping in with a load of new ideas. This unit functions perfectly well as it is.'

Rob smiled and said, 'You're right. Andy will be promoted sooner rather than later. And don't worry about the MCIU. It will continue to operate in the correct way; we'll make sure of that. Do you fancy a couple of beers?'

Danny nodded. 'A quick pint sounds perfect. It will have to be just the one though. I don't want to be too late home. I like to see little Hayley before she goes to sleep.'

'That's what I like to hear. I was just the same when my kids were small. I always wanted to be home before they went to bed. I'm in the happy position now that my boys are nearly grown up. In a couple of years, I'll be badgering them to take their old man down the pub for a few beers.'

Danny laughed as he slipped his jacket on and followed Rob out the door. He could almost taste the cold Guinness already.

3

10.30 pm, 3 June 1987
Talbot Street, Nottingham

It was almost ten thirty when Stephen Meadows spotted Suzy Flowers walking out the doors and down the steps of Rock City, onto Talbot Street.

The concert had finished just after ten o'clock. Most of the fans had already spilled out of the large black doors and made their way down the hill and into the city centre. Stephen waited until he was sure Suzy was walking on her own before emerging from the shadow of the shop doorway.

He crossed the road and sidled up behind her. With a broad smile on his face, he said, 'Hello, S-s-suzy. Were the b-b-band any g-g-good?'

She was shocked to see him standing there. Seeing his huge smile, she smiled back, saying, 'Yeah, they were brilliant. Fantastic! Why did you fuck off, Stevie? I was only having a laugh. You know I didn't mean any of those things, don't you?'

He kept up the friendly charade, but inside, he was raging. He thought to himself, *Yeah, you were only having a laugh, but your fun was at my expense, as fucking usual.*

He said, 'I'm s-s-sorry I ran off, S-s-suzy. I just got a b-b-bit embarrassed, that's all. D-d-do you s-s-still want that ride home?'

Suzy slipped her arms around his waist and snuggled in against the chilly night. 'Of course I do, Stevie. Are you coming in for a nightcap?'

'Why d-d-dont you c-c-come b-b-back to mine tonight?'

'Sorry, babe, I can't tonight. I've got an important lecture first thing in the morning. I can make you a quick coffee at my flat if you want to come in?'

Stephen nodded. 'Okay, c-c-coffee sounds g-g-good. Come on, the van's in P-p-pilcher Gate car p-p-park. It shouldn't t-t-take us long if we get a move on.'

'I hope not, Stevie. It's bloody freezing.'

As he steered her towards the multistorey car park on Pilcher Gate, he thought to himself, *You should try wearing some clothes, you tramp.*

Fifteen minutes later, Suzy Flowers was sitting in the passenger seat of the Ford Transit van as Stephen Meadows drove into Denison Street from Hartley Road.

He stopped the van outside her bedsit.

As the van came to a stop, Suzy smiled and winked. 'Are you coming inside for that coffee?'

Without looking at her, he asked, 'Why did you m-m-make f-f-fun of m-m-me?'

Suzy giggled. 'I was only having a laugh. I didn't mean to embarrass you, babe.'

'And d-d-did you?'

'Did I what?'

'D-d-did you have a laugh?'

Suzy huffed loudly. 'Why are you being so fucking weird tonight? I can't be doing with all your bullshit. I'm going!'

Stephen Meadows then did something that, up until that exact moment, he would have deemed unthinkable.

He reached across and grabbed a handful of Suzy's peroxide blonde hair. He yanked her head back sharply as she tried to grab the door handle of the passenger door. She screamed once, then shouted, 'Get your hands off me, you crazy bastard!'

With the clenched fist of his right hand, he punched her once in the middle of her forehead. The force of the blow snapped her head back against the passenger-door window, knocking her unconscious.

He let go of her spiky hair and began removing the belt from his jeans. As soon as the belt was off, he reached over and grabbed her wrists, binding them tightly with the supple brown leather belt.

Having bound her wrists, he pushed her off the passenger seat down into the footwell, so she was out of sight.

He selected first gear and slowly drove the van back onto Hartley Road. He looked over at the top of Suzy's blonde head and said quietly to himself, 'Are you s-s-still having a laugh, you f-f-fucking s-s-slag?'

He turned on the cassette player and thrust in a cassette of the *Pyromania* album by Def Leppard.

As the heavy beat of the bass guitar throbbed through the van, Stephen Meadows smiled broadly. For the first time in his miserable life, he was the one in control.

4

11.30 pm, 3 June 1987
Ridge Hill, Lowdham, Nottinghamshire

An hour later, as he drove his van onto the driveway of the property at Ridge Hill in the village of Lowdham, memories came flooding into his brain. They were the same troubled recollections he always had every time he saw the property.

The large, detached bungalow was set well back from the country lane known as Ridge Hill. It was totally isolated, surrounded by farmland. The barley crop in the adjacent fields was now beginning to ripen after a prolonged spell of dry weather.

The large gardens at the front and rear of the bungalow were beginning to look neglected. Lawns that had once been fastidiously cut and trimmed were now over a foot tall. Flower beds, previously tended lovingly and full of colour, were now choked with dandelion, clover and groundsel.

The property had been occupied by Stephen Meadows for three months. It had been bequeathed to him following the sudden death of his parents. The beautiful bungalow had been his childhood home. When he had moved back there from his squalid, city centre flat, he had been conflicted. His mind was full of the many beautiful memories he had of growing up there, but they were thoughts that clashed heavily with the sorrow and sense of loss he now felt.

Both his parents had been full of unconditional love for their two children, and all his memories of them mirrored that love.

His father had been a pharmacist. A quiet man with a reserved nature, he rarely showed any outward affection. He had always supported Stephen in everything he did, in his own unassuming way.

His mother had been a full-time housewife. It was the unstinting pride in her home and her love of gardening that had kept the property and the grounds of the bungalow so pristine. Her feelings towards her children had always been far more overt than her husband's. She was extremely protective of both her son and daughter and rounded on anyone who tried to hurt them. She had realised early, when Stephen was still a very young child, that he was a vulnerable, sensitive boy. The dreadful stutter he was afflicted by meant he suffered mercilessly at the hands of playground bullies.

She had looked on angrily as this persecution had followed him throughout his childhood, then into adolescence and adulthood. She had endeavoured to protect and defend him all her life.

Her daughter Dawn, Stephen's younger sister, had been the love of her life. A hypoxic brain injury caused during her birth had caused her to suffer brain damage that necessitated twenty-four-hour care.

By some fluke, the cord had become wrapped around the

unborn baby's neck during birth, starving her of oxygen for several minutes.

Throughout her childhood and then through adolescence into adulthood, she had doted on her disabled daughter, doing everything for her, insistent that she should be cared for at home.

Stephen and Dawn Meadows' lives were both changed forever on that March evening when both parents had been snatched violently from them. The devoted couple had been celebrating their wedding anniversary with an intimate meal for two in the nearby town of Newark. As they returned home, the car they were travelling in had been involved in a head-on collision.

The mangled bodies of their beloved parents had to be cut from the wreckage of the Ford Escort. The massive impact had flipped the car upside down on the verge of the A46. The car's roof had been crushed. The severe injuries to the couple meant they had died instantly at the scene.

The driver of the other vehicle involved, a consultant surgeon at the Queen's Medical Centre, had survived the crash, sustaining only minor injuries.

Dr James McEllery had been driving a heavy Range Rover. This vehicle was far better equipped to withstand the impact than the much smaller Ford Escort. The consultant surgeon had been breathalysed at Newark Hospital after one of the police officers in attendance noticed that his speech was slurred and that his breath stank of liquor. McEllery had provided a positive breath test. A subsequent blood test revealed that he was almost double the legal limit.

McEllery was duly charged with causing death by dangerous driving and driving while above the legal limit. McEllery had appeared at the Magistrates Court in May. Through some obscure legal technicality, which Stephen didn't really understand, the consultant was found not guilty.

It had been just one more hammer blow for Stephen Meadows to take.

He had been unable to provide the same standard of care for his sister, Dawn, that his devoted mother had done all her life. Stephen had been forced to make the agonising decision to place his twenty-year-old sibling in permanent residential care at the Oaks, a specialist facility located just outside West Bridgford.

He had been unable to bring himself to visit her since making the onerous decision. He felt he had abandoned her and let her down.

After moving into the bungalow at the beginning of April, he had allowed the condition of the house and the gardens to deteriorate. He only occupied the lounge, his old bedroom, the kitchen and the bathroom.

He never ventured into any of the other rooms. The clothing and personal effects of his parents remained exactly as they had left them when they had gone out to celebrate on that fateful evening in March. The few anniversary cards they had received from friends remained on the mantelpiece in the living room.

His sister's room still contained all the specialist equipment she had needed to live as full a life as her disability allowed.

As he now drove the van to the rear of the bungalow, he tried to shrug off all those familiar melancholy memories.

There was a large outbuilding, which could be accessed from the rear of the bungalow through a single wooden door. The outbuilding had been built by his late father. He had used it as a workshop, to carry out his hobby of turning wood on a custom-built lathe.

When Stephen had moved back into the bungalow, he had emptied the workshop. He had replaced the lathe and woodturning tools with a sound recording deck. It was now his own makeshift sound studio, where he could play his music as loud as he wanted. A place where he could experiment, mixing different tracks and sounds.

When he was at home, this was where Stephen spent most of his time.

He had furnished the studio with a three-seater leather settee, a table and chairs. He had also placed a kettle, toaster and fridge in the room. It was now his favourite part of the property.

He parked the van behind the outbuilding and turned off the engine. In the silence, he could now hear Suzy Flowers groaning in the footwell of the passenger seat. He got out, walked round to the passenger door, and lifted the semi-conscious blonde out of the vehicle. He hoisted her over his shoulder and carried her inside the property.

Once inside the studio, he threw her roughly onto the wooden floor. He removed his leather belt from her wrists and began stripping her clothes from her. As soon as she was naked, she began to stir. He lifted her off the floor and sat her on a wooden chair. He then secured her tightly to the chair, using a thin nylon rope.

Once she was bound, he sat down on the settee behind her and stared at her naked back.

5

12.30 pm, 3 June 1987
Ridge Hill, Lowdham, Nottinghamshire

As Suzy Flowers gradually regained consciousness, she began to recognise her surroundings. Through distorted, hazy vision, she could see the record decks, the synthesizer and the posters on the walls. She had spent hours with Stephen, listening to rock music, in this room.

As she gained more of her senses, she suddenly realised how cold she felt. To her horror, she saw that she was now totally naked. She tried to move and couldn't. The very motion of moving her head to look down sent a flash of pain through her forehead. She suddenly felt nauseous and dizzy.

Taking a deep breath, she moved her head again. Much slower this time. As she looked down, she saw that she was sitting on a wooden chair and that her wrists had been tied tightly to the rail of the chair. She then tried to move her legs and realised that her ankles had been bound to the chair legs in the same way.

She struggled against the ropes that bound her wrists and ankles so tightly. When she realised she couldn't budge them, she began to cry.

Her sobs were interrupted by a voice behind her. It was a voice she instantly recognised.

'I s-s-see you're f-f-finally awake.'

Still not quite believing what was happening to her, Suzy said, 'Stephen?'

He got up from the leather settee, walked round the chair and stood in front of her.

She looked up at him and said angrily, 'Stephen! What the fuck do you think you're doing?'

He smiled and said softly, 'Oh, you know, j-j-just having a little f-f-f-fun.'

Suzy was enraged and shrieked, 'Untie me, you fucking freak!'

Stephen shook his head. 'We b-b-both know that's n-n-not happening. I j-j-just want you to have a little t-t-time to reflect on your actions b-b-before your c-c-cleansing.'

Suzy was now incandescent with rage. She began shouting, 'I'm going to the police, you mad bastard! You can't do this to me! Let me go!'

He laughed, then grabbed her face. His powerful fingers dug into one cheek, and his thumb into the other. He leaned forward until his face was just inches from hers, then shouted, 'Q-q-quiet reflection! B-b-bitch!'

Suzy could taste the blood in her mouth as his grip on her cheeks grew stronger. It felt as though he was going to keep squeezing until her teeth popped from her gums. She was powerless to stop him, and unable to scream.

Finally, he let go and pushed her head back.

He snarled the same word: 'Reflection!'

Suzy began to sob. Her injured mouth was hurting, and she spluttered, 'Please let me go, Stevie. I'm so sorry if I hurt you earlier. I love you.'

He laughed at her ludicrous pleading. 'I'm g-g-going now. D-d-don't b-b-bother to s-s-scream. No one will hear you. S-s-see you later, S-s-suzy.'

He walked out of the room, and she heard the key turn in the lock.

She began to cry louder; she knew it was pointless to shout for help. She knew exactly how isolated Stephen's bungalow was.

After five minutes, she stopped crying and began to take stock of her perilous situation. Her head was clearer now. She assessed the knots in the ropes that bound her and began to pull against them. It was impossible; she couldn't budge them. In desperation, she began to look for other ways she could free herself. Nothing obvious came to mind. She would need to think of a different strategy.

Suddenly, a possible escape plan came to her. When Stephen returned, she would come onto him and make him want to have sex with her. She knew he still had feelings for her. Why else had he bothered to strip her? He had wanted to see her body. That had to mean he still wanted her sexually.

Suzy smiled to herself. She felt confident that she would soon be able to coax him into releasing her when he saw what she was offering him. Then once he had untied her, she would make her escape and get the police to arrest the crazy bastard.

Her top lip curled into a sneer as she thought how easy it was going to be for her to dupe the stuttering moron.

She said softly to herself, 'Hurry back, you f-f-fucking f-f-freak.'

6

2.30 am, 4 June 1987
Gunthorpe Bridge, Nottinghamshire

Suzy Flowers lay bound and gagged in the back of Stephen Meadows' transit van. She was naked and felt bruised and battered after the short journey. Every time they had hit a pothole or gone around a bend, she had crashed into the metal sides of the van. She could feel blood trickling down the back of her head – a wound caused when she had been sent hurtling into the side of the van as the vehicle had swerved around a particularly sharp bend.

Every time she had clattered into the metal panelling, she could hear Meadows laughing from the front of the vehicle.

The plan she had hatched to seduce her captor, when he returned to the sound room at the bungalow where she was imprisoned, had failed miserably. She had tried everything, promised him everything. He had just laughed and called her a pathetic slut. He had then stalked around the studio, babbling on about her 'cleansing', before once again leaving her alone.

After what seemed like an age, he had returned with more ropes and a roll of sticky gaffer tape. She had struggled violently. Shaking her head from side to side, desperately trying to prevent him wrapping the gaffer tape over her mouth. She had failed. Very soon, she was snorting for breath through her nostrils. She'd quickly become breathless, and the lack of oxygen meant she could no longer struggle so hard.

Suzy had been left with no choice but to submit to him. First, he bound her ankles together. Then he had untied her wrists from the arms of the chair before quickly binding them together. Once she was securely bound and gagged, he had pushed her from the chair. She landed heavily on the floor, knocking all the breath from her body. She lay on her side, snorting heavily through her nose as she fought to get oxygen back into her lungs.

Her voice muffled by the sticky tape, she continually pleaded with him to spare her and take her home.

He had ignored her pitiful wailings and hoisted her over his shoulder in a fireman's carry. He carried her outside, where the cold night air had felt painful to her naked body. It had been pitch black and very cold. There was a new crescent moon high in the cloudless sky, but the celestial body offered little light.

He had opened the side door of the Transit van and thrown her from his shoulder roughly down onto the metal flooring inside. Staring down at her, he had snarled, 'N-n-not long now, b-b-bitch!'

That had been ten minutes ago. The journey in the back of the van had been so violent and horrific, it had come as a welcome relief when the vehicle suddenly came to an abrupt halt.

She had no time to wonder where she had been taken.

No sooner had the vehicle stopped than the side door was yanked open, and Stephen got inside, closing the door behind him. He made his way past her and moved to the back of the spacious van. She heard a clanking noise and recoiled in horror as Stephen approached her, carrying lengths of heavy chain.

She desperately tried to pull her feet away as Stephen started to wrap the heavy chains around her calves and knees. She couldn't prevent him securing the chains to her lower legs with more rope. In no time at all, she couldn't move her legs. The weight of the heavy chain links was too great.

Stephen yanked hard on the chains to ensure they were secure before turning towards Suzy. He put his face directly in front of hers and growled, 'It's t-t-time for your c-c-cleansing.'

He opened the van door and got out. Having checked that the area around Gunthorpe Bridge was still deserted, he reached inside the van and pulled her out. The chains wrapped around her lower legs rattled across the metal floor of the van.

Stephen Meadows was naturally strong and powerful. The effort required to lift the weight of the struggling woman and the heavy chains was nothing to him. He ripped the tape from her mouth and hoisted her up onto his shoulder. As he walked towards the grey stone parapet of the bridge, Suzy yelled, 'What the fuck are you doing? Put me down!'

Suddenly, she realised where she was, and the awful relevance of the heavy chains. In that horror-filled split second, she knew exactly what he was about to do. In the weak moonlight, she could see the river snaking away in the distance. In the darkness to her left, she could see the Unicorn public house. Ironically, it was where they had sat drinking beer on their first date. Her eyes widened and her heart raced as they reached the stone parapet, and she saw the black water of the river racing below.

She shouted, 'Don't do this! Please!'

Without saying another word, Stephen tipped Suzy and the chains from his shoulder, over the parapet of the bridge. The weight of the chains meant she fell hard and fast towards the black water.

He looked down from the parapet as Suzy Flowers hurtled towards her watery grave. He smiled with grim satisfaction as the heavy chains did their work and dragged the spiteful bitch down into the depths. He continued to watch for a few seconds after she had been dragged below the surface.

Satisfied that she couldn't escape, he got back in his Transit van and drove away from the bridge. As he made the short journey back to Lowdham, he thought about Suzy taking her first and last breath under the water.

The cold water rushing into her lungs, starving her brain of life-giving oxygen. The water would consume all of her. It would surround and envelop her body, smothering her very existence, nullifying her soul.

He smiled.

The cleansing would be complete. The water would see to that.

7

9.00 am, 10 June 1987
Gunthorpe Bridge, Nottinghamshire

PC Nick Kerridge had a concerned expression on his face as he looked out across the fast-flowing river. It had been a borderline decision when they'd first arrived at Gunthorpe Bridge that morning whether the training day should proceed or not.

Having made the telephone call the previous night to gain permission from the farmer who owned the land around the base of the bridge, PC Kerridge didn't want to call the dive off.

Nick was the supervisor for the four divers expected to train that day. He was a vastly experienced member of the Nottinghamshire Police Underwater Search Unit. He knew that even though the current was rapid below the bridge, the area could be dived safely using a line search pattern.

As soon as they had arrived at eight o'clock that morning, Nick had supervised the dropping of a line, weighted at intervals with fifty-six-pound weights, from the bridge. All the equipment needed for the training dives was in the caravan being towed by the police van.

Once the line was in place and on the bottom of the river, the divers began to get into their red-coloured dry suits.

As it was a training day, the four divers would take it in turns to traverse the river from one bank to the other. The current was strong and the river fast, so it was necessary for each diver to have a lifeline attached to his harness. This would always be held by the dive supervisor and a support diver.

The first diver into the river was a relative newcomer to the Underwater Search Unit. This would be PC Nathan Oxford's third training day since he'd completed his police divers' course in Northumberland.

As he pulled on the Interspiro AGA full-face mask, the novice diver was experiencing a mixture of excitement and apprehension. There was a demand valve connected to the two AGA air cylinders that were strapped to his back. He wore fins on his feet and had a heavy weight belt attached to his midriff, to help stabilise him in the fast-flowing water.

Once he entered the river, he would follow the weighted line on the riverbed and pull himself across the river. He knew that visibility at the bottom of the river would be less than a couple of feet because of the current. The riverbed immediately below the bridge was known to be a mixture of shingle and mud. He knew the fast-flowing water would disrupt the bottom.

Nick Kerridge tapped Nathan on the shoulder and shouted, 'Are you ready?'

The diver nodded and gave the *okay* signal, touching forefinger and thumb together, forming an O shape.

Nick said, 'Test your comms.'

Nathan spoke into the microphone that was built into the face mask.

'That's great, Nathan. You're coming through loud and clear. Tell me your rope drills: What's the signal for "get me up"?'

From behind the mask, Nathan grinned at his supervisor and said, 'Two heavy pulls on the line means "get me the fuck out of here".'

'Have a good dive, Nathan, and take your time. There's no need to worry about your air. You've got twin tanks, so you'll have ample time to make the crossing.'

The young diver nodded and began to make his way awkwardly towards the river. The heavy weight belt, combined with the fins on his feet, made movement on the bank ungainly and cumbersome. Two of the team were waiting on the far bank; the other diver remained with Nick to assist him.

When he reached the river, Nathan sat down, allowing his legs to enter the water first. He held onto the search line with his left hand and slowly eased himself down into the river. As soon as he submerged fully and was a yard or two away from the bank, he spoke into the face mask: 'Current doesn't feel as bad as it looks from up top, Nick. Visibility is only two feet or less. Commencing the crossing now.'

On the bank, Nick said, 'Remember what I said. There's no rush; you've got plenty of time. Don't forget that you're down there to search the bottom for items that have been thrown from the bridge.'

Nick made the reminder because he knew that all young divers tended to become engrossed in the actual dive rather than the search.

After Nathan had been under the water for six minutes, the radio crackled into life again. 'Nick, there's an old moped down here. It's near the first stanchion of the bridge. I can't see any registration plate, though.'

Nick Kerridge smiled. He already knew the moped was there. It had been left in the river as a test for the new divers. It acted as confirmation that they were actually searching as they made their way across the river.

He said, 'Well done, Nat. Keep going; you're doing great. How's the visibility out there now?'

'It's a little better. The bottom's mainly gravel near the middle.'

Another ten minutes passed, and the radio sparked up again: 'Nick ... are you there?'

Nick recognised the sound of rising panic in the young diver's voice. He replied calmly, 'I'm here, Nat. Is everything okay?'

'There's a body down here.'

'Repeat your last, Nat.'

'There's a body down here. I can see the feet and the lower legs; they're wrapped in chains.'

'How far out are you?'

'It's just before the second stanchion.'

'Is the body drifting in the current?'

'Not with all these chains around the legs. It's not going anywhere.'

'Okay. Turn around and make your way back to this side of the riverbank. We're going to have to start organising a recovery.'

'Will do.'

8

10.00 am, 10 June 1987
Nottinghamshire Police Headquarters

Danny Flint waited patiently outside the office of Detective Chief Superintendent Adrian Potter. Even when Bill Wainwright had been the Head of the CID, Danny had never enjoyed his visits to police headquarters. Now that it was the diminutive Yorkshireman Adrian Potter in charge, he positively loathed them.

At least with Bill Wainwright, there had been mutual respect. The dour straight-talking Scot was tough but reliable and always did the best for the men and women who worked for him.

Adrian Potter was the exact opposite: A career-driven individual who looked no further than his next promotion. Danny didn't feel able to trust him and felt constantly undermined by him.

There had been friction between the two senior detectives

from the moment Chief Constable Jack Renshaw had appointed Potter. The situation had become so bad in the weeks leading up to the death of Detective Inspector Hopkirk that Renshaw had found it necessary to have a face-to-face meeting with both men to try to establish a professional working relationship between them.

Since that meeting, Danny had done his utmost to maintain his professionalism and establish a good working relationship with his immediate supervisor. Danny had noticed there was now a lot less interference from Potter in the day-to-day running of the MCIU.

That uneasy status quo had all changed last week. Danny had received that ill-timed note from Potter, informing him that following the recent interviews, a replacement had been selected for the detective inspector vacancy on the MCIU. The vacancy that had been caused by the death, on duty, of his friend and colleague Brian Hopkirk.

Danny intended to resist this appointment. The last thing he needed on the MCIU was a Bramshill flyer with little or no experience of running a major crime enquiry. He also felt that Potter would have deliberately selected a detective inspector who he knew would report back to him. He had enough to deal with already, without worrying about having a spy in the ranks.

Danny would have usually engaged the secretary outside Potter's office in small talk while he waited. But he felt on edge today, and apart from the pleasantries spoken when he first arrived, he had remained tight-lipped, deep in thought.

The secretary broke into his thoughts, saying, 'Detective Chief Superintendent Potter will see you now.'

Danny stood and walked along the corridor to the office. He knocked politely on the door and waited.

A single-word instruction was shouted from within: 'Enter.'

Danny walked in and closed the door softly behind him. Potter remained seated behind his huge desk. Without speaking, he motioned for Danny to take a seat and continued reading the report he held.

After a couple of minutes, Potter placed the paperwork on the desk. He removed his glasses and said, 'It really is a most impressive record for someone with such little service.'

Without waiting for Danny to comment, he continued, 'I hope you haven't been waiting long, Chief Inspector. I was hoping your new detective inspector would have arrived by now. I'm sure she'll be with us shortly. I think she's going to be the perfect choice for the MCIU.'

Danny used the pause to say, 'About this appointment, sir. You know the tragic circumstances surrounding Brian Hopkirk's death, and how hard that tragedy hit everyone on the MCIU. I think it would have been far better for everyone's morale if we could have promoted someone from within the Unit.'

'Like Detective Sergeant Wills, I suppose? That promotion and appointment would have been out of the question. The interview panel agreed with me that Detective Sergeant Wills just doesn't have the requisite experience or skill set to undertake a command role yet. Yes, I agree he's a competent officer and a good detective. But the panel all agreed that he still has areas he needs to develop.'

'Just a minute, sir. Andy Wills is far beyond competent. He's an extremely talented detective, who already has vast experience of running serious crime enquiries on the MCIU. He's carried out the duties of acting detective inspector ever since Brian Hopkirk died, and he has been superb in the role. What areas does the panel think he still needs to develop?'

Before Potter could answer, the telephone on his desk rang. He snatched it up, listened for a moment, then said, 'Thank you. Send her straight in, please.'

Danny knew it was pointless to try to change Potter's mind. He was suddenly consumed by a feeling of dread as he waited to meet the officer who was about to be foisted upon him.

Danny stood as the door opened. A slim woman with long blonde hair tied back in a ponytail, wearing a dark-coloured business suit, walked in.

She looked at Danny, smiled and said, 'Good morning, Chief Inspector Flint.'

Suddenly, Danny's face broke into a huge grin. 'Tina Prowse. You're going to be my new detective inspector?'

The young woman smiled and said, 'It's Tina Cartwright now, sir. I got married three months ago.'

With a pained expression, Potter said, 'Do you two know each other?'

Danny registered the pained expression and said, with a half-smile, 'I'm sure you already knew that, sir. You've got Tina's file in front of you. Surely you read about her secondment to the MCIU as a detective sergeant. She worked on the Ben Mackay and Jimmy Wade cases with us.'

'Do I take it, then, that her appointment meets with your approval, Chief Inspector?'

Danny nodded. He was enjoying watching Potter squirm as his plan to upset the MCIU disintegrated.

Danny turned to face Tina Cartwright and said, 'It's definitely okay, sir. Tina's very well respected by all the detectives on the MCIU. I'm sure her appointment will be just what the department needs to lift everyone's morale.'

Tina said, 'Thank you, sir. I'm very much looking forward to joining the MCIU again. I loved my time working there, so thank you very much for the opportunity.'

'Don't thank me. It was the interview panel who recommended you, and the chief superintendent who facilitated your appointment.'

She turned to Potter and said, 'Thank you, sir.'

Potter was angry that he hadn't made the connection between Tina Prowse and Tina Cartwright. He should have realised that she had worked on the MCIU before. He grunted something barely audible, then said, 'I'll leave you to brief your new detective inspector, then, Chief Inspector Flint. That will be all.'

Danny nodded. 'Right you are, sir.'

Danny stood up and walked out, followed by Tina.

As Tina closed the door behind her, Potter's secretary approached Danny with a very worried expression on her face. She said, 'Chief Inspector Flint, I've just taken a telephone call from your office.'

'What is it?'

In a voice little more than a whisper, she said, 'A body has been found by the Underwater Search Unit in the river at Gunthorpe Bridge this morning. They suspect foul play. Detective Inspector Buxton is already on his way to Gunthorpe, but he's asked if you could join him there after your meeting.'

Danny nodded. 'Thanks, Amanda.'.'

He turned to Tina Cartwright and said, 'It looks like your "welcome to the MCIU" speech and briefing will have to wait. A body's been fished out of the River Trent at Gunthorpe Bridge. Let's go and see why the divers think it's a case of foul play, shall we?'

'As you say, sir. The welcome speech can wait.'

When they reached the car in the car park, Danny said, 'Well, that was a pleasant surprise. I knew I was getting a Bramshill flyer, but I didn't know it was you.'

'I could see that. I am a detective, you know.'

They both laughed; then Tina said seriously, 'I was really sorry to hear about Brian. He was such a lovely man. You are okay about my appointment, aren't you?'

'Brian's death was devastating for all of us. As you say, he was one of life's good guys. As for your appointment, I'm extremely happy. You're obviously aware of the underlying tension between Chief Superintendent Adrian Potter and myself?'

'I've heard whisperings. Nothing concrete, just gossip.'

'Disregard all the gossip you've heard. The bottom line is this, Potter doesn't like the concept of the MCIU. He considers it to be an expensive luxury. If the decision had been his to make, he would have got rid of the department in a heartbeat. Fortunately, for now at least, we still have the backing of the chief constable. That doesn't stop Potter trying to throw little spanners in the works every now and then.'

'You mean little spanners, like appointing a wet-behind-the-ears, know-nothing detective inspector fresh from Bramshill College to lead half of your Unit?'

Danny smiled at her self-deprecating comment. 'Yes, Tina. Exactly like that.'

'Well, sir, I'm only too aware of my shortcomings when it comes to operational experience. I'll always be prepared to listen to advice, but I have the rank. Which means I'll also be prepared to make the tough decisions when they're needed.'

'That's great to hear. You've joined us at a particularly good time. We're currently pretty clear, workwise, so it will give you time to settle into things.'

'Okay, sir.'

'When it's just the two of us, please call me Danny, okay?'

'Okay, Danny. One other thing, is Rachel Moore still on the department?'

'She most certainly is. I don't know how long I'm going to be able to hang onto her, though. Rachel passed her sergeant's exam last year, and I'm expecting her to be offered a promotion very soon.'

'That's brilliant. I really enjoyed working with Rachel.'

'Right. Jump in. Let's go and see what the river has delivered up for us.'

As Tina fastened her seat belt, Danny accelerated away from headquarters.

His spirits felt suddenly lifted. He was looking forward to introducing Detective Inspector Tina Cartwright to the rest of the Major Crime Investigation Unit.

9

11.00 am, 10 June 1987
Gunthorpe Bridge, Nottinghamshire

Danny parked the car outside the Unicorn public house. He walked to the back of the vehicle and opened the boot. He reached inside and took out a pair of Wellington boots.

As he put them on, he looked at Tina's flat shoes and said, 'Sorry, Tina. I think it's going to be muddy on the riverbank. I hope they aren't new.'

Tina grinned. 'They're not, don't worry.'

In the distance, parked in a field just below the arched bridge, Danny could see the trailer used by the Underwater Search Unit. There was activity alongside the trailer and near the water's edge.

Danny said, 'Come on. Let's find Rob and see what we've got.'

As they walked along the riverbank, approaching the

bridge, Rob Buxton saw them and walked slowly up the bank to meet them.

Behind him by the water's edge, Danny could see a black body bag that the divers had used to drag the dead body from the water. It had been an arduous task that had taken the efforts of all four divers. The heavy chains that had been used to weigh the victim down were still attached to the legs. The body had been a nightmare to retrieve from the soft river bottom.

Rob had a puzzled expression on his face as he approached them.

Danny said, 'Morning, Rob. You remember Tina?'

Rob smiled. 'Of course I remember her. How could I forget Detective Sergeant Prowse? What are you doing here, Tina?'

'Hello, Rob. It's DI Cartwright now; I got married three months ago. I've also been promoted and posted to the MCIU.'

Rob's smile grew wider. 'That's great news. Welcome back. We've got a tricky one for your first day, though.'

Danny said, 'What exactly have we got?'

'The deceased is a white female, looks to be in her early twenties. Heavily tattooed, piercings everywhere.'

Tina said, 'Everywhere?'

'She's naked. Whoever threw her in the river stripped her first. There's no doubt we're looking at a murder enquiry. The bottom of her legs, from the knee down, were wrapped in heavy chains. The weight took her straight to the bottom.'

Danny looked beyond Rob. He could see the scenes of crime team hovering around the black body bag, taking samples and photographs.

'Is there a Home Office pathologist travelling?'

'Seamus Carter's been contacted, and he's on his way. The

divers have only just managed to get the body out of the river. It's been a long job.'

'Okay. Well, we might as well wait here until Seamus arrives, then all examine the body together. Is the dive supervisor around? I'd like a word with him.'

'It's PC Nick Kerridge who's in charge of the divers, boss. I'll give him a shout.'

Rob shouted across to the gathered divers. PC Nick Kerridge began to make his way up the bank.

As he reached the top of the bank, he said, 'Nick Kerridge, sir.'

'Good morning, Nick. How was the body found?'

'We were diving below the bridge on a training exercise. PC Oxford was halfway across the river on the first dive when he found the body. She was located just before the centre stanchion of the bridge. Her lower legs were secured with heavy, industrial-looking chain links. I reckon she was thrown from the centre of the bridge. The weight of the metal links had taken her straight to the bottom. Even in this fast-flowing current, those chains weren't budging an inch. It took all of us well over an hour to get her and the chains off the bottom and out of the river.'

'How long do you think she's been in the water?'

'That's never an exact science, sir. I've seen a lot of bodies pulled from the water; I would think this one's been in about a week.'

Rob said, 'Will the pathologist be able to narrow it down any?'

Danny said, 'I doubt it. The temperature in water is quite different. Nick here would probably be just as accurate as the pathologist.'

Nick nodded and said, 'Well, we're about to find out. This looks like the pathologist now.'

Danny looked over his shoulder and could see the huge

shape of Seamus Carter negotiating the slippery, muddy path.

As he drew level, Danny said, 'Good morning, Seamus.'

'Good morning to you, Detective. What have we got?'

'Rather than us all constantly slipping and sliding up and down the bank, making it even more treacherous, we waited for you. Let's go and see, shall we?'

The pathologist followed the three detectives and the dive supervisor back down the bank until they all stood around the black body bag. The scenes of crime officer had unzipped the bag, exposing the dead woman.

The woman's body was bloated and alabaster white. The colours of her numerous tattoos were vivid and stark against the pale, puckered skin. Her eyes were opaque and lacked any colour. The eyelids appeared frayed, damaged by the attentions of small fish.

Danny could see that the chains binding her legs were covered in blue engineering paint.

He turned to Rob. 'What do you make of the colour of the chains?'

Rob shrugged. 'Other than that they look industrial, who knows? They're big heavy links.'

Danny turned to Seamus. 'How long do you think she's been in the water?'

The big pathologist squatted down and pinched the flesh on one arm between his forefinger and thumb. He said, 'About a week; a day more or day less. It's always hard to tell.'

Danny said, 'The dive supervisor, who oversaw her recovery, also thinks she's probably been in about that length of time.'

Seamus looked up. 'Well, in my experience, I've found that the divers are usually pretty accurate. Have scenes of crime photographed how the chains have been secured?'

Rob answered, 'Yes. They've got numerous shots showing how the ropes are securing the chains to her legs.'

The pathologist turned to Danny and said, 'In that case, would it be okay to remove the chains before we take this poor woman to the mortuary?'

Danny nodded and turned to Rob. 'Make sure scenes of crime take photographs of each step as the chains are removed.'

Rob nodded and walked over to the scenes of crime officers.

Seamus said, 'I can't tell you anything else here, Danny. We need to get her in for a post-mortem examination. Have the undertakers been requested to attend?'

Hearing the question, Rob shouted across, 'Undertakers will be here in fifteen minutes.'

Seamus said, 'Great. Let's get these chains removed, then. I'll see you at the City Hospital later this afternoon. I'll try to be there for as near to four o'clock as I can.'

Danny nodded. 'Okay, that's great. We'll see you there. Do you remember Tina? She's our new DI.'

'I think we have met before. Maybe Worksop Hospital, a year or so ago?'

Tina said, 'That's right, we did. The male nurse from Rampton, who was killed when Jimmy Wade escaped.'

'That's it, I remember now. Welcome back, Tina. I mean this in the nicest possible way – hopefully, you won't be seeing me too often.'

Danny said, 'See you at four o'clock, Seamus.'

He then turned to Tina and said, 'Let's go. The quicker we get back to the office, the sooner we can start setting out priority enquiries. Are you happy to take this enquiry on as your first case, Tina?'

'Of course. That's what I'm here for, sir.'

10

11.30 am, 10 June 1987
Grassland near Rainworth, Nottinghamshire

The rattle of the matchbox in his trouser pocket was the only sound he heard as he walked across the deserted gorse meadow at the back of Rufford Colliery. Behind the industrial site, surrounding the grey slag heap, were acres of unfarmed grassland and gorse bushes. The terrain here wasn't suited to agriculture; it was undulating and rocky beneath the surface. The only plants that grew here were hardy gorse bushes with their bright yellow flowers and spiny foliage, and tall grasses that needed little water or nourishment to survive.

The recent sunny weather had made the long grass brittle and dry to the touch. It made a whispering sound as his knees brushed through it. He was dragging his feet as he walked up the slope of a hill, towards a stand of hawthorn hedges. The wind was fresh and gusting down the hill, bending the long grass and making his eyes water.

He knew the perfect spot for his adventure would be at the top of this hill. The thick hawthorn hedge would provide a perfect windbreak from the gusting breeze.

Today was the third time in a week that he had strolled onto this wasteland. The other visits had been made during the evening, when the sun was low in the sky. He had set out earlier today, as heavy rain was forecast for later. The route he had taken into the gorse hills had taken him across already blackened, charred ground. The burnt stubble was visible evidence of his other visits. The weather hadn't been ideal on the last occasion. It had been a baking hot day, but there was no wind. He needed the power of the wind to really release the beast.

Having reached the summit, he sat down beneath the hawthorn bushes and looked down the hill. He took a few minutes to get his breath back after the steep climb. In the distance, he could see the rows of red-brick houses that made up the small mining village of Rainworth. The headstocks of the nearby colliery stood like a silent colossus, towering above the landscape.

He took one long last look around the rugged landscape to make sure he wasn't being watched. Satisfied there was nobody else about, he took the screwed-up newspaper sheets from his pockets and placed them carefully at the base of the dried stalks of long grass.

He took out the Swan Vesta matchbox. He rattled the contents before sliding open the box and removing three of the red-headed matches. He held the matches between his forefinger and thumb before dragging them sharply across the sandpaper strip. As the matches ignited, he felt the same thrill he always felt as flame burst from the inanimate wooden stalks. They were suddenly transformed from a dead, inert splinter of wood into a living, spitting animal.

Shielding the matches with the palm of his other hand, he leaned forward and held the small flame beneath the screwed-up paper.

He watched spellbound as the flame caught the paper and quickly spread to the bone-dry grass. In less than a minute, an area the size of a bedsheet was burning. He stepped back into the shade provided by the hawthorns and watched the fire slowly creep its way through the long grass.

Suddenly, the creeping fire was given energy and speed as the wind gusted and fanned the small flames. Within seconds, those fledgling flames grew in height and began racing across the open field. They rushed down the hill, consuming gorse bushes as they sped out of control, towards the colliery buildings in the distance.

With a growing sense of fascination, his eyes followed the dancing flames that were now almost three feet tall. A huge smile enveloped his face as the flames reached the only tree on the hill. A twenty-foot silver birch, which had been a local landmark for years, was first surrounded and then engulfed by the fire.

The smile disappeared as his enjoyment at watching the tree being devoured by the beast was suddenly cut short. He could now hear sirens in the distance. The smoke from the grass fire was now thick enough to be seen from the village. Somebody had obviously alerted the fire brigade.

Taking a final look over his shoulder at the blackened smouldering field and the flames still racing down the hill, he smiled and put the matchbox back in his pocket.

He turned, walked through a gap in the hawthorn hedge, and made his way through the woods, away from the fire. He knew these woods like the back of his hand. Walking in this direction would bring him to the village of Forest Town.

It would be a long walk back to his home in Rainworth. It was a lovely warm day, and he had nothing else to do. As he made his way through the woods, away from the latest grass fire he had started, his thoughts immediately turned to the next fire.

He still enjoyed seeing flames engulfing and destroying grass and shrubs, but it was starting to lose its thrill.

He needed to experience a bigger fire. His needs were escalating. It was no longer enough for him to light a grass fire and run away. He made his mind up as he tramped slowly through the woods; the next fire would be bigger. He would stay and watch the firemen as they attempted to tackle the havoc he had unleashed.

As he walked, he smiled and rattled the matchbox in his pocket. He could already feel a rising sense of excitement and anticipation.

11

4.00 pm, 10 June 1987
Ridge Hill, Lowdham, Nottinghamshire

Stephen Meadows' mind was in turmoil.
Part of him recoiled at the horror of what he had done, but a bigger part of him rejoiced in it.

The same feelings he had experienced in that dark doorway outside Rock City were once again coursing through his body. It felt like a surge of electricity pulsing deep within him. It had made it impossible for him to sleep. He had paced the floor of his makeshift sound studio, staring intently at the wooden chair Suzy had been tied to.

As the afternoon wore on, and the rain began to fall heavier outside the bungalow, Stephen came to a decision.

His mind was now made up. The conflict that had been festering inside, troubling him, had now completely disappeared. He grabbed a notepad and pen from the side of the mixing decks and sat cross-legged on the leather settee.

With a sense of urgency, he began to scribble names down on the notepad. Everyone who had ever ridiculed, bullied or harmed him throughout his short life was added to the list.

When he finished writing the list of names, he was overwhelmed by a feeling of nausea. He suddenly felt dizzy, daunted by the enormity of the task he was setting himself. He knew it was the right thing to do. The sense of empowerment and strength he had felt as he watched Suzy Flowers slip beneath the dark waters of the River Trent was something he had never experienced before. The memory of those feelings reassured him. He knew he was taking the correct path.

He intended to right every wrong he had ever suffered. The guilty would pay for making his life the miserable existence it had been thus far.

Once his head had cleared, he glanced down at the notepad. There were now several names scribbled on the paper.

He stared hard at the first four: Sarah Milfoyle, Rex Poyser, Pete Slater and Dr James McEllery.

He would deal with the other names on the list later. In the short term, these were the four individuals whose faces blighted him every day. The memories of the suffering they had caused him were the most raw and painful to bear.

For him to be truly free of those painful memories, they would all need to be cleansed by the river.

He glanced at the clock on the wall. It was rapidly approaching four o'clock. He suddenly felt drained. He needed to sleep before he started work tomorrow.

Work.

It was no longer the joy it had once been. He had been happy employed as a sound technician at Castle Sounds, on Maid Marian Way in the city. He had started working there straight from school, doing what he loved above everything else. It had been a privilege to work alongside rock musicians every day. Listening to the wonderful sounds from the drums and the lead and bass guitars. Using his skills to make those sounds even clearer, sharper, more precise. He loved his job and had been extremely good at it. That was why it had been so damaging to him when he had been forced to leave.

One of the names on the list was solely responsible for him being forced out of Castle Sounds. The manager, Rex Poyser, had bullied him mercilessly, every day. Ridiculing the standard of his work, turning his colleagues against him, until he had been left with no option but to resign from the job he loved.

Stephen had learned later that shortly after he left his position, Poyser had employed his live-in girlfriend as the new sound technician.

Poyser would pay dearly for his actions.

He needed to be cleansed.

Work for Stephen Meadows was now extremely mundane. A simple, mind-numbing driving job delivering parcels. Every day was the same. He would drive the white Transit, with the red arrow logos on the side panels, along the same route from his home to East Midlands Airport.

He would then have a coffee in the staff canteen at the Red Arrow Couriers depot with the other drivers before loading the van with forty to fifty parcels. He would then spend the rest of the day driving to various locations around the county, dropping off parcels. As soon as the van was empty, and the last parcel had been delivered, he would head for home.

The thoughts of his mundane work depressed him. To take his mind off work, he began concentrating on the names on his list.

He had no intention of delaying; he would locate the first

person on the list in the next day or so. He knew he would have some amateur detective work to do first. Once she had been located, he would then work out the best way to snatch her up and prepare her for cleansing.

It was going to be no easy task to locate and abduct the abominable Sarah Milfoyle.

There was one other thing he felt he needed to do before starting to exact his revenge.

As soon as he finished work tomorrow, he would visit the Oaks at West Bridgford. It was time for him to make peace with his sister, Dawn.

12

3.00 pm, 11 June 1987
The Oaks Residential Care Home, West Bridgford, Nottingham

The nurses at the care home had been surprised to see Stephen Meadows. They had welcomed him and given him a positive update on the condition of his sister, Dawn.

The feelings of guilt had weighed heavily on him as he had driven his delivery van down the long driveway to the home.

The property had once been the grand country house of a Lancastrian mill owner who had made a fortune in the woollen textile industry. The grounds and the surrounding gardens were still impeccably maintained. His parents had taken out a bespoke insurance policy that would provide care for Dawn in the event of their death.

The thought of that insurance policy went a small way to assuage some of the guilty feelings felt so acutely by Stephen.

His parents must have known that he would be unable to care properly for Dawn in the same way they had all her life. That was why they had taken out the policy.

The nurse who had given Stephen the update on his sister's condition had then escorted him through the vast home to his sister's private rooms.

After the nurse had left the siblings alone in the room, Stephen had sat quietly in a chair, just staring at his sister.

She was asleep, sitting up in her custom-built wheelchair. On good days, she had some mobility, but these had become less and less over the years. Most of her time was now spent either in the wheelchair or in bed.

Stephen noticed a trickle of saliva escape from the side of Dawn's mouth and start to roll down her chin. He stood up and stepped forward. Grabbing a tissue from the box on her bedside cupboard, he tenderly wiped the spittle from his sister's face.

He saw her eyes flicker once before they opened.

He could see there was recognition in her expression. He smiled at her and said tenderly, 'Hello, Dawny.'

Today wasn't a good day; Dawn could only respond with several grunts. She became animated in the chair, tensing and untensing her muscles.

He leaned forward and put his arms around her. He held her close and whispered, 'I'm sorry you had to come here. I'm going to make them all pay for what they've done to us.'

He kissed her once on the cheek and said, 'I'll come back and see you soon, Dawn.'

13

4.00 pm, 10 June 1987
City Hospital Mortuary, Nottingham

The decomposing, bloated body of Suzy Flowers lay on the stainless-steel bench in the centre of the room. The examination room at the Nottingham City Hospital mortuary was a cold, stark environment. The walls were painted brilliant white; the floor tiles were a dark grey. The overhead strip lighting had an unrelenting brightness that caused Danny to squint when he first walked in.

Seamus Carter and his assistant, Stephanie were already standing by the side of the bench.

As Danny and Tina walked towards the bench, Seamus said, 'I would advise you not to get too close for this one.'

Danny knew exactly what he meant. He had attended the post-mortem examinations of drowning victims in the past and knew what to expect. Now that the body had been out of the water for several hours, the level of decay – and the smell that went with it – was all too evident. The waxy white flesh on the cadaver had the faintest green tinge. The fragile skin had begun to pare back where the divers had grabbed arms and legs during their struggle to recover the body from the riverbed.

The smell from the putrefying flesh was already starting to seep beyond the Vicks vapour rub that Danny had placed beneath each nostril. As he breathed in again, he involuntarily took a step back away from the bench.

The only other people in the examination room were Tim Donnelly, from the scenes of crime department, and DC Jeff Williams, who was performing the role of exhibits officer.

Seamus said, 'I think we're all here now. Let's make a start, shall we?'

Danny nodded. 'Whenever you're ready.'

The pathologist stroked his bushy beard as he made his visual inspection. He spoke aloud into a Dictaphone as he walked around the examination bench. He paid attention to the lower legs and pointed out the areas where the putrefying skin had started to come away, stating for the recording device that this was as a result of the diver's actions and where the chains had been removed. He said to his assistant and Tim Donnelly, 'You both need to get some photographs of this area. Although they look like injuries, it's just where the degraded skin and flesh has pared away from the underlying skeleton. All these marks are as a result of the heavy chains that were attached.'

He described the woman physically and continued to make comments as he made his visual inspection: 'The deceased is a white female, age approximately twenty to twenty-five years. Well nourished, slightly overweight, approximately five feet three inches tall. Heavily tattooed, with several piercings in her ears, nose and nipples. Externally, I can't see any obvious injuries that could have caused this young woman's death.'

Danny said, 'Before you start your examination proper, I would like Tim to get photographs of each of her tattoos and piercings. These could help us to identify her.'

Seamus nodded. 'No problem. Take as long as you need, Tim.'

He turned to Stephanie and said, 'We'll need to be incredibly careful how we move her. After the amount of time she has spent in the river, the structure of the skin and underlying tissue is very poor.'

As Tim busied himself getting the photographs, Tina said, 'Do you have any more thoughts on exactly how long she's been immersed in the water?'

The big pathologist looked thoughtful for a moment. 'I would stick with my first impression on the riverbank. I think around a week.'

With the photographs all taken, Seamus started the internal examination. He paid close attention to the lungs and the brain, taking samples as he worked.

As he neared completion of the examination, he said, 'Okay. The cause of death is drowning. She was alive and fully conscious when she went in the water. Whoever did this knew there would only be one outcome. There was no way she could have freed herself from those chains.'

'So definitely murder?' said Tina.

'Oh yes. There are marks around her wrists that were hard to spot because of the water damage to the skin. These show that she was bound for quite a length of time before her death.'

Danny said, 'Will you be able to get fingerprints?'

'It will be tricky, but I'm sure we can. My assistant, Stephanie, is an expert at obtaining latent prints. She seems to have a much gentler touch than I do.'

'I'm just thinking about identification, Seamus. What about dental records?'

'We can sort that out as well. It will have to be done by X-ray, but we can do it.'

'That's great. When can you let me have your report?'

'I think we'll be quite late finishing up here, getting the samples for toxicology, fingerprints and the dental work you want. Can I say sometime tomorrow afternoon?'

'That's great. Thanks.'

Danny turned to Jeff Williams. 'I'm sorry, Jeff, looks like being a late finish for you as well.'

Jeff said, 'No problem, boss.'

Danny and Tina left the examination room and made their way through the hospital. Neither spoke as they walked along the busy corridors. Both detectives allowed themselves time to process what they had just witnessed. It was only when they finally got into the car that Danny said, 'First impressions?'

'My first impression is that whoever did this has an inner rage. He wanted that woman to suffer. It's not a rage that manifests itself in physical violence; otherwise there would have been a lot more injuries. This is a very cold and calculating individual.'

'And how do you propose we catch this individual?'

'I think whoever did this knew her in one way or another.'

'So, priority enquiries?'

'First and foremost, identification. We need to find out who she is as soon as we can. We need to try to find any witnesses at the deposition site. CCTV? Missing persons files?'

'Okay, let's get back and start getting the teams organised. It's been quite a first day, Tina.'

14

6.00 pm, 10 June 1987
MCIU Offices, Mansfield, Nottinghamshire

The main briefing room at the MCIU offices was packed. Rob had already gathered the team for the debrief.

Danny and Tina walked in and joined Rob at the front of the room.

Danny said, 'Firstly, I want to introduce you all to Detective Inspector Tina Cartwright. Most of you will remember Tina from the time she spent here as a sergeant. Tina will be taking over the everyday command of Brian Hopkirk's team. So, any problems or issues you may have, from now on, you take them directly to her.'

Tina scanned the room and found the smiling face of DC Rachel Moore.

Danny said, 'Right. Let's get down to business. The enquiry into the body found in the River Trent at Gunthorpe this morning is to be treated as a murder enquiry. The circumstances were such that it was always going to be so, but Seamus Carter has just confirmed it at the post-mortem.'

Danny turned to Tina. 'Perhaps you could give the team a general overview of the enquiry so far?'

Tina took a deep breath and said, 'The naked body of a white female in her early twenties was found by our Underwater Search Unit this morning. She was in the river immediately below Gunthorpe Bridge. All indications point to her being put in the river between a week and ten days ago. When the woman's body was recovered, it became obvious that she had been weighted down by chains secured to her lower legs. These chains were large, linked, and very heavy. There is an unusual blue paint on the links.'

Tina paused and waited to see if anyone wished to make a comment. When the room remained silent, she carried on. 'I've just come back from the post-mortem. The pathologist has confirmed that the cause of death was drowning. More significant was his confirmation that this young woman was still alive and fully conscious when she was thrown from the bridge into the river. The divers are of the opinion that she has remained in one place due to the weight of the chains. This is important because it means she was thrown into the river from the centre of Gunthorpe Bridge.'

Danny said, 'Thank you. Right, everyone. Our top priority is to identify this young woman as soon as we can. Rob, I want you to delegate three detectives to start trawling through missing persons reports. Tina will give you a full description of the woman, and there will be photographs from the post-mortem to assist in this. Tim Donnelly has assured me those albums will be ready by morning. We may get lucky and achieve an identification through fingerprints or dental records, but I don't want to waste time if they come back negative. Start the misper enquiries within force, and gradually work out to surrounding forces.'

Rob nodded. 'I'll get that started this evening.'

Danny turned to DC Helen Bailey. 'I'd like you to concentrate fully on any CCTV that may be available. I know the deposition site is in a rural setting, but there may be traffic cameras in the area. Check the main roads around Gunthorpe and Lowdham for vehicles seen during the hours of darkness, either approaching or leaving the direction of the bridge. I think it's a fair bet to say this was done after licensing hours, as the Unicorn pub overlooks the river at the deposition site.'

Helen said, 'I'll have a drive over to the bridge this evening, while it's still light, and start jotting down some possibles.'

'Thanks.'

Danny turned to Tina. 'We'll have a chat about a possible press release and setting up a vehicle checkpoint near Gunthorpe Bridge in the next few days. We need to see if we can turn up any witnesses.'

Addressing the room, he said, 'Okay, everyone, let's get started. Let's find out who this young woman was as soon as we can, please.'

15

6.00 pm, 10 June 1987
Dale Lane, Blidworth, Nottinghamshire

He had waited patiently outside the telephone box on Dale Lane at Blidworth for at least ten minutes. The fat woman inside had been chatting for ages. Her high-pitched, shrill voice could still be clearly heard across the street. He thought to himself, *Hurry up, you gobby cow!*

He stayed hidden behind a dirty, flatbed truck that had been parked on the grass verge by builders working on the house opposite. It was vital that the mouthy woman didn't see him waiting to use the public telephone.

Eventually, she finished her call and pressed the button to return the coins she hadn't used. From the cover of the truck, he watched as the grossly overweight woman waddled away from the red phone box.

From the cover of the truck, he glanced around the street. Satisfied that nobody else was in the vicinity, he crossed the road and stepped inside the phone box. Using a handkerchief, he lifted the receiver and used a pencil to dial the emergency three nines system.

After a couple of seconds, a woman's voice came on the line: 'Emergency. Which service do you require?'

He put on a panicked voice: 'Fire brigade! There's a house on fire! Appleton Road at Blidworth!'

Calmly, the operator said, 'Did you say Appleton Road, Blidworth?'

'Yes. You need to hurry.'

'The fire brigade have been alerted and are on their way. Can you give me your name, please?'

He slammed the telephone down on the cradle and stepped out of the telephone box. He ran the fifty yards from the phone box to the junction of Dale Lane and Park Avenue. There was a wooden bench at that location. The bench had a brass memorial plaque on the back, commemorating the life of Councillor Agnes Fraser, whoever she was.

Not really caring who had provided the bench, he sat down and looked at his watch. It was exactly six o'clock.

In the distance, he could hear the blaring two-tone sirens approaching.

There was no house fire. He had made the emergency call to test how long it would take the first fire engines to arrive. He knew the nearest fire station was in the nearby market town of Mansfield.

He heard the roar of diesel motors and saw the first fire engine turn onto Dale Lane from Mansfield Road, quickly followed by a second.

He stared at the grim faces of the firemen inside the appliances as they were driven at speed from Dale Lane onto

Park Avenue. The driver of the second appliance revved the engine loudly as he changed gear to negotiate the sharp bend. A cloud of black diesel fumes belched from the exhaust as the powerful engine propelled the appliance up the hill, towards Appleton Road.

He glanced at his watch; it was now twelve minutes past six.

It had taken twelve minutes for the fire engines to arrive. Taking account of the traffic at this time of day, he took off three minutes. He planned to make the fire engines do a similar journey in the dead of night, when there would be little or no traffic to slow them down.

He settled on nine minutes.

That would be the length of time it took the fire brigade to travel from Mansfield to Blidworth after somebody had reported the fire he intended to start.

As he sauntered back along Dale Lane towards Mansfield Road, the fire engines swept by again. He imagined the disgruntled firemen inside, cursing the idiot who had called them out to a false alarm.

He watched as they sped away.

Beginning the long walk back to his home in the neighbouring village of Rainworth, his mind drifted to his next move. It was time for him to get serious. Grass fires and dustbin fires had been great at first, but he found them tiresome now. It was time for him to unleash the beast in a far more spectacular way. The next fire he set would be a building of some sort.

He daydreamed about what sort of property that would be. Maybe a factory unit or someone's house. He would continue his search around the village. When he saw the perfect property, he would know immediately.

His head was buzzing with excitement as he thought

about the firemen tackling the blaze he intended to start. This time, he intended to stay close enough to see the action.

The darkness of night would be his friend and conceal him.

16

6.30 am, 11 June 1987
Mansfield, Nottinghamshire

'I'm sorry, sweetheart. Did she wake you?'

Danny turned to his wife and grinned. 'Do you mean now or at three o'clock this morning?'

'I meant now; I saw you stirring earlier when she needed her feed.'

'Don't worry, Sue, it's what babies do. They can't tell us if they want feeding or their nappies changing. They just wail.'

'Well, mister, talking of nappies, your daughter's ready for hers to be changed. Can you oblige while I make us both a coffee?'

Danny took his five-month-old daughter from her mother's arms and began making baby noises to soothe her. It still felt alien to him, holding this tiny vulnerable person in his big hands. At least he had got beyond the stage where he thought she would break every time he picked her up.

He quickly changed her nappy, and with a clean bottom and a full tummy, Hayley soon began to feel heavier in his rocking arms.

Danny walked over to Sue and whispered, 'Has she dropped off?'

Sue nodded and whispered back, 'Pass her to me, and I'll put her down. She looks fast asleep.'

Danny said quietly, 'I'll do it.'

He walked over to the carry cot in the lounge and gently placed Hayley inside. He put a soft blanket over her and watched as she gently sucked on her bottom lip for a few seconds before settling completely.

He walked back into the kitchen and sat down next to Sue at the breakfast table.

Sue took a sip of her weak, decaffeinated coffee and said, 'Ah, peace at last.'

Danny took his wife's hand and said, 'Are you okay? Are you getting enough rest?'

'I'm fine, sweetheart. I get my head down when she does.'

He glanced at the carry cot. 'She's so beautiful. I could stare at her all day.'

'What do you expect? She takes after her mother.'

'I can't argue with that.'

Sue smiled. 'No, you'd better not, either.'

She took another sip of her drink and asked, 'Have you got a busy day?'

'It's going to be full on today. A woman's body was found in the river yesterday. It was pretty clear from the outset that she'd been murdered.'

'That's awful; the poor woman.'

'I've other news as well.'

Sue looked intrigued. 'Go on.'

'I've finally been allocated a replacement for Brian.'

Sue looked worried before saying, 'And?'

'Don't look so worried. It's all good. The new detective inspector is Tina Prowse, who worked with us before. Well, she's Tina Cartwright now. She got married recently.'

'Yes. I remember her – blonde hair, petite, very smart.' Sue chuckled before continuing. 'Isn't she one of those Bramshill flyers that you're always moaning about?'

Danny grinned. 'Yeah, she's been on the accelerated promotion course, but I won't hold that against her. Seriously, she's perfect for the Unit. She's extremely hard-working, smart as a whip – and most importantly, she isn't going to be a spy for Adrian Potter.'

'Does that mean you might start smiling a bit more now? I haven't seen much of that lately.'

Danny gulped the last of his coffee, winked and said, 'I can't promise that, sweetheart. I'd better get to work. We can't have the boss being late, can we?'

'That'll be the day, Chief Inspector. Be careful.'

Danny blew a kiss towards his baby daughter fast asleep in the carry cot, then bent over and kissed his wife. 'See you later, sweetheart. I shouldn't be too late.'

17

8.30 am, 11 June 1987
Minster School, Southwell, Nottinghamshire

Stephen Meadows was feeling lucky.

He had expected it to be a difficult task trying to locate Sarah Milfoyle. He knew very little about the teacher who had made his life a misery throughout his school days.

He had driven to the Minster School at Southwell in his Red Arrow Couriers delivery van. It was his intention to say that he had a parcel on the van for her, but the label that had her home address on had been spoiled. He was going to spin a story to the school secretary that he knew she had been a teacher at the school, as he was an old pupil, and he wondered if the school had an address for her.

As he drove to the school, he had been forced to admit that it was a pathetic plan.

Luckily for him, it was a plan he would never have to use.

As he drove his Transit van into the school's car park, he saw the target of his pent-up hatred getting out of a red Mini with a white roof.

He was puzzled. He thought she had retired years ago.

Sitting in his van, he stared through the windscreen at the woman. It was her, alright. There was no mistaking Sarah Milfoyle.

The same unruly mess of wispy, ginger hair, which had been put up in a messy bun. The wire-rimmed spectacles, perched on the end of her pointed, ratlike nose. The same garish, bright red lipstick that bled into the lines on her top lip.

She was even dressed how he remembered her. Still wearing a scruffy two-piece tweed suit that was stretched tightly over the bulges of fat around her waist.

Just looking at her again made him feel nauseous.

He didn't want her to see him, but he needed to make sure she was here for the day. He got out of his van and walked behind her, avoiding eye contact. He followed her as far as the main doors of the school. He stopped outside the open doors and listened as Sarah Milfoyle engaged the school secretary in idle chat.

In that familiar whining voice that he had grown to despise, he heard her say, 'Good morning, Mavis. It's going to be another lovely day.'

The school secretary smiled and said, 'It's far too nice to be in school all day, Ms Milfoyle.'

'Very true, my dear. I'll be finishing at three o'clock today, and hopefully the sun will still be shining.'

'Let's hope so. Enjoy your day.'

There was a heavy sigh before the teacher replied, 'I doubt I'll be enjoying my day much. I'm teaching English literature to 3B all day. I declare, there isn't a brain cell among them!'

She chuckled at her own witty aside as she walked into the school.

Stephen Meadows had heard enough; he would be back in the school car park at three o'clock, ready to follow the little red Mini. He needed to establish where Sarah Milfoyle was living.

He smiled as he walked back to his delivery van. Today was turning out to be an exceptionally good day.

18

3.00 pm, 11 June 1987
Sherwood Avenue, Blidworth, Nottinghamshire

He felt elated and excited.

After wandering the streets of Blidworth village for hours, he had finally found the perfect place. It was the last building on Sherwood Avenue, a street on the outskirts of the small mining community. The property he had selected was a semi-detached house, with smashed windows and an overgrown front garden.

The property obviously hadn't been occupied for years. Paint was peeling from the window frames, and there were gaping holes in the roof where tiles had slipped and never been replaced.

He couldn't believe he'd never noticed the property before. It was perfect for him to step up to the next level and set a fire that was something bigger than yet another field of dry grass or a waste bin.

He took one last look around to make sure nobody was watching him before slipping through the small rusting gate into the front garden. Once through the gate, he was hidden from view by the large unpruned bushes in the front garden. He pushed through the thick bushes to the rear of the house.

He couldn't believe his luck. The only barrier between the back garden and the open farmland behind the property was a small wooden fence that was in a state of disrepair. The dilapidated fence really offered no barrier at all. He made his way to the back of the house and tried the back door. It was locked.

Every pane of glass in the windows at the rear of the house had been smashed. Taking care not to cut himself, he began to remove shards of glass from one of the kitchen windows. He chose a window that would be big enough for him to climb through once the dangerous pointed glass that remained in the frame had been removed.

He took out each individual piece and laid it down on the overgrown lawn. As soon as the opening was free of glass, he manoeuvred himself through the space and into the building. It was a squeeze, but not too bad.

Once inside, he waited. He strained to hear any noises emanating from deeper within the building.

There was nothing.

He found himself in what had once been the kitchen. Only the rusting sink unit gave its previous role away. There were no cupboards or appliances left in the room. The linoleum floor was wet. Puddles still lay where previous rainfall had worked its way in through the broken windows.

He sniffed the air and wrinkled his nose. The building reeked of damp and decay. There were no interior doors left in the property. They had all been stolen soon after the building had become unoccupied.

With a growing sense of excitement, he made his way

through the building. The damp was causing the wallpaper in every room to peel from the walls, and the floorboards creaked beneath his weight. Fearing they might be rotten, he moved to the edge of the rooms and sidled his way around, keeping his back to the walls.

After checking the rooms downstairs, he made his way up the staircase.

The bedroom walls were covered in black mould caused by water that had penetrated the leaks in the roof. There were still one or two pieces of abandoned bedroom furniture too decrepit to be of use to anyone.

The entire building felt damp. The walls were sodden; the threadbare carpets that had been left in the bedrooms squelched underfoot.

As he made his way back down the stairs, he was deep in thought. He knew that matches and newspaper would not be enough to release the beast in these damp conditions.

He would need an accelerant to start the fire.

The green plastic petrol can in the garage at home was three-quarters full of fuel. He would need to bring that with him later. Having examined the building, he knew the best place to set the fire would be beneath the wooden staircase. It was the one location that contained dry, flammable material. The staircase was made of wood, and the carpet that covered the stairs was the driest in the house. He knew it was the only place in the entire house where a fire would take hold.

Firelighters and rags soaked in petrol left in that area would burn fast and set light to the carpet. There was a good chance that as the fire became bigger, and the heat more intense, it would then spread through the damp house.

He felt a surge of excitement beginning to course through his body as he thought about what the night would bring.

With a broad smile on his face, he slipped back out of the same window he had entered by. He stopped by the wall for a few minutes. As soon as he was sure he wasn't being watched, he ran down the overgrown back garden and climbed the rickety fence onto the farmland.

It was a half-hour walk through the ripening barley crop back to Rainworth.

He would return to the house later, under the cover of darkness.

It was time to take his obsession to the next level.

19

3.30 pm, 11 June 1987
MCIU Offices, Mansfield, Nottinghamshire

Danny and Tina were sitting in Danny's office, discussing the content of the press appeal they had planned. They were hoping that by heightening the public's awareness, they would locate possible witnesses and generate new lines of enquiry into the murder of the unknown woman at Gunthorpe Bridge.

There was an urgent knock at the door.

Danny shouted, 'Come in!'

DC Jeff Williams walked in and closed the door behind him. 'You need to hear this, sir.'

'Go on.'

'I took the fingerprints obtained by Seamus Carter's assistant to the fingerprint department for comparison before I went off duty last night. They promised me they would do the job as a top priority. They've just phoned. We have an identical match.'

'That's brilliant, good work.'

'The dead woman is Suzy Flowers. She was arrested for a public order offence and assault last year. Apparently, as she was being detained, she slapped the arresting policewoman across the face. She was charged, and her fingerprints taken. The address she gave at the time of her arrest was in Salford, Manchester. I've made a check on the voters register, and the only person listed for that address is Mavis Flowers.'

'Thanks, Jeff. I want you to find DI Buxton. Give him my regards and tell him to get his team who were working on the missing persons reports to start finding out everything we can about Suzy Flowers.'

DC Williams nodded and left the office.

As the door closed, Danny turned to Tina and said, 'This is a massive breakthrough. I didn't expect us to identify the victim so soon. While we concentrate on researching Suzy Flowers here, I want you and Rachel to travel up to Manchester this evening. If Mavis Flowers is our victim's next of kin, we need to notify her sooner rather than later.'

'Will do.'

'Take your time with the relatives, Tina. It's a tricky tightrope that we all have to walk. You'll need to be sympathetic to their loss, but at the same time, ensure you get all the information they can give you about Suzy.'

'Will do.'

20

3.30 pm, 11 June 1987
Minster School, Southwell, Nottinghamshire

Sarah Milfoyle was raging.

Twenty minutes she had been kept waiting in that stuffy classroom.

Waiting patiently for that ignoramus to apologise for his unruly conduct in her lesson. The boy was just one of many in that class who had little or no respect for authority.

Well, Nick Towle wouldn't get away with it in her lesson, not while ever she was in charge.

She had made the thirteen-year-old stand with his hands on his head, facing the corner of the classroom, until he had muttered an apology for his disruptive behaviour. Deep down, she knew that the little shit would still behave the same way tomorrow and the day after.

Towle was a lost cause as far as schooling was concerned.

His life would never amount to anything; education was wasted on him.

It was the realisation that all she had really achieved was to make herself twenty minutes late finishing work that was contributing to her already foul mood.

As she walked out of the main doors of the school, the secretary bade her a pleasant afternoon. Sarah Milfoyle begrudgingly acknowledged her, answering only with a barely audible grunt. She marched up the driveway and stomped towards the car park. With every step she took, she wondered why the hell she had agreed to come back as a locum teacher.

The answer was a simple one.

Sarah Milfoyle had been retired for four years and had found herself bored beyond belief. The novel she had always promised to write in her retirement had proved to be an elusive, impossible dream. So, when the opportunity arose to resume work as a supply teacher, to cover sickness and maternity leave, she had – with some reluctance – agreed.

Although she had reservations, she had been grateful for the approach made by the headmaster of the Minster School. Days like today made her doubt the sanity of her decision.

Having reached her red Mini, she got in and slammed the door.

She needed to get home. She could then make herself a nice cup of tea, settle down in her beautiful back garden, and enjoy what was left of the afternoon sunshine.

As she started the car, she thought to herself, *To hell with Nick Towle, and to hell with the Minster School.* She selected first gear and accelerated out of the car park.

Sarah Milfoyle had always been a bad driver, with little consideration for other road users. Today was no different. She drove straight out of the school driveway onto the road, causing an articulated lorry to brake hard to avoid a collision.

She drove away from the school at speed, totally unaware of the curses shouted after her by the lorry driver, who had narrowly avoided a disastrous collision.

She was also oblivious to the white Ford Transit van that was following her along the winding country lanes.

It was a ten-minute drive along the B6386, from the Minster School at Southwell to her small cottage on Blind Lane, in the picturesque village of Oxton.

Without any indication, she suddenly swerved her Mini from the B6386 onto Blind Lane. Two hundred yards behind her, the Ford Transit mirrored her manoeuvre.

Stephen Meadows drove slower onto Blind Lane, purposefully hanging back so he could just keep the Mini in sight. Once again, without any indication, the brake lights lit up on the small red car as it was driven from Blind Lane through a set of open wooden gates onto a wide gravel driveway.

Meadows stopped his van opposite the entrance. He watched as the Mini was brought skidding to a halt on the gravel outside the secluded stone cottage.

The cottage was one of the last properties on Blind Lane. It stood alone, fifty yards before the entrance to the Green Dragon public house.

He watched as Sarah Milfoyle got out of her car and walked to the front door. He saw her use a key to access the cottage. The driveway led to a large turning circle that was also made up of loose pea gravel.

He was still unsure if Milfoyle lived in the cottage on her own. Other than the fact she was a teacher, Meadows didn't know anything about the overweight, middle-aged woman who had made his school days a misery.

He sat in the van with the engine running. He closed his eyes, and a plan began to formulate in his mind.

Blind Lane was deserted. The pub at the end of the lane was closed, and there was nobody about.

Horrendous images of his school days flashed into his mind.

He could hear Milfoyle's strident voice ordering him to stand and read aloud in front of the class. She knew all about his bad stammer, but relished the chance to ridicule him at every opportunity. She even made him repeat the passages that accentuated his stammer.

On one occasion, as he read aloud from the Herman Melville classic *Moby Dick*, she had referred to him as 'Stuttering Steve', in front of all his classmates. As a result of that one insensitive remark, from that day on, every pupil in the Minster School referred to Meadows as 'Stuttering Steve'.

The thought of those torturous lessons, being forced to read aloud and subsequently falling victim to the ridicule caused by his stammer, sent a shudder through his body.

He began to experience similar feelings to those he had felt when he'd run from the laughter outside Rock City.

That feeling grew and grew until suddenly he opened his eyes. He selected first gear and drove his van purposefully through the open gates and down the gravel driveway towards Milfoyle's cottage. He manoeuvred the vehicle so the sliding side door was facing the front door of the cottage.

He jumped out of the van and knocked loudly on the heavy wooden door.

A woman's voice shouted, 'Just a minute!'

He recognised the shrill tone of the voice.

The heavy door was flung open, and Sarah Milfoyle stood facing him. He was tongue-tied for a second, and with an arrogant, impatient tone, she snapped, 'Well, don't just stand there with that gormless expression on your face! What do you want?'

Galvanised by her rudeness, he said, 'P-p-parcel for M-m-milfoyle.'

'That's me. I'm Sarah Milfoyle.'

'It's heavy. Is there anyone at home who c-c-could help me g-g-get it out of the van?'

With a growing sense of irritation, she said, 'No! There's nobody here but me. Can't you manage it? That's what you get paid for!'

Meadows' heart was racing. He knew what he had to do.

He said, 'If you c-c-could just g-g-give me a hand, p-p-please?'

She stomped forward, muttering under her breath, 'This is ridiculous! I'll be writing in a complaint to your company.'

He opened the sliding door on the side of the van. As she looked at the mass of parcels on the floor, she failed to notice the delivery driver step behind her.

Seizing his moment, Meadows punched her hard on the back of the head. The force of the heavy blow knocked her unconscious, and she fell face first into the van, landing in a heap on the parcels. He immediately stepped forward, scooped up her legs and shoved her bodily into the van. She was sent sprawling over the unopened parcels, her tight tweed skirt riding up over her thighs.

He reached inside his jacket and grabbed two plastic cable ties, quickly securing her wrists and ankles.

He slammed the side door of the van shut and walked towards the open front door of the cottage. He rolled the sleeve of his sweatshirt down until it covered his hand, then slid his covered hand into the letterbox and used it to pull the heavy door shut. He heard it close and lock on the Yale latch.

He walked slowly back to the van, looking around to see if there was anybody watching him. He got in and drove the vehicle slowly down the driveway; he was relieved that as his vehicle emerged onto Blind Lane, there were no other vehicles on the road, and no pedestrians on the narrow footpath. He was less than fifteen minutes away from his home at Lowdham.

As he drove away from the cottage at Oxton, he realised that he felt none of the conflict he'd experienced when he abducted Suzy Flowers. This time, everything felt right.

He felt strong. He felt empowered.

He knew those feelings would continue to grow within him after the cleansing of Sarah Milfoyle.

21

8.00 pm, 11 June 1987
Highfield Road, Salford, Manchester

'What number was it, Rachel?'

'It's number twenty-five. I think it's the one over there, with the red door.'

Tina Cartwright glanced across the narrow street at the terraced housing. 'I see it. Pull up outside, and we'll see if anyone's home.'

Rachel parked the CID car outside the house and switched off the engine. She turned to Tina. 'I always hate this part of the job. It doesn't matter how many times I do it, I'll never get used to it.'

Tina nodded. 'Me too. Come on, let's get it done.'

Both detectives got out of the car and stood outside the front door. Tina grabbed the black, ornamental knocker and rapped loudly on the front door.

A woman's voice shouted from inside, 'Just a minute.'

The door was opened by a woman in her mid-fifties. Her grey hair was in curlers under a sheer, lilac-coloured headscarf. She was quite short, and her plump figure strained against a tight, flowery housecoat.

Tina said, 'Hello, I'm Detective Inspector Cartwright, and this is Detective Constable Moore from Nottingham CID. We're looking for Mavis Flowers.'

A worried expression replaced the warm smile that had first greeted the detectives. 'I'm Mavis Flowers. You said Nottingham. Is this something to do with my daughter?'

Tina nodded. 'May we come in, please?'

Mavis Flowers nodded and said, 'Of course.'

The two detectives were shown into a small lounge at the front of the two-up-two-down terraced property.

Tina said, 'Mrs Flowers, is the daughter you mentioned Suzy?'

'Yes, what's happened? Is she alright?'

'I'm deeply sorry to have to tell you this. Suzy has been found dead in Nottingham.'

Mavis sat down heavily on the settee as the shock of what she was hearing hit her.

Rachel sat down beside the distraught woman. She said, 'We're so sorry, Mrs Flowers. Is there anyone else here with you?'

'No, lass, I live here on my own now. I lost my husband two years ago, and my son lives in Lincoln.'

'Is there a neighbour?'

'You could try the house next door, but one. My friend Betty lives at number twenty-nine.'

Rachel put an arm around the trembling woman and said, 'I'll go and see if Betty's at home. Tina will stay here with you.'

Rachel stood up and left the house.

Tina sat down opposite Mavis Flowers and said gently, 'I know it's terrible news for you to take in, but can you tell me why Suzy was in Nottingham?'

Shaking her head, the distraught woman said, 'I don't understand this at all. She's studying fashion at university down there. She's going to be a fashion designer.'

The realisation that she had spoken about her daughter as if she were still alive suddenly dawned on the older lady, and tears began to flow.

In between sobs, she asked, 'What happened, Detective? Was it an accident?'

'We think that somebody deliberately harmed Suzy.'

'You mean she was killed? Murdered?'

'I'm sorry, Mrs Flowers, but yes, we do.'

Rachel arrived with the neighbour, Betty, just as the floodgates opened and Mavis broke down completely.

Rachel had told Betty why the detectives were there. She sat down next to Mavis and put her arms around her friend to comfort her.

Tina asked, 'Would you like us to contact your son for you, Mrs Flowers?'

She sobbed a reply. 'Yes, please. His new address is in the notepad by the phone.'

Betty said, 'Her son's name's Geoff. He's a lecturer at the university in Lincoln.'

Rachel picked up the notepad in the hallway and flicked through the pages of numbers. She found the entry for Geoff Flowers and noted down the address and telephone number.

Tina said, 'We'll get the police in Lincoln to go and see your son. They'll deliver the news in person, not over the telephone.'

Rachel said, 'I know this is all a massive shock, Mavis. Do

you feel up to answering a few questions about Suzy? If you can, it will really help us.'

Without looking up, Mavis nodded. 'I'll try, love.'

Rachel said, 'What's the name of the university where Suzy was studying?'

'Nottingham Trent, I think.'

'Do you have Suzy's address in Nottingham?'

'She was living in a bedsit; the address is in the same notepad, sweetie.'

'How long has she been at the university?'

'Just over a year now. She loves it. Loved it, sorry.'

Once again, the tears came. Rachel realised the questions would soon have to stop.

'Do you know the names of any friends she had made, or if she had a boyfriend?'

'Our Suzy never made many friends. She was always different, and that puts most people off.'

'Any boyfriend that she spoke to you about?'

Mavis shook her head. Rachel could see the woman's body juddering as the shock of the news took hold. She knew the questioning had to stop; she said, 'We're going to leave you with Betty now. I'll leave you our names and contact numbers. If you have any questions later, don't hesitate to call either of us, at any time. Okay?'

Without looking up, Mavis Flowers nodded.

Tina said, 'We'll contact Geoff tonight and ask him to call you straight away.'

Mavis mumbled, 'Thanks, lass. I'll be okay. Betty's here; she'll stay with me.'

Rachel made a note of the address in Nottingham where Suzy Flowers had been living up until just over a week ago, and the two detectives left the house.

As they got back in their car, Tina said, 'Let's find the nearest nick and make the phone call to Lincoln. I think it would be a good idea if we can get the son to come to Nottingham to make the formal identification, rather than that poor woman.'

Rachel nodded. 'I agree. I don't think Mavis should have to go through that ordeal. Let's hope the son agrees to do it.'

22

2.00 am, 12 June 1987
Sherwood Avenue, Blidworth, Nottinghamshire

He stood in the shadows, watching.

There had been no problems getting back into the derelict semi-detached house. He'd crawled through the same window into the kitchen he had used before. Once inside, he had waited and listened. The air was still; there wasn't a sound.

The house had felt even more damp and cold now that the frigid night air enveloped it. He had crept through the house until he reached the cupboard under the stairs. Once there, he balled up the sheets of newspaper he had secreted under his jacket. He made a small pile of paper and, on top of that, placed the old rags and cloths he had brought with him. He placed three barbeque firelighters at the bottom of the pile.

Finally, he had splashed petrol from the green plastic can

in the void under the stairs and all down the stair carpet. He knew that the heat from the burning petrol would soon make a difference to the cold air inside the house.

He checked his escape route one more time before igniting the slow-burning firelighters. The last thing he wanted to do was trap himself inside the building.

As soon as he was satisfied that all was well, he had stood in the darkness and struck a single match. The flame illuminated his face, his eyes sparkling with anticipation.

He bent forward and held the match below each of the firelighters, waiting for each one to catch before quickly stepping out from beneath the stairs.

No sooner had he emerged from the cupboard than the petrol vapours caught the flame, and the entire space below the stairs was engulfed in flame.

He smiled, then made his way through the house into the kitchen, where he climbed back out the window. He had planned to make his escape over the fields at the rear of the house, but something made him hang back. He wanted to make sure the house would be totally consumed by the beast.

Using the shadows, he made his way to the front of the house and hid in a neighbour's garden.

From his hiding place, he continued to watch the derelict semi-detached house.

For a few minutes, nothing happened. With rising excitement, he saw what he thought was a wisp of smoke emerging from one of the smashed windows at the front of the house. He could now see the first hint of an orange glow from within the house as the flames began to take hold of the wooden stairs. There were noises now – cracking and banging from within the derelict property.

With little warning, there was a very loud bang, and a hole appeared in the tiled roof. Flames started to lick through the opening.

As the fire took hold, and clay tiles started to crack and rain down from the roof, lights began to come on in the neighbouring houses.

Suddenly, a panicked scream filled the night air. It had come from the property attached to the derelict house. The flames had travelled swiftly through the adjoining attic space, and now the second property of the semi-detached build was also well alight. This house wasn't derelict, and it was occupied.

The upstairs windows of the second house cracked open. Given life by the sudden influx of air, huge flames erupted from within the bedrooms. The burning curtains flapped through the broken windows. He heard the voice of an old man shouting for help again.

He was obviously trapped inside one of those bedrooms, with no way of getting out.

From his hiding place in the garden, he heard footsteps running along the street. He then heard someone shout in a panicked voice, 'It's old Joe's house, it's on fire! Has anybody called the fire brigade?'

A different voice from across the street shouted, 'I've already called them. They're on the way.'

The first voice shouted back, 'Has anyone got a ladder?'

Before an answer came, there was an almighty bang, and the entire roof of the building – both sides of the semi-detached house – collapsed, sending a shower of sparks and smoke towards the heavens.

The crowds on the street watching the drama unfold grew bigger. He took the opportunity to sneak out from his hiding place and mingle with them. He remained at the back of the crowd, knowing that everyone's eyes would be focused on the burning houses in front of them. He inwardly rejoiced as the first fire engines arrived.

He watched as the fire crews raced around, getting ready

to enter the inferno and battle the flames. A police car and an ambulance also arrived on the street. Then the local press arrived and began taking photographs of the dramatic scenes.

Because he was standing behind everyone and out of sight, he allowed a broad smile to play across his lips. The beast he had unleashed was now raging through the two houses, devouring everything and everybody in its path.

Once again, he listened intently to the conversations of the people looking on around him. One woman sobbed, 'Poor Joe. He must be a goner.' Another woman answered, 'You never know, sweetheart. The firemen might get him out.'

A third, more assured voice said, 'He's got to be dead. That roof collapsing on his bedroom like that. The poor old sod wouldn't have stood a chance.'

He gloried at the power of the animal he had let loose, and slinked further into the shadows, to continue watching the unfolding drama.

23

2.40 am, 12 June 1987
Sherwood Avenue, Blidworth, Nottinghamshire

After concentrated and gallant efforts by the firemen in attendance, the fire had finally been brought under control.

Station Officer Sid Jackson was a worried man. There had been persons reported when they first arrived. None of his BA crews had found anyone alive.

As another pair of firemen left the building and were chalked off the tally board, Jackson approached them and said, 'Any sign of a casualty yet?'

One of the exhausted firemen said, 'I'm afraid so, boss. We've just located a body on the ground floor. He was wedged beneath a settee. I think he probably tried to hide from the flames under there. He's burnt from head to foot. I just hope he passed out from the smoke first.'

With a grim expression, Jackson said, 'Who's bringing the body out?'

'Our air was almost out. Tim and Dave have just gone back in with a body bag. They won't be long.'

The senior fireman made his way over to the police car that was parked on the street. The constable was standing outside the car, with his elbows resting on the roof, looking at the smouldering houses. In a low, even voice, Jackson said, 'We've located a body inside the right-hand side of the property. My men are in the process of bringing him out.'

The policeman replied, 'That house was owned by Joe Sinclair, a retired miner. He was seventy-odd years of age; he didn't deserve to go like that. The neighbouring house was derelict. I've spoken to a couple of people on the street, and they reckon the derelict house was alight first.'

'That doesn't sound good. There are any number of reasons why occupied houses catch fire; not so many for derelict ones. We could be looking at an arson. If we are, your lot could have a murder to investigate.'

'Right, sir. I'll inform our control room and get the CID to come out.'

Jackson allowed a disgusted look on his face and said, 'Can't you do something about those bloody vultures?'

He pointed across the street at the three press cameramen, who were busy taking photographs of the destruction.

Jackson continued, 'In a few minutes' time, my men are going to be bringing out a dead man in a body bag. I would prefer it if they didn't take fucking photographs of them doing it. Can't you get them to piss off?'

Stung into action, the young police officer strode across the street and said, 'That's enough photographs, gents. The fire brigade has recovered a body, and I don't want you taking photos as they bring him out. Have a little respect, please.'

The photographers all nodded and turned away from the burned houses. Instead, they began taking pictures of the anguished faces on the street, watching the dramatic scenes as they unfolded.

24

8.00 am, 12 June 1987
MCIU Offices, Mansfield, Nottinghamshire

Danny Flint sat in his office with Rob Buxton, discussing the fatal house fire at Blidworth.

Danny said, 'Scenes of crime have been at Blidworth all morning, working alongside the fire brigade's fire investigator.'

Rob said, 'I've never heard of a fire investigator.'

'No. It's a new initiative being trialled by the fire brigade. Tony Parrish was a station officer for twenty-odd years before he retired last month. The fire brigade's hoping that his expertise will enable us to investigate crimes of arson in a much more capable way.'

'Sounds like a bloody good idea.'

There was a knock on the door. Danny shouted, 'Come in.'

The door opened, and a short, stocky man with crew cut,

steel grey hair walked in. He was dressed in navy blue overalls, carried a clipboard, and reeked of smoke.

He said, 'Chief Inspector Flint, I'm Tony Parrish, the fire investigator.'

Danny stood up, shook hands with Parrish and said, 'Grab a seat, Tony. Can we get you a drink?'

'No, thanks, I've not long had a coffee. Please excuse the smell. The smoke and soot tend to stick to fabric. I'd prefer to get straight down to it and let you know what I've found at Sherwood Avenue this morning. The seat of last night's fatal fire was in the derelict property next door to the property occupied by your victim, Mr Sinclair. There's ample evidence to show that an accelerant was used to start the fire in the cupboard below the stairs. There's also evidence of petrol flash on the walls, where the staircase would have been. This flaring blackens the walls deeper. It's caused when the vapour from petrol ignites.'

'So it's definitely arson?'

'One hundred percent. Unfortunately, there was no wall between the loft spaces. So as soon as the fire took hold in the derelict property, it spread along the roof space, burning the wooden trusses and joists before moving down and taking hold in the upstairs rooms of the adjoining property. My guess is that because the occupied house was so much drier than the derelict one, the fire took hold quicker on that side, weakening all the remaining roof joists. Eventually, the entire roof collapsed, and the fire was unleashed throughout the rest of the property.'

'Bloody hell. So, do you think we could be looking at a murder enquiry?'

Tony Parrish said, 'I can't tell you how to do your job, Chief Inspector. What I can tell you is that the fire was started deliberately. Was it set with the intention of killing the old man? I don't know.'

Danny said, 'Thanks. Please call me Danny, okay? When can you let me have your written report, please?'

'Will do, Danny. I'll prepare a full report that will evidence my findings, and I can get it to you in the next day or so.'

'Have you ever seen anything similar?'

'I've seen plenty of similar scenes in business properties. Not so many in dwelling houses. It's a method usually employed by people torching properties to make false insurance claims.'

Danny turned to Rob and said, 'Find out who owns the derelict property. I want to know if anyone had a vested interest in burning it down. What time's the post-mortem for Joe Sinclair scheduled for?'

Rob replied, 'Will do. The post-mortem's booked for two o'clock this afternoon at the City Hospital.'

Danny was thoughtful, then said, 'I think we should treat this as a murder enquiry until the evidence shows something different. Tony, do you want to attend the post-mortem this afternoon?'

'If you don't mind, Danny. Throughout my service, I've seen a lot of burns victims. I might be able to spot something that doesn't look quite right.'

Danny said, 'Okay, that could be especially useful. We'll all travel down together this afternoon. Rob, tell Glen Lorimar to start looking at the two properties on Sherwood Avenue. By the time we get back from the hospital, I want to know who owns them, who their insurance companies are, and what policies are held on both dwellings.'

As Rob and Tony left the office, there was another knock on the door, and Tina Cartwright walked in.

Danny said, 'How did you get on in Manchester?'

Tina said, 'We arrived up there at eight o'clock. So, as it wasn't too late, I decided to try the address straight away. We spoke to Mavis Flowers, who lives alone at that address. Mavis is Suzy's mother.'

Danny looked worried. 'How did she take the news?'

'She was obviously terribly upset. Before we left, Rachel arranged for a neighbour, who's a good friend, to come and sit with her.'

'Is she travelling down to do the formal identification?'

'No. Mavis has a son, Geoff. He's Suzy's brother and a lecturer at Lincoln University. We arranged for the Lincoln police to go and deliver the death message to Geoff Flowers last night. He contacted his mother straight away after getting the news. After a brief chat, they've agreed it would be better if he made the formal identification. He's travelling over to see me this afternoon so we can do the formal identification.'

'That's good. It's probably better if he does it. What could Mavis Flowers tell you about her daughter?'

'The main thing was the reason why Suzy was in Nottingham. She was a student, studying fashion at Nottingham Trent University. I intend to start getting enquiry teams into the college today, to see if we can find people who knew Suzy. Mum said that Suzy didn't make friends easily, so we may not get too much from the university.'

'Any knowledge of a boyfriend?'

'Nothing.'

'That's good work. Keep me updated of any developments, please. The Suzy Flowers murder enquiry will be down to your team alone now. We had a fatal house fire at Blidworth last night that was arson, so Rob's team will be committed on that investigation.'

'No problem. I'll keep you informed of any progress.'

25

2.00 pm, 12 June 1987
City Hospital Mortuary, Nottingham

The bright white light of the examination room was in sharp contrast to the dark, sombre mood that lay heavily in the room.

The charred, blackened remains of Joe Sinclair lay on the sterile, stainless-steel bench. Glen Lorimar was poised, ready to perform the role of exhibits officer for the post-mortem. Danny Flint and Rob Buxton stood beside Tony Parrish on one side of the bench, ready to observe and make any relevant notes. A scenes of crime photographer took photographs of the deceased from all angles.

The body lay on its back in the classic pugilistic pose typical of burns victims. The only areas of the body that hadn't been touched by the flames were the legs below both knees. The flesh that remained there was scarlet red, contrasting sharply with the rest of the blackened remains.

The pathologist began her gruesome but essential task by doing a thorough external examination. When she had finished, she turned to Danny and said, 'I can't see any obvious marks of violence or ligature marks. The damage caused to the outer skin is extensive, but I would still expect to see telltale signs of ligature marks on the lower layers of the dermis.'

Danny nodded his head.

Forty-five minutes later, the post-mortem was nearing completion. As she finished, the pathologist said, 'The cause of death was asphyxia brought about by extensive smoke inhalation. This man was dead before the flames reached him. His brain had been starved of oxygen, and his vital organs had all shut down. All the burns you can see happened post-mortem.'

Tony Parrish muttered under his breath, 'Thank God for small mercies.'

Danny said to the pathologist, 'Have you got all the samples you need for a full toxicology report?'

'I have. I've also taken skin samples from both hands, requested by Mr Parrish, to test for any traces of an accelerant.'

Danny glanced at Tony Parrish with a questioning look.

Tony said, 'I've known arsonists to fall foul of their own insurance scams before. This will just help you to rule out Joe Sinclair as a suspect.'

Danny nodded. 'Okay, thanks.'

He then turned to the pathologist and said, 'How soon can you let me have your report?'

'I should be able to get it to you within the next couple of days. I don't think there will be anything in it you don't already know. This man died as a direct result of the fire at his home. I doubt the toxicology or skin samples will show anything different.'

Danny turned to Tony Parrish. 'Does it all appear that cut and dried to you?'

The arson investigator nodded. 'Yes. I'm afraid it does.'

26

11.45 pm, 12 June 1987
Ridge Hill, Lowdham, Nottinghamshire

Sarah Milfoyle felt like she had been strapped onto the hard wooden chair for an eternity. Her entire body ached, both from the cold and being immobile for so long.

When she had first regained consciousness and found herself bound and naked, in what looked like a music studio, she was at first unbelieving, then terrified. She replayed the events repeatedly in her mind.

The last thing she could remember was the imbecilic delivery driver asking her to help him carry a parcel from his van into the house.

She recalled being struck from behind, and that was it. When she had regained consciousness, she was in her current predicament and nursing a massive headache. She had shouted herself hoarse before accepting the fact that nobody could hear her anguished cries for help.

As the hours had dragged by, the inevitable happened. She could hold her bladder no longer and urinated where she sat. She had sobbed as she felt the warmth envelop her thighs.

Questions raced through her mind. *Who had done this to her? There was something familiar about the delivery driver? About the way he spoke, that annoying stutter?*

The answer came crashing into her brain. The delivery driver – her abductor – was Stuttering Steve. The dim schoolboy she had been unable to teach a thing when he was a pupil at her school.

As soon as she realised who had done this to her, the fear she had been feeling disappeared. Instead, she became angry and indignant. *How dare he?*

Her thoughts were banished by the sound of heavy footsteps approaching. The door burst open, and standing in front of her was Stephen Meadows.

She screamed at him, 'Meadows, you wretch! What the hell do you think you're doing?'

He stepped forward until he was barely an inch away from her face. Without raising his voice, he said one word: 'C-c-cleansing.'

Full of indignant rage, she screamed, 'What the hell are you talking about, you idiot? Untie me this instant.'

Meadows turned around and walked out of the room, returning minutes later with a length of heavy chain linking.

Sarah Milfoyle looked horrified at the chains. Realising that her bluster and shouting was having no effect, she changed tack.

In a subservient voice full of humility, she said, 'Come on, Stephen. Let's stop all this nonsense. I'm very cold, and I want to go home. I'm so sorry for what happened at school all those years ago. I didn't mean to cause you any harm.'

Meadows fixed her with a cold stare. He said quietly, 'And d-d-do you think there's b-b-been any?'

Milfoyle looked puzzled. 'Any what?'

'D-d-do you think there's b-b-been any harm?'

'I don't know, Stephen; I wouldn't have thought so.'

'You really d-d-don't have a c-c-clue how m-m-much of a m-m-misery you m-m-made life at school for me, d-d-do you?'

Ignoring his comment, she pressed on. 'Please, Stephen. Untie me; there's a good lad. Give me back my clothes. I'm an old lady. I shouldn't be sitting here like this. Don't worry. I promise I won't tell anyone what's happened.'

'I'm n-n-not worried at all. After your c-c-cleansing, I know you won't t-t-tell anyone.'

He stepped forward. 'I'm all d-d-done t-t-talking. It's t-t-time.'

'Time?'

Without speaking, he untied her from the seat. He then quickly bound her hands behind her back. She tried to struggle, but was too weak and ineffectual to prevent him doing what he wanted. He bound her knees and ankles together with thin cord, then began to wrap the heavy chains around her fat legs. He pulled the chain links tight, pinching her skin and making her yelp with pain.

She protested throughout, shouting at him to stop and to let her go.

Ignoring her protests, he finished binding the length of heavy chain, making sure it was secured tightly to her legs. He then lifted her bodily from the chair and hoisted her over his shoulder. She weighed a lot more than Suzy Flowers. The weight was nothing, though, for the immensely powerful Meadows.

Finally, Sarah Milfoyle stopped shouting.

The angry, demanding shouts had now been replaced by tearful, frightened sobbing. Between the sobs, she asked, 'Where are you taking me?'

As he threw her down into the back of the Transit van, he growled, 'You'll s-s-soon s-s-see,' before slamming the door.

She shrieked, 'You can't do this to me, Meadows!'

27

4.00 am, 13 June 1987
Lady Bay Bridge, Nottingham

It was a foggy morning; the drive from Lowdham into the city of Nottingham had been painfully slow.

Stephen Meadows had wanted to drive the van at speed through the winding streets so he could hurl his prisoner around in the back of the van, adding to her already considerable discomfort. The thick pea-souper fog shrouding the roads had put paid to that idea.

He had secured Sarah Milfoyle by wrapping the heavy chain links around her fat calves and knees. He had used a strong nylon rope to securely bind her wrists. After putting her in the back of the van, he had gagged her with brown gaffer tape after becoming sick of listening to her constant whining and pleading.

The large stands of the Nottingham Forest football

ground loomed out of the fog. He knew he was close to the river, close to the bridge. It would soon be time for the disgusting bitch to be cleansed.

As he approached the bridge, he cursed. He had forgotten that access to the parapets from the road was restricted by iron girders. There was no way he would be able to stop the van in the centre of the bridge and move Milfoyle from the van to the parapets. He parked the van at the end of the bridge and sat quietly, weighing up his options.

He got out of the van and looked along the footpath that spanned the bridge. He could see the narrow gaps in the girders that separated the footpath from the road. The metal railings of the parapet were only three feet high. So it would be no problem for him to lift Milfoyle over them and drop her down into the river. The problem would be getting her from one end of the bridge to the centre without being seen.

He locked the van and walked onto the bridge. It was fifty paces to reach the middle. Even though her legs had been weighted with the heavy chains, Meadows knew he was strong enough to carry the fat teacher that distance. He was less confident about being exposed for the length of time it would take him to do it. If another vehicle drove by or a pedestrian walked onto the bridge, he would be totally compromised.

He leaned over the metal railings. Through the swirling fog, he could see the black river water rushing underneath. The motion of the fast water was mesmerising. It seemed to be cajoling him into action. He could almost hear the river urging him to get on with it.

With his mind made up, he stalked back to the van. He took one last look around him and unlocked the doors. Sliding open the side door, he reached inside and grabbed Milfoyle's legs. He dragged her to the doorway and then hoisted her over his shoulder, into a fireman's lift.

She was now bellowing into the gaffer tape. Whatever it was that she was shouting was muffled and incomprehensible. Ignoring her strident protests, he started to stride out onto the bridge, counting out the fifty paces. The weight of the chained woman was more than he had expected. After thirty paces, the physical exertion was making him breathe hard. He paused for a second, took three deep breaths, then continued.

As soon as he had counted out fifty steps, he stopped and threw the woman onto the hard pavement. She landed on her back, her head whipping back and smacking into the unforgiving pavement. She let out a groan, and her eyes rolled back into her head.

Meadows ripped the gaffer tape from her mouth. She didn't stir. The blow to the back of her head from the pavement had rendered her unconscious.

Not wanting to delay any longer, he screwed up the gaffer tape and hurled it over the parapet and down into the water below. Grabbing the unconscious woman below her armpits, he lifted her up to the railings. He manoeuvred her weighted legs over the railings first, still gripping beneath her arms. As soon as her entire body was on the other side of the railings, he shoved her forwards.

He watched as she disappeared, falling into the grey swirling fog. There was a massive splash as Sarah Milfoyle's heavy body hit the water below. There was no way he could see exactly what had happened. He was satisfied by the loud splash that she was now in the river. He started to walk slowly back to his van, safe in the knowledge that the chains around Milfoyle's legs would be dragging her to the bottom of the river. She would soon be taking her last breath, inhaling the cold, black water.

With her cleansing now complete, Meadows felt good.

He got in his van and started the engine. As the powerful

diesel roared into life and he drove slowly away, his thoughts were already turning towards his next target, Rex Poyser.

28

7.00 am, 13 June 1987
MCIU Offices, Mansfield, Nottinghamshire

The MCIU briefing room was full. Every detective on the Unit was present for the briefings on the two quite different murders they were now investigating. There was a gentle hum of conversation among the gathered detectives as they chatted about the individual enquiries they had been tasked with.

Danny said, 'Quiet. I want to get started. We've got another busy day ahead of us.'

He turned to Tina. 'Can you give us an update on the Gunthorpe Bridge enquiry?'

Tina said, 'I can now confirm that our victim is a young woman called Suzy Flowers. Her brother, Geoff, came to see me yesterday, and he formally identified her at the mortuary. We are now aware that Suzy was twenty years of age and a student at Nottingham Trent University, where she was studying fashion and design. We began making tentative enquiries there yesterday. Now that we have a formal identification, these enquiries will continue and be more in depth today. I want the detectives tasked with carrying out these enquiries at the university to concentrate on finding any associates of the victim. Her own mother has described how Suzy found it difficult to make friends, but there must be someone she confided in. It's also a priority to establish if Suzy had a boyfriend, or if she was involved in another relationship. Let's try to ascertain what she did when she wasn't studying. What were her interests? How did she spend her free time? You all know what we need, so let's start making some progress.

'We now know that Suzy rented a bedsit on Denison Street in Radford. We'll be conducting a full forensic search of that property, along with scenes of crime, this morning. As you're all aware, currently we only have the deposition site. We still need to identify the scene of her murder, if possible. The teams who made a start on investigating Suzy's background yesterday, I want you to continue that today. I want you to work alongside the enquiry team at the university. I want to know who her friends were, both here and back home in Manchester. Let's not close our minds to the possibility that this murder could be connected to people she knew in her hometown. We're still searching the area around Gunthorpe to try to locate any possible CCTV. Today, we will be concentrating on the towns you would drive through when approaching the bridge. Does anyone have any questions?'

The room remained silent.

Danny said to Tina, 'Now that we have that formal identification, we'll need to discuss the details of the press release to go out later today. Is there anything else you need from me?'

'I'd like to do a stop check of vehicles travelling over Gunthorpe Bridge at various times in the next few days. It could be a useful way to find any possible witnesses. You never know, somebody may have driven by a vehicle that had stopped in the centre of the bridge. I may need some help getting uniform staff to assist us.'

Danny made a note in his enquiry book. 'I'll make a phone call to the relevant division and see if they can spare us any staff. Can you let me have a list of times you want to carry out the vehicle checks?'

'Will do, boss.'

Danny paused, then said, 'Right. Let's move on to the fatal house fire at Blidworth. Rob, can you give us all an update?'

Rob Buxton said, 'First and foremost, the fire has now been confirmed as arson. We will be treating the death of Joe Sinclair as a murder enquiry. The fire investigator, Tony Parrish, has identified that the seat of the fire was in the neighbouring derelict property. His examination of the scene has ruled out it being a small fire started by a homeless person or a tramp that subsequently got out of control. The reason being, he's found overwhelming evidence that an accelerant was used. The derelict property wasn't watertight. It would have been very cold and damp. The investigator has found that significant amounts of accelerant, probably petrol, were used. It had been poured above and below the staircase, with the sole intention of destroying the property. Unfortunately, because there was no dividing wall in the loft space of the semi-detached property, the fire quickly took hold of all the wooden trusses in the lofts of both properties. This subsequently caused the entire roof to collapse.

'The deceased was, as I said, Joe Sinclair. He was seventy-three years of age and a retired miner. He lived alone at the rented property. We have so far concentrated our enquiries on the landlords of both the properties. Initial enquiries have discovered that in recent months, Mr Sinclair made numerous complaints to both his landlord and the council about the state of disrepair of the adjoining house. These complaints ranged from kids causing further damage and being a nuisance, to the proliferation of vermin in and around both properties. Nothing was ever done; his complaints were all ignored. We will be continuing to delve deeper into the current finances of the company that act as the landlords for the property. Specifically, I want to establish what insurance arrangements they have in place. Tests made during the post-mortem ruled out any physical involvement by the deceased in setting the fire. I will allocate two of you to start investigating the background of Joe Sinclair, today. I still haven't ruled him out of this enquiry. It's entirely possible that he was pissed off enough about living next door to such a dump that he paid somebody else to set the fire, not realising what the outcome would be. We all need to keep an open mind about this case.'

Danny said, 'So, that's it, everybody. You've all been assigned your individual tasks to complete. Let's get cracking. Tina, come and see me about the press release before you leave.'

29

9.00 am, 13 June 1987
Hardwick Avenue, Rainworth, Nottinghamshire

He splashed cold milk on his cornflakes, then reached for the sugar bowl, getting the usual two full spoons of sugar, which he sprinkled generously all over the yellow cereal. As he pushed his spoon into the bowl, he stared at the photograph in the newspaper that he'd left open on the table.

He smiled and then began to chew the crunchy, sugary breakfast cereal as he read the report corresponding to the photograph of the blazing house in neighbouring Blidworth. He continued to read the article as he ate his breakfast. It was far more satisfying than the cereal packet he usually read. This was all about him. This was his handiwork. He felt a glow of self-importance that he hadn't felt for a long time.

It felt good to be someone significant for a change.

He allowed his eyes to linger over the part of the article

that described how the elderly resident of the house had failed to escape from the blazing inferno. How he had subsequently been found dead by the searching firemen after they had bravely fought the blaze and extinguished the flames.

He scoffed and muttered aloud, 'Hmph! Always the brave firemen!'

He finished his breakfast and placed the empty bowl in the sink. He knew it would be washed and put away by someone else. He picked up the newspaper and walked into the living room of the semi-detached house. He was alone, so he could take his time. He grabbed the large pair of scissors from the drawer of the sideboard and began, very carefully, to cut out the photograph and report from the newspaper.

He replaced the scissors and took the rest of the newspaper out to the kitchen, where he threw it in the bin. There was nothing else in the useless local rag that would interest him.

He took the newspaper cuttings upstairs to his bedroom. From the drawer where he kept his underpants and socks, he took out a scrapbook and a small tube of Pritt Stick glue. He spread open the first page of the scrapbook and glued the newspaper clippings inside.

Once they were in place, he read them again, transfixed by the image of the blazing house.

The sense of excitement he felt looking at the picture made his mind up for him. He had been considering whether to find another suitable property to burn, and he grinned widely as he finalised the decision in his head. He would start looking for the next perfect property, the next place to unleash the beast, as soon as possible.

There were still far too many blank pages in his scrapbook that needed to be filled.

30

2.00 pm, 13 June 1987
The Oaks Residential Care Home, West Bridgford, Nottingham

Dawn Meadows was wide awake, sitting in her wheelchair, staring out of the large bay window, when Stephen was shown into the room by a nurse.

The nurse said, 'I'll leave you two to it. You know your way back to the desk when you've finished your visit, don't you?'

Stephen nodded and said, 'Yes. Thanks.'

The nurse closed the door, and Stephen walked across to the window. He sat on the wide windowsill and said, 'How are you today, Dawny?'

Without moving her head, her eyes flickered towards him. She tried her best to communicate, but it came out as a series of grunts and shrieks. Stephen knew that if he listened carefully enough, there would be words in amongst the sounds.

He heard the word *why* several times.

He held his sister's hand, which was bunched in a constant fist, and said, 'Because Mum and Dad died. I had to let you live here so you could be looked after properly. Mum isn't here anymore. I'm sorry.'

Her eyes filled with tears, and she looked back out the window.

Stephen held her hand tighter. 'I've made a start, Dawny. I've sorted out that bitch of a teacher who made my life hell at school. She's sorry now.'

He felt his sister tense up. Her eyes stared at him again, and another torrent of sound gushed from her mouth.

The only word he could understand was *what*.

He smiled and said, 'I've taken care of her. I've changed her so she can't hurt anyone else. I put her in the river, where she'll have to stay quiet forever.'

His comments were met by a crescendo of noise from his sister. It got louder and louder and was unintelligible.

Suddenly, her eyes rolled back, and she started to shake violently.

Stephen had seen it often enough at home. His sister was having an epileptic fit. He raced to the door, opened it, and shouted, 'Nurse!'

Within seconds, the nurse who had shown him into the room returned and immediately went to the aid of his stricken sister.

She was joined by a doctor clutching a syringe. He plunged the syringe into Dawn's arm and waited for the drug to take effect.

The violent convulsions subsided and eventually stopped altogether. Dawn's eyes were once again open, but were now staring vacantly ahead.

The doctor turned to Stephen and said, 'Your sister will be okay now.'

Stephen said, 'What was in the syringe?'

'Your sister is on a regime of epilepsy drugs. She's currently prescribed Epilem Chrono, phenytoin and phenobarbitone to help control her seizures. Do you know what brought it on?'

'No. We were just talking.'

'It's probably the emotion of seeing her brother again. She's really missed her family, Stephen.'

'I know she has. It's been difficult for me after my parents died.'

'I understand. Please don't be put off visiting her again.'

'I won't be. I'm all she's got now. I need to be here for her.'

'She needs to rest now. Come and see her again soon, won't you?'

'Don't worry. I'll be back to keep her informed.'

31

2.00 pm, 13 June 1987
Nottinghamshire Police Headquarters

Such was his reluctance to attend the hastily arranged briefing with Detective Chief Superintendent Adrian Potter, Danny had made the usual twenty-minute drive from Mansfield to headquarters last for just over thirty minutes.

It was, unfortunately, part of his role as the head of the Major Crime Investigation Unit to keep the head of the CID informed of all developing murder enquiries.

Danny parked his car and walked into the headquarters building and up the stairs to the command corridor. He knocked politely on Potter's office door and wasn't surprised to hear the usual haughty response, delivered in the man's South Yorkshire accent, 'Enter!'

Danny walked in and said, 'Good afternoon, sir. I wanted

to update you on a couple of new enquiries we're currently investigating.'

In his effeminate, whining voice, Potter replied, 'The woman in the river and the old man in the house fire?'

'Yes, sir. Suzy Flowers, a twenty-year-old student studying at Nottingham Trent University, and Joe Sinclair, a retired miner.'

'And how are things progressing?'

'Early days. But we're making good headway into all the priority enquiries.'

'So, nothing really to report yet? No spectacular breakthroughs on either case?'

There was the usual heavy sarcasm in Potter's comment that Danny so detested. Over the months, he had learned to ignore it. After a pause, he said, 'Nothing at the moment, sir. My staff are all working diligently to expedite the enquiries into both tragic cases.'

Potter looked over his glasses, which perched precariously on the end of his pointed nose, and said, 'My, my, Chief Inspector Flint, that was proper headquarters language. Have you been on a course?'

Danny ignored the sarcastic, rhetorical question and said, 'There is something you could possibly help with.'

'And what's that?'

'We would like to set up vehicle road checks at various times on Gunthorpe Bridge, to try to generate possible witnesses. We're struggling with staff numbers for such an undertaking, and the chief superintendent on the Division that covers the bridge is dragging his heels over my request. I wondered if you could possibly gee him up a bit?'

Potter was thoughtful, then said, 'I'll make the call, but we all have to be mindful of the fact that divisional commanders always have the final say on how their staff are utilised.'

I'll take that as a no, then, thought Danny.

Potter continued, 'Is that everything, Chief Inspector?'

In a comment mirroring Potter's sarcasm, Danny replied, 'Yes, sir. I'll keep you informed of any spectacular breakthroughs we make.'

Without waiting for a response, Danny stood up and left the office.

32

6.00 pm, 13 June 1987
Castle Sounds, Lister Gate, Nottingham

Stephen Meadows shuffled uncomfortably on the hard wooden bench on Lister Gate. He stared, unblinking, at the door next to the window of the Timpson Shoes shop. The nondescript, scruffy red door led upstairs to the Castle Sounds Recording Studio, which was owned by some long-forgotten '60s pop idol, but managed by Rex Poyser.

Spurred on by the earlier visit to see his sister, he had decided to act immediately. The quicker he dealt with those who had caused them all the pain, the quicker he would be able to concentrate on looking after his sister. Meadows had parked his delivery van in the same car park where Poyser always left his midnight blue Triumph Stag. It was a private car park that only a few people knew about. It only had ten spaces and was situated behind a dance school on nearby Isabella Street. The owner of the dance school allowed it to be used by employees of Castle Sounds in return for free music tapes.

He knew that Poyser would be leaving work soon. He had already seen the lanky Rastafarian's young blonde girlfriend leave thirty minutes ago.

As he sat reminiscing about working at Castle Sounds and thinking about Poyser, Meadows became more and more enraged.

It had been solely because of the continuous bullying by Rex Poyser that Meadows had resigned from the job he loved. Every single minute of every single day, Poyser had found a reason to criticise or belittle his work in front of the other staff who worked there.

It was totally unfair and unfounded criticism. He had always been brilliant at his job as a sound engineer. His ability on the mixing decks was second to none, yet he had been singled out for abuse and ridicule by Poyser. At first, he had thought it was because their musical tastes were so different. Meadows was fanatical about the heavy rock scene, whereas the aging Poyser, now in his late forties, loved reggae and soul music.

It soon became obvious that it had nothing to do with their varied tastes in music, and everything to do with Poyser's personal agenda. There was a rumour among the staff that Poyser had begun dating a very sexy, very glamorous sound engineer. The gossips said she was twenty years his junior and was applying pressure on him to find her a job at Castle Sounds.

After enduring the hatred and the awful moods within the workplace for three months, Stephen couldn't stand it any longer. One week after his parents had both been killed in a car accident, when he was at an exceptionally low ebb and suffering badly with severe depression, he had handed in his resignation. He no longer felt able to cope with the spiteful nastiness and hatred dished out by Poyser.

His colleagues had been shocked. Several of them had taken him to one side and told him it was a mistake, and that he should withdraw his resignation. He had instantly regretted the decision to quit, and the very next day tried to take back his resignation. Poyser had just laughed in his face. He told him that he had already filled the position with a talented young sound engineer called Angela Thomas.

The same Angela Thomas he had been fucking for the last six months. With Meadows gone, Poyser had been able to install his blonde bimbo girlfriend directly into the sound engineer's role.

It had been a humiliating experience for Meadows and one that he now felt compelled to repay, with interest.

The scruffy door to Castle Sounds opened and snapped Meadows back from his thoughts. He saw the tall, skinny Rastafarian emerge from Castle Sounds and begin striding along Lister Gate, his long dreadlocks halfway down his back.

He recognised Rex Poyser immediately. It was a dull, cloudy day, but the middle-aged manager of Castle Sounds still wore the wraparound sunglasses that never left his head. Meadows suddenly had an image flash into his brain of Poyser sleeping, still wearing those bloody ridiculous sunglasses.

He got up from the bench and walked briskly to catch up with Poyser. He caught him up, then remained ten yards behind him. Meadows followed him through the narrow alleyway that led behind the historic St Nicholas church and out onto Maid Marian Way. Once across the dual carriageway, he followed Poyser through the grounds of Nottingham College towards the castle. As he turned into Isabella Street and into the small private car park, Poyser was totally unaware of Meadows' presence.

The car park was empty except for Poyser's Triumph Stag and the Red Arrow Couriers delivery van parked in the corner. As Poyser fumbled in his camel-coloured Crombie coat for his car keys, Stephen moved in. He slipped the heavy wrench he had been carrying from his coat pocket into his hand.

He took one last look around, then stepped forward and smashed Poyser on the back of the head with the wrench. The force of the blow knocked Poyser forward, into the side of his Triumph Stag. Before his target could do or say anything, Meadows stepped forward again and landed a heavier blow on the top of the man's head.

The weight of the wrench and the force of the second blow knocked Poyser out cold. His long, skinny legs collapsed beneath him.

Meadows moved fast now, dragging the unconscious man over to his van. He unlocked the van and opened the sliding door on the side. It took no effort to lift the painfully thin Rastafarian from the floor and throw him into the back of the van.

Meadows climbed inside the van and began using plastic tie wraps to secure Poyser. He made a quick examination of the head wounds he had inflicted. There were two small cuts that were both bleeding slightly, and swellings beginning to puff up beneath the cuts. Neither of the injuries would cause a threat to the man's life.

The last thing Meadows did was to place sticky brown gaffer tape across Poyser's mouth. He made sure that his prisoner's nostrils were clear of the cloying tape so he could still breathe.

He didn't want to do anything that would prevent him from cleansing the bastard properly later.

He opened the sliding door slightly and looked around the car park before getting out. Seeing that the car park was still deserted, he got out and walked to the driver's door. Just as he was about to get in the van, he saw Poyser's car keys on the floor. He picked them up, grinned, and hurled them over the fence. Chuckling to himself, he said, 'You won't be needing these anymore, you snide bastard!'

He got in the van, started the engine, and slipped a cassette into the tape player. As the throbbing rock sound of his all-time favourite band, Deep Purple, vibrated the sides of the van, he drove slowly out of the car park and headed for home.

33

8.00 pm, 13 June 1987
Ridge Hill, Lowdham, Nottinghamshire

Rex Poyser tried to take in his surroundings. He had blurred vision, but could just make out that he was inside what looked like a very amateur recording studio. He tried to make sense of what had happened to him. His head was aching badly, and he felt physically sick. Every time he moved his head, he gagged and dry retched.

He could remember being struck from behind, and that first blow knocking him into the side of his car. That had been followed instantly by a second, even harder blow. Then everything had gone dark.

He had been conscious for ten minutes now. Slowly he was becoming more aware; his senses were returning. He had quickly realised that he was now totally naked and tied to a wooden chair. The chair had been placed in the centre of the room. He struggled against the bindings, but the nylon rope that had been used to secure him was strong, and any sustained movement against the thin rope quickly burned his skin. He realised that his efforts were futile, and that he couldn't move.

There was a strange sensation around his ears. They felt closed in, as though they had been wrapped in something. There was the feeling that something had been wrapped tightly around his head. That wrapping, whatever it was, was being used to hold something in place against each of his ears.

He shook his head to dislodge whatever it was, and instantly regretted it. The wave of nausea that swept over him made him retch, and he almost vomited.

He allowed his head to clear, then shouted, 'Hello! Is there anyone there? Help!'

He repeated his cries for help until his voice grew croaky, and he realised just how thirsty he was.

He was shocked as the door immediately in front of him was opened with a loud bang. A man walked into the room, and Rex Poyser let out an audible gasp as he recognised the man standing in front of him.

Feeling a wave of anger rising inside him, Poyser shouted, 'Meadows! What the fuck are ya doing, man? Untie me now, ya bloodclaat!'

Meadows grinned. 'Hello, Rex. Are you having a g-g-good t-t-time?'

The lanky Rastafarian sucked his front teeth and snarled, 'What the hell are ya talking about? What good time is dis? Rassclaat! Are you fucking mad!'

'D-d-don't b-b-be like that, Rex. I've even arranged to p-p-play s-s-some of your favourite m-m-music through the headphones f-f-for you.'

Poyser now realised that the things held in place against his ears were headphones.

Meadows said, 'D-d-do you realise how d-d-difficult it was to g-g-get the g-g-gaffer tape to s-s-stick to your f-f-fucking d-d-dreadlocks? You always were an ungrateful b-b-bastard.'

Poyser strained against his bindings and snarled, 'Fuck off, Meadows. When I get out of here, you're fucking dead. I know people who will seriously fuck you up, man!'

Meadows laughed out loud. 'D-d-do you, Rex? D-d-do you know p-p-people? D-d-do you know anyone who's g-g-going to g-g-get you out of this shit?'

Poyser was silent.

'N-n-no. I d-d-didn't think s-s-so. Just shut the f-f-fuck up and enjoy the s-s-sounds I've g-g-got lined up for you. I d-d-don't know if you'll enjoy this f-f-first t-t-tape. It m-m-might need Angela, your f-f-favourite s-s-sound engineer, to refine the s-s-sound quality a little. What d-d-do you think?'

Without waiting for a reply, Meadows walked over to a tape deck and switched it on. The sound of an Iron Maiden track filled the room.

He turned the volume down and said, 'I'll p-p-play it through your headphones s-s-so you c-c-can hear it c-c-clearly. Rex, you're g-g-going to l-l-love this.'

The heavy metal sound suddenly filled Poyser's head, and he winced at the volume.

Meadows said, 'S-s-sorry, Rex. You know these t-t-tracks are always b-b-better p-p-played loud.'

With that comment, he slowly increased the volume to maximum. Poyser screamed in agony as the deafening music perforated both his eardrums.

The Rastafarian tossed his head from side to side violently. Desperately, trying to dislodge the headphones. It was futile; they were taped fast. The deafening noise through the headphones, combined with his head injury, meant that the action of shaking his head violently caused Poyser to retch repeatedly until he was violently sick. He vomited all over his bare legs.

Meadows laughed and continued to play track after track, all at the same deafening, strident volume. The pain became so intense that Poyser passed out. Blood started to trickle from beneath the gaffer tape as his inner ears started to bleed.

Meadows turned the music off and slapped Poyser's face until he stirred.

As soon as he was awake, Meadows stood directly in front of him and screamed, 'Are you s-s-sorry now, you b-b-bastard?'

Poyser could see Meadows' lips moving, but he was now so profoundly deaf that he couldn't hear a word he was saying.

Meadows didn't wait for an answer. He shouted, 'I will c-c-cleanse you s-s-soon, Rex. I think we s-s-still have t-t-time for s-s-some m-m-more m-m-music.'

He stepped back to the tape deck and switched the music on again. The volume through the headphones was as loud as before, and Poyser began screaming.

Stephen Meadows laughed as he walked out of the room. He had decided that Poyser could suffer a little longer before his final cleansing.

34

9.00 pm, 13 June 1987
Finningley Road, Mansfield, Nottinghamshire

He had been walking for a couple of hours, and his feet were starting to ache. The weight of the items in the plastic carrier bag was beginning to make the handles bite into the palm of his hand.

At least the bag would be lighter when he walked home afterwards.

Night was beginning to close in now, and all the streetlights on the Bellamy Road estate were coming on. As he walked along the roads, and lights were switched on but curtains not drawn, he could see people inside their homes.

He came to a row of brick-built bungalows. He could see by the handrails alongside the front doors that these dwellings were sheltered housing for old-age pensioners. On the opposite side of the road to the bungalows was an eight-foot-high hawthorn hedge. He backed into the hedge and continued to observe the bungalows.

A light came on in one of the properties. He could now clearly see the two elderly occupants inside, moving around their lounge. He began to smile, and placed the plastic carrier bag, containing the green can full of petrol, at his feet.

He was smiling because he had finally found his target. It would soon be time for him to release the beast again. He could see the letterbox in the front door, where he would pour the petrol. He just needed to wait until all the lights in the bungalow were turned off. Once the lights were out, he would wait another half an hour. Only then would he move in and start the fire.

He took the petrol can from the bag and swung it back and forth, humming gently as the contents sloshed around inside.

The lights would soon go out.

It would soon be time.

35

2.00 am, 14 June 1987
Kelham Bridge, Newark, Nottinghamshire

Stephen Meadows parked his van in the small layby next to Kelham Bridge. He switched off the engine and reflected on what he was about to do. Rex Poyser was an ignorant bastard, simple as that. He deserved everything that was coming to him.

Now that the engine had been turned off, he could hear the middle-aged Rastafarian bumping around in the back of the van. His wrists and ankles were bound tightly with nylon rope, and heavy chains had been wrapped around his skinny legs.

Meadows had been extra careful when he strapped the chains on. The man's legs were so skinny it was difficult to prevent the heavy metal links from sliding off. Poyser was now gagged with gaffer tape that had been wrapped completely around his head. Only his eyes and nose remained clear of the sticky tape.

It was time.

Meadows got out of the van and had a good look around. It was a cold, clear night. There were no clouds, and a bright moon cast a muted white light over everything.

He slid the side door open and grabbed Poyser by the ankles. Screaming into the cloying gag, the man began to struggle violently. Meadows tried to grip him, but he was as slippery as an eel and kept evading his grasp. Losing patience, he stepped inside the van and punched Poyser hard in the face. Meadows' clenched fist made a crunching sound as it connected with Poyser's jawbone. He saw the man stop struggling and go limp.

Not wasting any more time, Meadows snatched the skinny man out of the van and placed him over his shoulder. Poyser was so tall and thin that his hands and feet weren't far from the ground as he draped over Meadows' shoulder. He weighed far less than Sarah Milfoyle had. It was no effort to carry him, and the chains that bound him, out to the centre of the old stone bridge.

He sat Poyser down on the low wall that formed the parapet of the bridge, and turned him slowly around. Eventually, his legs, with the chains still strapped to them, were dangling over the edge of the wall, hanging down towards the water below.

Meadows didn't wait. He just tipped Poyser off the wall and down into the river. There was an enormous splash as the skinny black man hit the water, the heavy chains instantly dragging him below the surface.

From the bridge, Meadows looked down at the black water momentarily, then turned and walked back to his van.

36

2.00 am, 14 June 1987
Kelham Bridge, Newark, Nottinghamshire

Jimmy Birch had just finished rebaiting his ledger rig and was about to cast out into the centre of the river. He was fishing about fifty yards upstream from the bridge and was startled by the loud splash. He immediately looked to his left and saw a man walking from the centre of the bridge, away from the Fox public house.

Jimmy cast out his bait and placed the rod back onto the rod rest. He heard the rumble of a diesel engine and looked back towards the bridge. He was just in time to see a large van crossing the bridge, travelling from the Newark side towards the Mansfield side.

He decided to fish for another couple of hours, then call the police when it started to get light. There was a phone box on the other side of the river, near the entrance to the Fox pub car park.

What he had just witnessed all seemed a little odd. The man he had seen walking on the bridge had definitely thrown something heavy into the river. He wasn't sure if the police would be interested in what he'd seen. Anyway, that phone call could wait. Right now, Jimmy was far more focused on getting one of the large chub in this part of the river to go for his bait.

37

2.00 am, 14 June 1987
Mansfield, Nottinghamshire

Sue Flint gently shook her husband's shoulder, to rouse him from his sleep, and said, 'Danny, wake up. It's the control room inspector. He needs to talk to you urgently.'

Danny sat up in bed, wiped the sleep from his eyes, and took the telephone from Sue. He said groggily, 'Danny Flint.'

'Sorry to call you at this hour, sir. There's been another fatal house fire.'

Danny was now wide awake. 'Where?'

'Finningley Road on the Bellamy Estate in Mansfield.'

'You said fatal house fire. Who's died?'

'The property that was set on fire is a bungalow – sheltered accommodation for the elderly. After the blaze was put out, firemen discovered two bodies inside the burned-out property. We believe the deceased to be Douglas and Joan Cooper, the residents. They were both in their late seventies.'

'Anything to suggest arson?'

'According to our officers at the scene, the sub-officer from the fire brigade seems pretty certain that the fire's been started deliberately.'

'Okay. I'm going straight to the scene. I want you to contact Detective Inspector Buxton and instruct him to join me there. Tell him to contact Fire Investigator Tony Parrish and ask him to attend the scene, as well. Have you contacted the on-call scenes of crime team yet?'

'Not yet, sir. You're my first call.'

'Okay. I want you to contact them straightaway and ask them to liaise with me at Finningley Road.'

'Will do, sir. Is there anything else you'll need at the scene?'

'Not right now. I'll decide on the home office pathologist when I'm on scene. Thanks.'

Danny put the phone down and sat quietly on the bed, trying to absorb everything he had just been told. The main thought that kept rushing into his brain was the one that scared him the most. If this fire was also started on purpose, was he now hunting a maniac who was deliberately killing people by fire?

Sue walked into the bedroom, carrying baby Hayley in one arm and a mug of hot coffee in the other. She handed Danny the coffee. 'I take it you've got to go into work?'

Danny took the coffee and nodded. 'There's been another house fire. Did the telephone call wake her?'

'No. I was feeding her downstairs when the telephone rang beside me. I nearly jumped out of my skin!'

Danny grinned, took a mouthful of coffee, and then walked to the bathroom. He washed his face and hands, cleaned his teeth, then walked back to the bedroom and started to get dressed.

Sue, now sitting in bed, had started to breast-feed Hayley again. She said, 'Was anybody hurt in the fire?'

'Two people have died. I think it's a bit too much of a coincidence to have two fatal house fires in a couple of days.'

'Do you think this fire was started deliberately, as well?'

'Hard to say right now. I'll know more later.'

He finished the Windsor knot he was tying and pushed the necktie up to his collar before stepping over to his wife. He bent forward and kissed the top of Hayley's head, then kissed Sue on the lips. 'I'll see you later, sweetheart.'

Sue put her hand to his cheek and said what she always said: 'Be careful, darling.'

Danny nodded and walked out of the room.

Five minutes later, he was in his car and speeding through the deserted streets of Mansfield, towards Finningley Road.

38

2.30 am, 14 June 1987
Finningley Road, Mansfield, Nottinghamshire

The smell of acrid smoke still hung heavily in the cold night air. Now that the fire was out and there was only one fire tender still on the street, the large crowd of onlookers was starting to drift away.

The press photographers were still on the scene. They were busily walking up and down Finningley Road, taking photographs of the burned-out shell of a bungalow that used to be the home of Douglas and Joan Cooper.

Danny walked over to the photographers, identified himself and said quietly, 'Make sure you take photographs of the people watching the firemen, please.' He took their details and said, 'I'll be in touch in a few days for copies of all your photos. Thanks, guys.'

The photographers nodded. They immediately turned their attention to the crowds and started snapping.

The first to arrive after the call-out was Tony Parrish. He found Danny talking to the uniform sergeant who was supervising the scene.

Tony interrupted, saying, 'Morning, Danny. What do we know so far?'

'Thanks for getting here so quickly, Tony. Nothing much yet. Can you find the sub-officer in charge and see if he'll let you inside the bungalow to have a look? He's told my sergeant that the scene is still off-limits to the police.'

'I'll go and find him. If they won't let you in, there must be an issue with the gas or electricity. I'll see what I can find out. Give me a couple of minutes.'

As Tony Parrish walked off, Danny saw Rob Buxton arrive. He walked over to the car.

As soon as he got out, Rob said, 'Arson?'

Danny replied, 'Could be. The control room inspector suggested to me that it was. Tony is around here somewhere. He's having a conversation with the sub-officer in charge. We'll see what he says.'

'Another big crowd, I see.'

'I know. I've asked all the press lads to make sure they get photographs of the rubberneckers, and that we'll be in touch to obtain copies.'

'Good call.'

'I've held off calling out the home office pathologist until it's confirmed as arson.'

'Looks like we're about to find out,' said Rob as he saw a grim-faced Tony Parrish walking back towards them.

'We can go inside in another ten minutes. They're just waiting for the electricity to be safely switched off. The fuse box inside has been irreparably damaged by the fire, and there are bare wires everywhere.'

Danny said, 'Does he think it's arson?'

'He does, and I totally agree. He showed me the shadow

splash in the hallway near the front door. It's the classic petrol-through-the-letterbox scenario. This fire's definitely been started deliberately.'

'What about the occupants?'

'They were both still in bed. Looks like they were overcome by the toxic smoke as they slept. The fire did reach the bedroom, and they've both got burns to the exposed areas of their bodies. Their heads and arms are a mess. The bedclothes burned, but they kept the flames away from their skin. You'll see what I mean later, at the post-mortems.'

'Thanks, Tony. Rob, can you organise three forensic suits for us, from the scenes of crime team when they arrive? I'll grab the sergeant's radio and get a home office pathologist travelling.'

As he walked over to the uniform sergeant, Danny's thoughts immediately turned towards the investigation process. He looked around him. He was standing in the middle of a large housing estate. The house-to-house enquiries alone were going to be a massive undertaking. Then there would be the trawl for any CCTV. He began to think of the victims, and wondered if they had any connection with Joe Sinclair, the retired miner killed in the first fire. The most worrying thing, though, was the lack of an obvious motive for the crimes. Why would somebody want to burn down houses and kill old people in their beds?

Having made the radio call, Danny walked back over to Tony Parrish. 'What do you think? Are the two fires linked?'

'If I were a betting man, I would say yes. Petrol has been used to start both fires. All the victims are elderly, so stand less chance of escaping the fire, and both premises seem to have been selected rather than chosen at random.'

'Why do you say "selected"?'

'Come with me. I want to show you something.'

Danny followed Tony as he walked away. The fire investigator talked as he walked. 'Part of my job is to try to think like the arsonist. I try to imagine how I would set the fire, how I would select the property. I've had a look around the area and found this. I think it's significant.'

The fire investigator had stopped near the hawthorn hedge that overlooked the burned-out bungalow.

'Look here.'

Tony squatted down and pointed at a muddy area below the bushes. There were boot prints clearly visible in the mud.

'I think our arsonist stood here, watching the bungalow. He was waiting for the old couple to go to bed before setting the fire.'

'I'll ask scenes of crime to get casts and photographs of the boot prints. Do you think whoever did this stood watching the people inside? Saw that they were elderly and lit the fire anyway?'

Tony nodded. 'I think they did. I also think that you have an extremely dangerous individual to find. Whoever's doing this enjoys what they're doing.'

Danny was thoughtful, then said, 'Do you think there'll be more fires?'

'Unless we catch him, yes.'

'Let's get this area taped off before it gets trampled on. I want to get inside the bungalow and start work as soon as the sub-officer gives us the nod.'

39

10.00 am, 14 June 1987
MCIU Offices, Mansfield, Nottinghamshire

Danny and Rob were discussing possible lines of enquiry into the latest arson.

Rob said, 'I've fired a call in to the Special Operations Unit. They can provide us with two sections to undertake the house-to-house enquiries on the Bellamy Estate. I've got Simon Paine already out on the estate mastering the streets and houses, so everything will be ready for the special ops lads when they arrive.'

'That's good; that estate is huge. It could take a couple of weeks to finish.'

'I know. I've instructed DC Paine to use the attacked bungalow on Finningley Road as the centre and to work out from there. That way if there's anything significant, we should pick it up quickly.'

'Who's on CCTV?'

'Phil Baxter's already out there trawling the streets to try to find any CCTV. He hasn't reported anything yet, but it's still early.'

'Have scenes of crime finished at the bungalow?'

'Just. Tim Donnelly called me just before I came in here.'

'Anything?'

'Nothing startling. It's the usual story – fire and forensics don't mix. He'll have an album of photographs available later today.'

'What time are the post-mortems arranged for?'

'They will begin at three o'clock this afternoon, at King's Mill Hospital mortuary.'

'Do we know the Coopers' next of kin yet?'

'Yes, sir. They had a daughter, Sophie Arnold, who now lives in Stevenage. Hertfordshire Police have been to her home address and informed her personally about what's happened.'

'Is she coming here?'

'Sophie and her husband will be arriving tomorrow morning.'

'Okay. I'll make sure I'm available to see them. Do you know what time?'

'They indicated to the cops in Stevenage that they'll be here at ten o'clock.'

'Thanks. Can you think of anything else we need to do?'

'The only other thing that needs looking at is what you mentioned earlier, trying to establish if there are any possible links between Joe Sinclair and the Coopers. I've got Fran Jefferies looking at the victimology on both fires. If there's anything there, Fran will find it.'

'Anything further on the landlords who own the properties involved at Blidworth?'

'I think that enquiry has run its course, boss. There's

nothing dodgy about either the landlords or the insurance company that we can find.'

'Okay. Just make sure that there are no links between them and the Coopers before you close it down.'

'Right. Will you be going to the post-mortems this afternoon?'

Danny shook his head. 'I'm not going to be able to. I've got to speak to Potter and arrange a press conference for later. Will you be able to take Tony Parrish with you?'

Rob nodded. 'I'll pick him up on the way to the hospital.'

'Keep your team motivated and working. We need to catch this nutter. I don't think he's going to stop until we do.'

Rob stood up and left the office.

As soon as he closed the door, Danny picked up the phone. The phone was answered on the second ring. 'Detective Chief Superintendent Potter.'

Danny said, 'Good morning, sir. It's DCI Flint. I wanted to update you about another fatal house fire during the early hours of this morning, at Mansfield. Two elderly residents, Mr and Mrs Cooper, were killed in their sheltered bungalow.'

'I see. Is this another arson attack?'

'All the early indicators are that it is.'

'Is it linked to the Blidworth fire?'

'Not yet, evidentially. It's a bit too much of a coincidence, though, don't you think?'

'Hmm, I've never been one to bother much about coincidence. I prefer hard evidence, myself.'

'There are distinct similarities at both crime scenes, sir.'

'But we're not crying "serial arsonist" just yet, are we, Chief Inspector?'

'I think we should consider a press release so people are alerted to that possibility.'

Potter was quiet for a minute. He said, 'I agree. Hold a press conference and make it a general appeal for witnesses at both fires. Don't link them specifically, and finish the conference with some input from that fire investigator you've got working with you. Ask him to give out some general fire safety information and remind people to stay vigilant. If you do it right, you'll get the message out there without the panic. Can you do that?'

'Of course, sir. I'll call the press liaison officer and get something set up for this evening.'

'Good. Keep me informed.'

The phone went dead.

Another startling and informative conversation. Danny shook his head and replaced the telephone before dialling the number for the press liaison officer.

40

11.30 am, 14 June 1987
MCIU Offices, Mansfield, Nottinghamshire

Tina Cartwright was busily reading through the reports from the previous night's vehicle stop checks at Gunthorpe Bridge. Every negative report she read worsened her already bad mood.

When the telephone on her desk rang, she virtually snatched it from the cradle and said, 'DI Cartwright. Can I help you?'

The voice on the phone said, 'Good morning, ma'am. It's Sergeant Hudson in the control room. I've just picked up a report that was made to Newark Police Station at four thirty this morning. I don't know why you weren't flagged up straight away, to be honest, but I thought you may be interested in the content of the call.'

Now intrigued, Tina said, 'Go on, Sergeant.'

'A man by the name of James Birch made a call to say that

he was fishing when he saw a man throw something into the River Trent from the bridge at Kelham.'

Tina could feel the anger rising within her, and she fought hard to compose herself before answering. She took a deep breath and said, 'I think it's fair to say that's something I would be interested in, Sergeant Hudson. What are the details?'

'I'm afraid the details I've got here are all a bit sketchy. The officer who went out to see Birch has made a note on the message log that states that there was no description of the man involved, and that Birch couldn't say what had been thrown from the bridge, other than it caused a large splash.'

'Okay. Give me the details for Birch.'

'James Birch, thirty-one years. He lives at Briar Cottage, Church Lane, Kirklington.'

'Do we have a telephone number?'

'Sorry, no. Birch made the initial call from a telephone box at Kelham, and the officer hasn't taken his home number.'

Again, Tina felt her anger rise at the sloppy work. 'What's the name of the officer who attended?'

'PC 118 Jack Reynolds.'

'Thanks; leave it with me. Mark the log with the correct time, that I've been informed, please. I'll be speaking with PC Reynolds later.'

Tina hung up. She walked across the room and knocked on Danny's office door.

Danny said, 'Come in.'

Tina walked in and said, 'Have you got a second?'

'Of course, grab a seat. How are you settling in?'

'Fine. Everyone's been immensely helpful and welcoming. I know you're full on with the house fire enquiries right now, but I've just had an interesting telephone call that may be relevant to the Suzy Flowers enquiry. I thought you should know about it.'

'Go on?'

'Well, it might be nothing, but a man reported seeing someone throw something into the river off Kelham Bridge during the early hours of this morning. I was wondering if we could task the Underwater Search Unit to search below the bridge to see if they can find whatever it is that was thrown in.'

'Do we have any other details?'

'Unfortunately, no, we don't. The cop who attended initially hasn't exactly covered himself in glory. He's done a sloppy job, to be honest. To make things worse, the control room have only just let me know about the call. I've got the informant's details now, so I'm going to his home address to talk to him.'

Danny was thoughtful for a minute, then said, 'I'll call the Underwater Search Unit and ask them to get a search organised. Go and see the informant, get as much detail as you can from him. When you've done that, call me straight away so I can pass it on to the Underwater Search Unit supervisor.'

'Thanks, boss.'

'Let's hope the divers don't find what we're both thinking they might. Call me as soon as you've seen your informant.'

'Will do.'

Tina walked out and closed the door behind her. She saw Rachel Moore sitting at her desk and said, 'Rachel, have you got any car keys?'

Rachel nodded. 'Yes. Are we going somewhere?'

'Grab your coat. We're going to see a fisherman at Kirklington.'

41

12.30 pm, 14 June 1987
Briar Cottage, Church Lane, Kirklington, Nottinghamshire

As the CID car was driven onto Church Lane, Tina looked at the row of ancient stone cottages that ran along one side of the lane, down towards the thirteenth-century church St Swithun's. The square tower of the ancient church stood over the cottages like some vast stone sentinel.

Tina reflected on the last time she had approached a cottage in a car with Rachel. The cottage had been South Lodge at Retford. Moments later, the psychopath Jimmy Wade had tried to kill Rachel before he was shot dead by a police sniper.

She kept her thoughts to herself and said, 'I think that's Briar Cottage. The second one along the row.'

As Rachel brought the car to a stop, Tina said cheerfully,

'Right. Let's go and find out exactly what Mr Birch saw, shall we?'

The two detectives got out, and Rachel knocked loudly on the cottage door.

There was no reply.

Rachel knocked again, louder this time. Still no reply.

Just as she was about to start banging again, she saw the door in the neighbouring cottage open. An elderly man came out and said, 'Are you after Jimmy?'

Tina walked over, showed the man her identification, and said, 'Police officers. We're trying to contact James Birch.'

The old man smiled and said, 'Aye, lass, Jimmy. He was out fishing all night, so he won't hear you. He'll be asleep in bed, with his earplugs in.'

Tina said, 'It's important that we speak with him right now.'

'Just a second, lass.'

The old man went back inside his cottage and emerged a few minutes later. He turned to Tina and said, 'I've got a spare key for Jimmy's place, in case he gets deliveries when he's out. Wait here. I'll go and wake him up.'

Tina looked quizzically at Rachel as the old man let himself in and closed the door behind him.

A couple of minutes later he re-emerged, saying, 'Jimmy's just getting dressed; he'll be with you shortly.'

Tina said, 'Thanks for all your help.'

The old man chuckled, and as he walked into his own cottage, he said, 'No problem, lass. You two are the prettiest coppers I've ever seen.'

Tina laughed, looked at Rachel, and said, 'I'm not proud. I'll take a compliment wherever I can get one.'

Rachel smiled, but the smile quickly disappeared as the door to Briar Cottage opened. A very dishevelled-looking Jimmy Birch stood there, in a tatty brown dressing gown and threadbare slippers. He tried to smooth his unruly, blonde hair down with his hand, then said, 'Old Tommy said you were cops. What's wrong?'

Tina said, 'I'm Detective Inspector Cartwright, and this is Detective Constable Moore. We're from the Major Crime Investigation Unit. We need to ask you a few questions about the call you made to the police earlier today. Can we come in for a second?'

'Of course, sorry. Where are my manners? I was fast asleep. Come in, come in.'

Jimmy Birch showed the detectives into the cosy lounge of his cottage and said, 'Major Crime? That all sounds very serious.'

Tina said, 'Don't worry, Mr Birch, you're not in any trouble. We just want to know exactly what it was you saw this morning.'

'I've already told everything to that uniform copper. The one who came out to Kelham Bridge this morning?'

Rachel said, 'I know, and I'm sorry for the inconvenience. We'd just like to hear it for ourselves; that way we'll know if it was something important. Would you mind?'

'Okay. No problem. Let me see, I'd been fishing for a couple of hours, so I reckon it was between two o'clock and half past two this morning. I was fishing from the Newark bank. The bridge was to my left as you look at the river. I was about to cast out, so I had my back to the bridge – I'm right-handed, you see – when I heard an almighty splash.'

Rachel said, 'How far away from the bridge were you standing?'

'About fifty yards, I suppose.'

'What did you do when you heard the splash?'

'It was so loud, it startled me. I spun around to see what it was.'

'And what did you see?'

'There was a man leaning over the bridge, looking down at the water. He was looking down for a few seconds; then he stood up and walked across the bridge towards the Newark side.'

'When you first saw him, whereabouts on the bridge was the man standing?'

'Slap bang in the middle, I reckon.'

Tina said, 'Please excuse my ignorance, Mr Birch. Are there any streetlights on the bridge?'

'There's a couple, but the lights aren't great.'

'Did you get much of a look at this man?'

'Not really. It was dark, and he was quite a distance away from me.'

Both detectives remained silent. The silence prompted Birch to elaborate on his 'not really' comment. Eventually, he said, 'The only thing I can remember is that he had long dark hair.'

Rachel said, 'That's great. What do you think this man threw into the river?'

'I've no idea. It must have been fairly heavy, though, because it made one hell of a splash.'

'So, after the splash, you see this man walk from the middle of the bridge back towards the Newark side. Then what?'

'I carried on fishing. I don't mind telling you, my heart was still pounding, though. The splash had really made me jump.'

'Did you see anything else?'

'Only the van.'

Tina said, 'Excuse me? What van?'

'As soon as the man had disappeared from my view, I heard a diesel engine start up. A couple of seconds later, I saw a van being driven over the bridge, towards Mansfield.'

'What can you tell me about the van?'

'It was white.'

'That it?'

'Yeah, it was only there for a second. It looked like a Transit or similar. That sort of size, and definitely white.'

'Thank you so much, Mr Birch. That's been extremely useful. Are you alright for time? I'd like DC Moore to take a written statement from you now.'

'No problem; I'm off work today. I've got nothing else planned, only catching up on my sleep.'

'Thanks.'

Tina turned to Rachel. 'I'm going to drive over to the police station in Southwell while you're getting the statement. I need to let the boss know what we've got here. He can then press on with organising the Underwater Search Unit to start searching the river below Kelham Bridge.'

Rachel said, 'Here's the keys. I just need to get some statement forms from the car before you take it.'

Rachel turned to Jimmy Birch and said, 'I'm just getting some statement paper from the car, Mr Birch, then we'll make a start. It won't take long.'

Jimmy said, 'I'll put the kettle on. Tea or coffee?'

Rachel said, 'Coffee, white no sugar, would be great, thanks.'

The two detectives walked out to the car. Tina said, 'I won't be long, Rachel. I'll pick you up here in half an hour, tops.'

42

5.30 pm, 14 June 1987
MCIU Offices, Mansfield, Nottinghamshire

Danny was preparing what he was going to deliver later at the scheduled press conference. It would be held in the canteen at Mansfield Police Station, at six thirty. Danny was adding the final touches to what he wanted to say.

He glanced at his watch. Time was getting on, and he still needed to brief Tony Parrish about the part he wanted him to play at the press conference. Tony was with Rob Buxton at the post-mortems for Douglas and Joan Cooper, the elderly victims of the latest house fire.

Just as Danny was thinking the post-mortem examinations were taking a long time, there was a polite knock on his office door. He shouted, 'Come in.'

Rob and Tony walked in, both men wearing grim expressions.

Danny said, 'Grab a seat, gents. What was the outcome?'

Rob said, 'Pretty much as Tony had expected. The pathologist confirmed that both victims died as a result of suffocation. There were burns on the heads and arms of both bodies, but these were all post-mortem. It was the toxic smoke in the bungalow that killed them.'

Tony explained, 'The problem is, an awful lot of everyday household items give off an extremely toxic smoke when burnt at a high temperature. There's a plastic foam that's commonly used in soft furnishings – settees, armchairs, that sort of thing – that gives off cyanide gas when on fire. The fire brigade is working hard with furniture manufacturers on this issue, but it's going to be a long job.'

Danny said, 'Did the pathologist find any other marks of violence on the bodies?'

Rob shook his head. 'Nothing. They just went to bed, went to sleep and never woke up.'

Danny muttered under his breath, 'Because of that maniac.'

He wrote the initial findings of the post-mortems into his enquiry log and said, 'When will we get the pathologist's report?'

'It was Professor Hargreaves doing the examinations, and you know how slow he is. He assured me that he would have them to us by the day after tomorrow.'

'Keep on top of that, Rob. Don't be frightened to chase him up if you have to.'

'Will do.'

'Tony, before you went to the post-mortems, you had a couple of hours at the bungalow on Finningley Road. Any other observations?'

'Only that I can now positively identify the seat of the fire. It was immediately below the letterbox in the front door. Judging by the extensive shadowing on the walls in the hallway, I think our man used a hell of a lot of accelerant. There's distinct shadowing along the entire length of the hallway, which suggests that he poured a lot of petrol through the letterbox before igniting it. The shadowing is caused when the petrol vapour ignites before the liquid. It convinces me even more that the two fires were started by the same individual. There's one more worrying aspect that occurs to me.'

'Go on.'

'It's fair to assume that the death caused in the Blidworth fire could have been unintentional.'

'How so?'

'Well, the fire was set next door. It could be that the arsonist never expected both properties to catch fire. This fire, however, was deliberately set in a property where the arsonist stood and watched the occupants. The worrying thing is that he set the fire in such a way that there could be no escape for the victims.'

'Christ Almighty. You're saying that you think this arsonist is now deliberately setting out to kill people? That's a hell of an escalation.'

'It's just my personal view on developments, based on what I see. I could be wrong.'

Danny was quietened by the theory. His mind was in turmoil, wondering how the hell he was going to stop this maniac.

'Do you stand by what you said this morning, that you think there will be more fires?'

'I'm afraid so, yes.'

'A press conference has been arranged for six thirty this evening, downstairs in the canteen. Are you available to come and give some general fire safety input at the end of the conference?'

Tony nodded. 'Of course. There were no smoke alarms in the bungalow on Finningley Road. I'm not saying they would have made any difference to the outcome, but if smoke alarms had been fitted, the Coopers may have at least had a chance of survival.'

'Thanks, Tony. I appreciate it. I've got to somehow balance warning the public that this maniac is out there against causing some sort of mass hysteria.'

Rob said, 'Just a thought: Is it worth setting up extra foot patrols around old-age pensioner complexes for the foreseeable future? If our man is deliberately targeting the elderly, we might intercept him.'

'Good idea. I'll talk to the divisional commander and see what uniform resources are like. I'll mention there will be increased patrols in the press conference as well. It may help to reassure the public.'

Rob said, 'The divisional commander may want to consider utilising the Special Constabulary if they're willing to help out.'

There was an urgent rap on the office door, and Tina Cartwright opened it. She apologised for the interruption and said, 'The control room have just phoned the office. The Underwater Search Unit have found another body, below Kelham Bridge.'

Danny said, 'Bloody hell. We need to get out there and see what they've got. Rob, will you stand in for me at the press conference?'

Rob nodded.

Danny said, 'I've written down what I was going to say anyway, and you're fully up to speed on all the ongoing enquiries.'

'No problem, boss. Me and Tony can handle it. I'll talk to the divisional commander about that staffing issue as well.'

'That's great. Thanks, Rob. One other thing, while we're travelling to Kelham, can you speak to the control room? Tell them to contact Seamus Carter and ask him to meet us at

Kelham Bridge. It will be useful to have the same pathologist at the scene. That way, we'll know in quick time if this body is linked to the killer of Suzy Flowers.'

Rob reached for the telephone. 'I'm on it.'

'Thanks. Have you got transport, Tina?'

'Rachel's ready with a car.'

'Let's get out to Kelham Bridge and see what we've got.'

43

6.45 pm, 14 June 1987
Kelham Bridge, Newark, Nottinghamshire

Danny looked down at the tall, skinny figure lying in the black plastic body bag on the riverbank. He turned to Tina and said, 'The chain linking around the legs looks identical.'

Tina nodded. Seamus Carter said, 'I've been doing some investigations around the chains that were recovered from Suzy Flowers. I initially thought the blue paint was indicative of an industrial use, but from my research, it seems that it's more likely to be part of farm machinery.'

'That's interesting. I'd got them pegged as being industrial as well. Tina, I want these chains fast-tracking through the Forensic Science Service, to see if they're an identical match to those used on Suzy Flowers.'

Seamus squatted down and made a closer examination of the body. As usual, he spoke his findings into his Dictaphone.

He said, 'The body is that of a middle aged male, possibly late forties, early fifties. Afro-Caribbean in appearance, with long dreadlocks. The body has been stripped naked. There are no obvious marks of violence to the torso.'

He shifted position, easing the weight of his enormous bulk from his knees, then continued, 'The legs are bound with chains, and the wrists with a nylon fibre rope. He has been gagged extensively with brown gaffer tape.'

He reached into his bag and took out a pair of scissors. He deftly cut away the gaffer tape, revealing the head of the deceased.

He then examined the head closely, saying, 'There appears to be some sort of injury to both ears, and major contusions to the back and top of his head.'

Rachel was standing to one side of the body bag and looked closely at the ears of the victim. She turned to Seamus Carter and said, 'What's that jellylike substance oozing from his ears?'

'It looks like the inner ear and eardrums have been severely damaged. I've seen similar seepage from the ears of divers who've died from the effects of decompression sickness. So it could be from the pressure of the water.'

Rachel shouted across to the divers, as they removed their equipment from the edge of the riverbank: 'What's the depth of the water below the bridge?'

One of the divers shouted back, 'Out in the middle where the body was found, it's about fifteen feet deep.'

Rachel shouted back, 'Thanks.'

Seamus said, 'That's way too shallow to have caused the bends. I'll probably know more when I can examine the ears closely during the post-mortem.'

Danny said, 'Do you think it was the body being thrown from the bridge that caused the splash our witness heard?'

'From the decomposition rate, I would say so. It's obvious

that this body hasn't been in the water that long. The dive supervisor will probably confirm this.'

As Seamus Carter made his preliminary verbal examination, Tim Donnelly and his scenes of crime technicians were taking photographs of the deceased and bagging up samples removed from the dead body.

Seamus said, 'Danny, do you have any objections if we remove the chains prior to transportation again?'

Danny looked at Tim. 'Have you got everything you need?'

Tim nodded, and Danny said, 'Okay, start unwrapping the chains from around his legs. Take photographs of every stage, please.'

The technicians got to work and began untangling the mass of chain links from around the legs as photographers constantly snapped away in the background.

Tina said to Seamus, 'Where should we ask the undertakers to take the body?'

'At this time of night, Newark Hospital mortuary will be empty. It's also probably the closest. I'll contact my office and ask them to make the arrangements at the hospital. Shall we say nine o'clock tonight?'

Danny nodded. 'That's fine. I'll see you there. Tina, Rachel, are you both okay to attend as well?'

Tina said, 'Of course. I'll just need to make a phone call home first.'

Danny said, 'Me too. Welcome to the world of major crime investigation.'

Seamus said, 'I can finish up here with Tim and arrange transport with the undertakers when they arrive, if you want to go and make those calls.'

'Okay. Thanks. We'll see you later, at Newark Hospital.'

As the detectives made their way from the riverbank, back to their car, Tina broke the silence by verbalising what she was thinking: 'I'll need to get a team out here first thing in the morning to make a start on the house-to-house enquiries. I never realised there were so many houses dotted around this area.'

Danny said, 'I know. It's deceptive, isn't it? I've driven over this bridge countless times and never really noticed all the houses set back from the road.'

Warming to her theme, Tina continued, 'I'll also need a full trawl for any CCTV opportunities. We may be able to obtain some footage of the van seen by the witness. I doubt there's been that many white vans going over the bridge, or being driven between Newark and Mansfield, at that time of night.'

'You're right, Tina. And if we can find and identify that van, we may very well find our killer.'

44

9.00 pm, 14 June 1987
Newark Hospital, Nottinghamshire

The burly Irish pathologist had taken a long time examining the lungs and respiratory tract of the body pulled from the river earlier that evening.

He finally turned to the watching Danny, Tina and Rachel, and said, 'He's the same as the Gunthorpe Bridge victim. He was still alive when he was thrown into the river. The cause of death is drowning.'

Samples were then taken for toxicology before Seamus turned his attention to the deceased's damaged ears. After making incisions to expose the inner ears, he said, 'Both eardrums have been perforated. No, it's more than perforation. It's closer to obliteration. The damage to both inner ears is very severe and extensive.'

Rachel said, 'Well, the divers confirmed it couldn't have

been caused by the pressure of the river water. Any ideas what may have caused it?'

Seamus was silent for a moment, trying to recall something. When it came to him, he said, 'The only other time I've seen anything like this was a post-mortem I carried out on an aircraft engine technician who had been killed in an industrial accident at East Midlands Airport. That poor man had been pulled into a jet turbine that he was testing and become trapped. He had lost his ear defenders as he was sucked into the engine. It was the horrific injuries to his torso that killed him, but his inner ears had been extensively damaged by the tremendous noise of the jet engine, which had continued to run.'

Danny said, 'So you think being exposed to a loud noise over a period of time could have caused all this damage?'

'It's the only other time I've seen such injuries. The noise involved would have to be extremely loud and prolonged to have caused that amount of damage.'

'Okay. At the riverbank, you mentioned the injuries to the top and back of the head. Were they significant?'

'When I examined the skull, neither of the wounds had caused a fracture, but they were nonetheless significant injuries. Either one could have caused the deceased to lose consciousness.'

'Anything else you think is significant?'

'I haven't found any other significant injuries on the body. There's some slight bruising on one side of his jawline that could have been caused by a punch. There are no tattoos, operation scars, implants or broken bones that could help with your identification. I'll obtain fingerprints and make dental impressions before I finish up.'

'Thanks. When can you let me have your report?'

'As soon as I get the toxicology reports back, I'll send you the full report. The preliminary finding is what I've already said: The cause of death was drowning.'

Danny turned to Rachel. 'Are there any other exhibits you need to bag and label before we go?'

'Everything's done, boss.'

Danny turned back to the pathologist, who was busy getting fingerprint impressions, and said, 'We're off now. Talk to you soon.'

'Right you are, Danny.'

The three detectives left the examination room, leaving Seamus and a mortuary technician alone with the body.

As they walked back to the car, Danny said, 'We need to go public on this. These murders are linked, and we're no further on, really. We need to try to get a breakthrough from somewhere. We're going to need the public's help to catch this killer.'

Tina remained tight-lipped and nodded.

Danny asked, 'What's your top priority now?'

Tina said, 'We need to identify this victim and then ascertain if there's anything that links him to Suzy Flowers.'

'Right. Let's get to it, then.'

45

8.00 am, 15 June 1987
MCIU Offices, Mansfield, Nottinghamshire

There was a knock on his office door, and Danny shouted, 'Come in!'

The door opened. Tina and Rob walked in, clutching their enquiry logs in one hand and a mug of coffee in the other.

Danny said, 'Grab a seat. I want to go through the two enquiries with you both, to see exactly where we are. We need to drive things forward; I think these enquiries are in danger of stalling, and I want to make sure we aren't missing something. Let's start with the fires.'

Rob opened his log and said, 'Two dwelling house fires, both started using petrol as an accelerant. The first at Blidworth; the second in Mansfield. All three victims are elderly. Joe Sinclair from Blidworth had no next of kin, and enquiries so far have found no reason why he should be targeted. The landlord of the property is no longer of interest. We found nothing to connect him in any way with the fire. The house-to-house enquiries at Blidworth, carried out by the Special Operations Unit, haven't turned anything up at all. We are running out of viable enquiries to push this investigation forward. As you know, fire and forensics don't mix. We've got nothing back from scenes of crime, and although Tony Parrish has been a massive help in identifying the fact that the fire was arson, he can't really help us any further.'

He paused to see if Danny had any questions. When none were forthcoming, he continued, 'Moving on to the second fire on Finningley Road ... Once again, both the victims were elderly – Douglas and Joan Cooper. It's still early days on the house-to-house enquiries, but so far, they've drawn a blank. Again, it's probably too early to be definite, but we can find no link between either Douglas or Joan Cooper and Joe Sinclair. I might know more after I've spoken to the daughter this morning. Sophie Arnold will be here at ten o'clock, to make the formal identification. I'll talk to her afterwards and see if she's aware of any link between her mum and dad and Joe Sinclair. I'll also try to ascertain if her parents had any enemies, or if they had been involved in any recent disputes with anybody. Certainly, the enquiries we've made so far haven't found any.'

Danny interrupted: 'I wanted to meet Mrs Arnold when she came in today, but I've been summoned to headquarters at ten o'clock, for a meeting with Potter. You'll have to speak to Mrs Arnold without me. Will that cause any issues?'

'Okay. She wasn't expecting to see you, so there won't be a problem. That's about it for the Mansfield fire.'

'Forensics?'

'Again, there's no forensics from the scene itself. Footwear impressions have been made of the footprints found by Tony. There's nothing to identify the brand of footwear. Tim Donnelly has informed me that all he can say for definite is that they were made by a work boot of some kind. The size is quite small – probably a size seven or eight.'

'Thanks. How did you get on with the divisional commander last night?'

'Surprisingly well, actually. He liked my idea about using the Specials. He contacted the local Special Constabulary chief inspector while I was there. Between them, they've agreed to provide ten officers to make foot patrols at night around local OAP housing. He's agreed to put the extra night patrols on for one week initially, then review it.'

For the first time that morning, Danny smiled. 'That's great. You must be very persuasive. You've got far more out of him than I usually get. Is there anything else we can be doing to push the enquiry forward?'

'I'm still hopeful that the house-to-house enquiries will turn something up. As you know, the Bellamy Estate is massive, so there's still the potential for a witness to be found.'

'Has anything come in yet from the press appeal last night?'

'Not yet. I emphasised the point about providing more foot patrols, and Tony did a brilliant piece on fire safety.'

'One last thing. Have we got copies of all the photographs taken by the press, of the crowds of onlookers?'

'They've arrived this morning.'

'Are there many?'

'A rough estimate? Fifty or sixty.'

'Okay. I want you to make sure everyone on the Unit gets to see them, sooner rather than later. Work your way through the photographs and see if there are any faces that you or your team may recognise. I want you to pull photographs of convicted arsonists who live in the surrounding areas from the Local Intelligence Office and compare them to the faces in the crowds.'

Rob nodded and made notes.

'Tina, where are we with your enquiry?'

'All our efforts this morning will be focused on identifying the second victim. The enquiries into the death of Suzy Flowers are stalling badly. All the enquiries we've carried out at the university have so far drawn a blank.'

'How come?'

'Suzy was well known by everybody, but it seems she wasn't very well liked. She has been described as arrogant, brash, and even a tart. She was a larger-than-life character alright, but also one nobody cared much for.'

'I see.'

'She doesn't appear to have any significant close friends, and nobody has mentioned anything about a current boyfriend.'

'Keep looking. Did you find anything at Radford?'

'The search of her bedsit in Radford didn't reveal anything significant. I've arranged for a press appeal to be held during the lunchtime news on the local television channels today. I've spoken to Suzy's mum on the phone again this morning. She's fine about us releasing her daughter's details to the media.'

'That's good. Let's hope that turns something up.'

Tina continued: 'I've tasked Andy Wills with trying to find any CCTV around the Kelham Bridge area, to see if we can get a sighting of the white van mentioned by James Birch. He's also mastering the house-to-house enquiries at Kelham. The Special Operations Unit will be available to commence house-to-house enquiries later this morning. I'm staying here this morning while I sort out the press appeal for the media. I've also got teams here trawling through missing persons reports to try to identify our latest victim. I want to make sure they are pushing things on. I'm still waiting to hear from Seamus Carter about the fingerprints and dental impressions.'

'Okay. It sounds like you've got everything covered. I'll chase Seamus on your behalf before I leave for the meeting with Potter at headquarters. What about the vehicle stop checks at Gunthorpe Bridge? Have they turned anything up?'

'Nothing has come from them at all. I was starting to get a lot of grief from the divisional commander over there, about wasting resources on what he called "a wild goose chase".'

Danny frowned. 'Anything else you think we need to be doing?'

Tina shook her head.

'Okay. Both of you need to keep pushing your teams. All of us in this room know that we're struggling for new leads. You mustn't let them see that. Keep them all motivated. Keep driving them hard, and something will turn up. Rob, concentrate on completing the house-to-house. I know it's an onerous task, but it could provide the breakthrough we need. Tina, concentrate on identifying the Kelham Bridge victim, and let's hope the press appeal brings some fresh leads. We need to locate that white van.'

The two detective inspectors got up and left Danny alone in his office. He stared at his own enquiry log, hoping some inspiration would leap from the pages.

It didn't.

As well as the two enquiries racing through his mind, his thoughts were also on this morning's unscheduled meeting with Potter. He pondered what possible reasons the detective chief superintendent could have for calling him into headquarters for such an urgent meeting. It had only been two days since Danny last updated him about progress.

Danny dismissed those thoughts and began concentrating on the two enquiries. He would find out what Potter wanted soon enough.

46

10.00 am, 15 June 1987
The Oaks Residential Care Home, West Bridgford, Nottingham

Stephen Meadows walked into the spacious reception and spoke to the nurse behind the desk. He hadn't seen her before, so he introduced himself and said, 'Good morning. I'm here to see my sister, Dawn Meadows. I'm not too early, am I? Only I've got the day off today. It's a beautiful morning, and I wondered if I could take her out in her wheelchair to get some fresh air.'

The nurse smiled. 'That sounds a lovely idea. Let me check with Dr Sanderson and see how Dawn's doing today. If you grab a seat, I'll call him. I won't be a minute.'

Stephen nodded and walked across the marble-floored foyer and sat down in one of the three leather bucket chairs.

He couldn't wait to tell Dawn his progress. How he had dealt with Poyser and was working on the next.

As he sat waiting, he suddenly felt torn about his actions. It had felt so good being able to despatch Milfoyle and Poyser. He had enjoyed dropping them both into the river. He had relished the sense of power it had brought him. For once in his long-suffering life, he had felt in charge. He was calling the shots, and it felt great.

But now, as he sat waiting to enjoy time with his sister, he felt conflicted. He knew that what he was doing was wrong and that if he got caught, he would be sent to prison for a long time.

Who would look after Dawn then?

Who would come to visit her?

If Dr Sanderson said it was okay to see her today, he would ask his sister what she thought he should do.

Maybe he should stop the cleansing altogether.

47

10.00 am, 15 June 1987
Nottinghamshire Police Headquarters

'Enter!'
It was the usual terse command that Danny had become accustomed to whenever he went to see Adrian Potter at headquarters.

He walked into Potter's office and closed the door. Potter looked over his glasses at him and said, 'Take a seat, Chief Inspector. I understand there have been more developments overnight.'

Danny sat down, crossed his legs and said, 'Yes, sir. The body of a middle-aged Afro-Caribbean male was recovered from the River Trent beneath Kelham Bridge yesterday evening.'

'Is it linked to the body recovered at Gunthorpe?'

'It would appear so. The man's legs had been weighted

down with chains that look identical to those used at Gunthorpe.'

'Do we know who the deceased is yet?'

'No, sir, but all our efforts this morning are concentrated on finding out who the man was.'

'So, you have a possible serial arsonist killing old people in the Mansfield area, and another potential serial killer deliberately drowning people in the river. How are enquiries progressing?'

'All my team are working flat out, sir. They are diligently following whatever leads we can generate.'

'But getting nowhere fast?'

Danny bit his lip and measured his reply. 'I'll admit, it's very slow going, but it's still early days. I believe we're making genuine progress on both enquiries.'

'The chief constable disagrees; he feels the enquiries are stalling. I had a meeting with him first thing this morning, where I personally briefed him on how each of the enquiries are progressing.'

There was nothing measured about Danny's next response: 'And are you the person best placed to provide that briefing, sir?'

'It's part of my role, Chief Inspector. The chief has agreed to my proposed initiative of bringing in an investigative expert to assist in these enquiries.'

'Excuse me? What investigative expert?'

'Professor Sharon Whittle, from Durham University, is a world-renowned expert in criminological psychology. She will be travelling down from Newcastle and joining your team first thing tomorrow morning.'

'With all due respect, I don't think that's necessary. What can a psychologist bring to these investigations?'

'Professor Whittle has studied profiling and the psychology of offenders, with the FBI at Quantico in the

United States. I would say she is eminently qualified to bring a fresh perspective and new ideas to your enquiries. If you could manage to keep an open mind for one minute, she could help you catch your killers.'

'I always strive to keep an open mind, sir. I'm yet to be convinced about profiling for criminal investigations.'

'Chief Inspector, I didn't call you in today to have a debate on the merits of alternative methods of investigation. The chief constable has already agreed with my suggestion. Professor Whittle will be arriving at ten o'clock tomorrow morning. Make sure you have everything ready at the MCIU offices so you can brief her on each enquiry upon her arrival. I have already sent her the control room logs for each offence, so she won't be coming in stone cold. She isn't coming here to sit blithely on the sidelines, Chief Inspector. You will cooperate with her fully, is that understood?'

'Understood, sir. I just hope you're right, and this isn't all going to be a huge waste of time and energy.'

Potter got to his feet and said angrily, 'That's enough negativity! I want to see genuine cooperation between you and Professor Whittle. The chief constable will be watching on with interest. That will be all.'

Danny got to his feet slowly and walked out of the office. As he walked back to his car, he scolded himself for being stubborn. He knew that both enquiries were floundering. Who knew; maybe this professor might see something they were all missing?

He sat in his car, started the engine, and said out loud, 'Keep an open mind!'

48

4.00 pm, 15 June 1987
Hardwick Avenue, Rainworth, Nottinghamshire

He pressed the rewind button and watched as the images on his television moved backwards at twelve times the normal speed. When he pressed play on the video recorder, the police press conference was just starting again.

This would be the third time he had watched it, in quick succession. He was alone in the house, so could take his time and enjoy his moment of celebrity. Even though nobody knew his name, they were beginning to realise what he was capable of.

He hit the pause button as the picture flicked from the stern-faced detective talking about the help the police needed, to an image of the charred, blackened remains of the bungalow on Finningley Road.

The more he looked at the gutted shell of the property, the more he marvelled at his own handiwork. He had released the beast in the most exquisite, perfect way. He knew that once the fire was alight, it was like the genie in the bottle. There was no stopping it, and no returning it to its captive state.

Staring at the flickering image on his television, his mind drifted back to the actual night. He could almost smell the rancid, black smoke that had poured out of the windows as the fire took hold. He had mingled silently with the crowds as they gathered, still clutching the carrier bag that contained the now-empty petrol can. The memories were delicious. Recalling how the firemen had tried so hard to slay the beast he had released.

He finished watching the press conference and switched off the television. He flicked the eject switch on the video recorder and took out the VHS tape, placing it inside the protective cover.

As he walked upstairs to put the video tape in the drawer next to the scrapbook, he was deep in thought. He'd been so engrossed in watching his handiwork on the video, that at first, he hadn't heard the detective talking about the extra patrols at night. He would now have to wait a few days before setting out again. He needed to be careful. He didn't want his growing importance to be suddenly stopped by an unfortunate encounter with some uniformed cop.

He would spend his time searching for the next perfect target, but during daylight. As soon as he saw the ideal property, he would know. If he couldn't find one that way, he would wait a few days and start searching again at night. He felt a surge of excitement building within him as he wondered if the selected property would contain more people to be sacrificed. He dearly hoped there would be people inside the building, as it made his significance and power even greater.

He lay on his bed and stared at the ceiling. Closing his eyes, he imagined giant flames sweeping through a building. He could hear the people inside screaming, and a smile played slowly across his face.

49

7.00 pm, 14 June 1987
Mansfield, Nottinghamshire

Danny walked back into the lounge, and Sue asked, 'Has she settled down okay?'

'Yeah, she's fast asleep now. She's doing those snoring, snuffling sounds that are so adorable. I've just been sat next to the cot, watching her bottom lip quiver as she breathes in.'

'That's good. I'm glad she's settled. Now perhaps you can tell me what's bothering you?'

'Bothering me?'

'Yeah. You've been quiet ever since you got home. I know something's bothering you, so spill the beans.'

Danny sat down next to his wife. He put his arm around her and said, 'Do you think I'm stubborn?'

'You've got a stubborn streak sometimes. Why?'

'Potter's arranged for a criminological psychologist to

work with the MCIU, investigating the fires and the bodies found in the river.'

'I know what a psychologist does, but what does a criminological psychologist do?'

'They study the patterns of behaviour demonstrated by criminals. They then use that information to detect serious crimes – or, at least, that's the theory of it.'

'And I can see that you're not convinced, sweetheart.'

'I don't know. I think I'm smarting more because I wasn't asked my opinion before it happened. It's yet another example of something being forced on to me by Adrian Potter.'

'So, who's this psychologist, and where are they from?'

'Her name's Sharon Whittle. She's from Newcastle, and she's a professor at Durham University. Apparently, she's worked with the FBI in America. I did some checking before I came home, and she's very well regarded.'

'Sounds like she knows her stuff. So why so gloomy?'

'I don't really know; I suppose I'm just feeling old and stuck in my ways. Is this the future of police investigation? Are we going to have a psychologist breathing down our necks on every enquiry? That's why I asked if you think I'm stubborn.'

Sue cuddled in closely to Danny and said, 'When's your professor arriving?'

'She's driving down from Newcastle tomorrow morning. We're having a full briefing at ten o'clock.'

'That quick, eh? I think you're just going to have to go with the flow on this one. Who knows? If she's as good as people think, she may even be able to help you. You said yourself that both enquiries were stalling a little.'

'I know, and you're right. I keep telling myself to keep an open mind.'

'And that's what you've got to do, sweetheart. Anyway, that's enough about work. Is there anything good on the box?'

Sue switched the television on and began flicking through the different channels. Danny stared at the screen, but kept hearing a small voice in his head, saying, *Keep an open mind.*

50

10.00 am, 16 June 1987
MCIU Offices, Mansfield, Nottinghamshire

Danny had arrived at work early, to warn Rob and Tina about Professor Whittle's arrival. A solemn-looking Danny now waited with his detective inspectors in the MCIU office. The telephone rang, and Danny answered the call. After a brief conversation, he put the telephone down and said, 'She's here, waiting downstairs.'

He stood up and put on his jacket. 'You two wait in my office. I'll go downstairs to meet her personally and bring her back up for the introductions and briefing. Have you both got everything?'

Rob nodded, and Tina said, 'Yes, boss.'

Danny walked down the two flights of stairs and went to the front counter of the police station. There was only one person waiting in the foyer. Standing near the front door, with a small suitcase at her feet, was a petite, slim woman with short ash blonde hair. As Danny opened the door to the station, the woman turned to face him.

Professor Sharon Whittle was in her mid-forties, but looked younger. She had the brightest emerald-green eyes that Danny had ever seen. They appeared larger than they were, as the professor wore rimless round spectacles that exaggerated the size of her eyes, making them even more striking.

Danny held out his hand and said, 'Professor Whittle? I'm Detective Chief Inspector Flint. How was your journey?'

She shook his hand, smiled and said, 'Please call me Sharon. I always feel ancient when people call me "professor". The journey was good, thanks. The roads were clear, so it was a comfortable drive.'

Danny smiled and said, 'Sharon it is, then. And please call me Danny. We'll go upstairs to my office so my two detective inspectors can brief you fully on the cases we're investigating.'

Danny picked up her suitcase, opened the door to the station, and said, 'This way, please.'

As they walked up the stairs, Danny said, 'Where are you staying while you're here?'

'I've booked into the Park Hotel on Woodhouse Road. Is it okay?'

'I've never stayed there personally. I'm told it's clean and tidy and that they do a particularly good cooked breakfast. How long do you expect to be staying here, Sharon?'

'I really don't know. The invitation from Adrian Potter was open-ended. He told me about the two enquiries. He said that there was a possibility that two separate offenders were responsible for the murders. I was quite excited by the prospect of working on two potential serial killer cases at the same time. As you can see, I gladly accepted his invitation.'

'Wasn't it a problem to get time off from the university?'

'Not at all. I work on a consultancy basis these days. My main body of work is lecturing psychology and criminology students at Durham. That said, I do have an understanding with the vice chancellor that if the right opportunity arises, I can leave without notice.'

'Do you see our enquiries as that sort of opportunity?'

'Serial killers are still a rare phenomenon in this country. So it makes a change for me, not to be jetting off to America to work.'

Noticing the wedding band she wore, Danny said, 'You must have a very understanding husband, as well. I'm not sure my wife, Sue, would like me working away all the time.'

'My husband is an industrial chemist who works on the oil rigs off Aberdeen, so we're both used to spending time apart.' She grinned. 'It seems to work for us, Danny.'

Danny could hear the slight hint of an American accent as she spoke, and he remembered what Potter had said about the FBI training.

'How long have you been doing this?'

'I've been a psychologist all my working life. I've specialised in criminological psychology over the last ten years.'

'Chief Superintendent Potter mentioned to me that you had some training in the United States?'

'Yes, I have. I was fortunate enough to spend two years studying with the FBI's Behavioural Science Unit. They are light years ahead of us in this country.'

'In what way?'

'They've really bought into the psychology of criminal behaviour; all their detectives are routinely trained to do their own profiling. Profiling is about so much more than physical description. Detectives in the States learn how to use behavioural tendencies, personality traits, geographic location, demographics and biographical features of offenders, as standard. It's a concept that just hasn't been accepted over here yet. What are your thoughts on the subject, Danny? After all, we're going to be working together on these cases.'

Danny said, 'I'm always willing to learn, and I always keep an open mind on things. I'm sure we'll get along fine, and hopefully you'll be able to help us. Now, how about a tea or coffee before we start the briefing?'

'A coffee would be great; I'm gagging for a drink.'

Five minutes later, with the introductions all done and beverages provided, Danny was about to start the briefing in his office when there was a knock on the door.

Danny shouted, 'Come in!'

Rachel Moore walked in and said, 'Sorry to interrupt your meeting, sir. I thought you'd want to know; I think we've now identified the victim at Kelham Bridge.'

Danny said, 'Go on, Rachel.'

'His name's Rex Poyser. He was forty-seven years old and is from the St Anne's estate in Nottingham. He was identified from the missing persons files. His girlfriend, Angela Thomas, reported him missing after he didn't show up for work two days ago, on the fourteenth. He didn't come home the night before that, but apparently that wasn't unusual. So she didn't report him missing until the fourteenth, when he didn't turn up for work at Castle Sounds, on Lister Gate in Nottingham. Poyser was the manager at the recording studio, so it was very strange for him not to be at work. Apparently, Angela Thomas also found his car, still locked up and in the car park where he'd left it, on the thirteenth.'

'How sure are we that he's our man?'

'The description's spot on. As you know, the deceased was quite striking in appearance. I've arranged for someone to pick up Angela Thomas and take her to Newark Hospital for a formal identification. I'm going to drive over now and meet her there.'

'I know it's probably too early to say, but is there any obvious link between Rex Poyser and Suzy Flowers?'

'I don't know yet, sir.'

'Okay, thanks. Let me know as soon as we have a positive identification. Oh, and Rachel, before you go to Newark, get someone to check the car park where Poyser left his car. There may be CCTV available. It's possible he was abducted from that car park, and I don't want to lose that evidence, if it's there.'

Rachel nodded and left the room.

Professor Whittle said, 'You do know there's already one, glaringly obvious link in both cases. A link that has nothing to do with the victims.'

Danny said, 'Go on.'

'Both your victims were found in geographically specific locations. They were both dumped from bridges into the river. If you try to see things through the eyes of the killer, the middle of a bridge is not a very bright place to dispose of a body. There's the very real risk of being seen by other drivers, as well as the chance of the bodies being discovered early. Yet our killer still dumped them there.'

'Your point is?'

'I was just wondering how many bridges there are over the River Trent?'

'Off the top of my head, I would say probably half a dozen.'

'Would it be possible to task your divers to search below the other bridges?'

'Do you think there are other victims?'

'It's eminently possible. For some reason, the killer seems to be drawn to the bridges. I haven't seen the post-mortem reports yet, but am I correct in assuming that both the victims were still alive when they went in the river?'

'Yes, they were.'

'I think that's also incredibly significant. He wanted them to suffer a painful, lingering death. Drowning is horrific; it's the stuff of nightmares. I think there's a strong element of payback in the way this man kills. So, the million-dollar question you need to answer is, exactly what is he paying them back for?'

Tina said, 'I understand what you're saying, but we haven't even formally identified the second victim yet. Let alone established a connection between the two victims.'

'I'm sure there will be a connection somewhere. When you find that link, the killer will become obvious. What about it, Danny? Can you organise your divers to search below the other bridges?'

'I'll talk to the Underwater Search Unit and see how quickly they can do it.'

He thought, *Keep an open mind, Danny; keep an open mind.*

Professor Whittle smiled benignly and said, 'Tina, why don't you start by telling me everything you've learned so far about Suzy Flowers?'

51

4.00 pm, 17 June 1987
The Oaks Residential Care Home, West Bridgford, Nottingham

Dr Sanderson was sitting in his office at the Oaks, deep in thought. He was extremely troubled by the recent downward spiral in the condition of one of his patients.

Dawn Meadows had remained in a stable condition ever since she had been placed in the specialist care home following the sudden death of her parents. That had all changed after her brother, Stephen, had started visiting her.

Every time the brother came to visit, he would speak at length in hushed tones to his sister. On each occasion, the outcome had been the same. For no apparent reason, Dawn would lapse into a severe epileptic fit. This had happened on three occasions now.

He had been so troubled by these recent events that he

had made an appointment to see Dawn Meadows' social worker, Heather Joyce, to discuss the matter.

There was a knock on his office door that dragged him from his thoughts. He shouted, 'Come in.'

The door opened, and a middle-aged woman wearing a pinstripe navy blue suit walked in. As she walked across to the doctor's desk, she smiled. Her face had a warmth and kindness that contrasted sharply with the short blonde hairstyle that saw one side of her head completely shaved. Her blue eyes held a fire within them that spoke of an inner determination and strength.

The two professionals knew each other well.

Heather Joyce said, 'Hello, Joel. You asked to see me about Dawn Meadows?'

'Grab a seat, Heather. Can I get you a coffee or something else to drink?'

As she sat down, she shook her head. 'I'm fine, thanks. What seems to be the problem? The last time I was here, Dawn had settled in wonderfully well. What's changed?'

'Her brother.'

'I know she has a brother. I spoke to him quite a lot after the parents died. I thought he held things together remarkably well at the time, considering what had happened and the subsequent farce of the court case.'

'I don't know anything about that. The problem I have is that after Dawn was first brought here, she saw nobody. There were no visitors at all, and that helped us to get her into a routine.'

'There were no visits because she has nobody left who could visit, apart from her brother.'

'I understand that, but we had her medications balanced just right. She had suffered no seizures at all and was responding very well. We had seen a vast improvement in her condition.'

'I sense a "but" coming, Joel.'

'But then her brother turned up out of the blue and began visiting her. That's when problems started for Dawn.'

'Why would a visit from her only living relative cause a problem? He's obviously taken some time to come to terms with the loss of his parents and only now feels able to support his sister.'

'Ideally, I'm sure that would be the case. The problem is that whatever it is he's saying to her during his visits, it is really affecting her state. After every visit, Dawn suffers a severe epileptic episode. I've had to significantly increase her dosages of the three drugs she was on, and it's not doing her any good. Obviously, I can't stop her brother visiting, but I am very concerned for Dawn.'

'And you've no idea what the brother is talking to her about?'

'No. Listen, I was so worried that the last time he was here, he wanted to walk with his sister in the grounds. I agreed solely so I could send a nurse out with them, hoping that she would be able to hear what was being said.'

'That's totally out of order, Joel. You can't ask your staff to eavesdrop on private conversations.'

Dr Sanderson paused, thinking carefully how to respond. He remained calm and said, 'Nobody was eavesdropping. I'm just extremely concerned that Dawn's condition will continue to deteriorate while ever her brother is having these conversations with her. Whatever it is he's saying, it's obviously upsetting her greatly.'

'Okay, I can see why you're concerned. All I can do is go and talk to the brother and see if I can shed some light on what it is he talks to her about.'

'Thanks, Heather. It's in everyone's best interests if we can stabilise Dawn again. Every epileptic seizure she has badly disrupts her cognisant ability. Her speech is already very bad;

after each seizure, it's virtually non-existent. We know from past studies that seizures erase short-term memory for patients. The bottom line is this: Her brother's visits are very bad for her health.'

'Leave it with me, Joel. I'll go and see him. I've got his home address back at the office somewhere.'

'Thank you.'

'Now, never mind a cup of coffee – do you fancy treating me to a proper drink at the Feathers in Bridgford?'

'Of course. It's good to see you again. I just hope you can get to the bottom of this little mystery.'

52

4.00 pm, 18 June 1987
Fiskerton Road, Bleasby, Nottinghamshire

Pete Slater cursed out loud as he drove the tractor along the narrow, winding Fiskerton Road, just outside the village of Bleasby. About fifty yards in front of him, and blocking the entire lane, was a white Ford Transit van. The driver had the bonnet of the van raised and his head buried in the engine compartment, obviously trying to repair some sort of mechanical fault.

Slater glanced at his watch. It was four o'clock. He had been working at White Moor Farm in Bleasby since just before six o'clock that morning. He was tired and hungry, and, because he was Pete Slater, he was irritable and in a foul mood.

Pete Slater was always in a bad mood; he was known for his foul temper.

He stopped the tractor and climbed down from the high

cab, mumbling obscenities under his breath. His mood worsened when he saw there was a passing place in the lane just behind the van. His muttering grew louder now. 'For fuck's sake! If your van was conking out, why didn't you pull in there!'

The driver of the stricken van never once turned around to see who had pulled up in front of his broken-down van.

Slater walked up to the van until he was standing right next to the driver, who still had his head under the bonnet. He said tersely, 'If it's fucked, mate, you should have pulled into the passing place. Not block the entire fucking lane.'

The driver of the van stood up from beneath the bonnet.

He stared at the farm labourer with a vacant expression before saying, 'I'm s-s-sorry. I think it's f-f-fixed now. I'll m-m-move it.'

Stomping back to his tractor, Slater shouted over his shoulder, 'Be quick about it. I haven't got all bloody day.'

Up until the tractor had come to a stop, Meadows had been all set to abduct Slater and cleanse him in the same way as Milfoyle and Poyser. It had been thoughts of his sister, suffering yet another bad reaction to his disclosure to her that he had cleansed Poyser, that had made him take the decision to abort the planned cleansing of Slater.

Hearing the throwaway comment from Slater, Stephen Meadows very nearly changed his mind again. He felt the weight of the heavy wrench in his overall pocket and seriously considered smashing the heavy tool across the back of Slater's head.

IT WASN'T the first about-face. Several times during the day, he had decided to stop the preparations, only to continue as the feeling of raw power he had felt as he cleansed Milfoyle and Poyser returned. It was an addictive, dark power. It made him yearn to make Slater pay in the same way as the others.

Eventually, the realisation that he needed to be around for his stricken sister had decided the constant conflict within his head, and he allowed Slater to walk away.

He got into the van and started the engine before reversing the vehicle into the passing space, allowing Slater's tractor to pass.

As the heavy farm machinery was driven slowly by, Meadows stared at the man in the cab. Memories of the night Slater and his cronies had beaten him up outside the Railway pub in Lowdham flooded back to Meadows as he watched the tractor travel slowly down the narrow lane.

Meadows had been out having a quiet drink on his own when Slater and four of his football hooligan friends had piled into the pub after yet another Nottingham Forest defeat. Slater was in an angry mood and recognised Stephen Meadows from school. He began mimicking his stutter and started flicking beer mats at him, trying to provoke a response.

Eventually, Meadows had asked Slater to stop, saying, 'P-p-please s-s-stop d-d-doing that!'

It had been all the excuse Slater needed. With the help of his friends, he had dragged Meadows outside the pub and subjected him to a prolonged and vicious beating. Meadows hadn't fought back; he had curled up in a ball, trying to protect himself from the boots and fists. The landlord had called the police.

By the time they arrived, the football hooligans, including Slater, had long gone. Although bruised, battered and humiliated, Stephen Meadows had refused to make a statement. Nobody else in the pub admitted knowing it had been Pete Slater who was responsible for the assault, for fear of future repercussions. Slater was well known in the area as a violent bully. Nobody wanted to cross him.

Unlike Milfoyle and Poyser, Slater had only crossed him once.

It was still with real reluctance that Meadows had allowed him to walk away. He had dearly wanted the bullying, ginger skinhead to pay, but he had come to realise that he needed to think about Dawn. His sister was now his priority.

There was still one name on the list that he knew his sister would want him to make pay. The man responsible for callously ripping their beloved parents away from them, and then cunningly using the courts to evade any justice.

The last man he desperately needed to cleanse was the orthopaedic consultant Dr James McEllery.

53

11.30 pm, 18 June 1987
Park Hotel, Woodhouse Road, Mansfield, Nottinghamshire

Sharon Whittle was sitting in bed in the comfortable room she had booked at the Park Hotel. She took off her glasses and placed them on top of the pile of intelligence reports on the bedspread. Her eyes were stinging. She suddenly felt very tired.

She had spent the entire evening reading intelligence reports about fires in the county of Nottinghamshire. She picked up the reports and her glasses from the bedspread and placed them on the bedside cabinet.

It had been another long, tiring day, working alongside Danny Flint and his team of detectives in the MCIU. The enquiries into the two investigations were both floundering. She understood completely why Adrian Potter and the chief constable had invited her to Nottinghamshire.

The fatal house fires were undoubtedly the work of a

serial arsonist. She knew from experience that the offender would have started by setting multiple smaller fires. That was the reason for the hours she had spent doing late-night research.

By trawling through the pile of intelligence reports, she had identified that there had been a disproportionate number of grass fires and rubbish bin fires in and around the town of Mansfield over the last six months. She had also found a larger-than-average number of hoax calls had been made to the fire brigade in that locality during the same time period.

It helped to show the pattern of behaviour expected from a developing arsonist. Frustratingly, that was all it showed. There had been no arrests for the smaller fires, and nobody had been investigated for making the hoax calls.

She squeezed the top of her nose where her glasses usually sat, before rubbing her sore eyelids gently with the tips of her fingers.

She put her head back on the headboard and closed her eyes.

Her thoughts now turned to the drowning victims and the other killer. She was convinced there would be other victims. She was also acutely aware that Danny and his team were still to be convinced by her methods and suggestions. So far, the searches by the police frogmen below some of the other bridges had found nothing. She could see, in the eyes of the detectives, that the level of scepticism about her work was rising steadily.

She reached over and turned out the bedside lamp, hoping that sleep would come quickly.

Tomorrow would be another stressful day.

54

2.00 pm, 19 June 1987
Ridge Hill, Lowdham, Nottinghamshire

Heather Joyce banged hard on the uPVC plastic, double-glazed door of the secluded bungalow. She was about to give up and start walking back to her car when she heard the rumble of a diesel engine.

She turned and saw a white Ford Transit van being driven slowly down the lengthy driveway, towards the bungalow.

The driver had obviously seen her standing there, as the vehicle suddenly came to an abrupt stop. The driver opened the door and jumped out.

As he walked towards her, Heather recognised him to be Stephen Meadows.

She offered her hand and said, 'Hello, Stephen. Do you remember me?'

She could see Meadows was struggling to put a name to

her face, so she said, 'I'm Heather Joyce. Your sister's social worker. I saw you at the trial of Dr McEllery.'

He nodded in recognition, then snarled moodily, 'Don't speak that bastard's name here.'

A little taken aback by the venom in the comment, Heather said, 'I'm sorry, Stephen. I didn't mean any offence.'

He ignored her apology and said, 'What do you want?'

'Can we pop inside for ten minutes? I need to talk to you about Dawn.'

A look that was a mixture of concern and fear flashed across Meadows' face, and he said, 'Is everything okay? Is Dawn alright?'

'Dawn is okay, but I need to have a chat about your visits.'

There was no invitation from Meadows to step inside the bungalow, and it was obvious to Heather that none would be forthcoming, so she didn't push it.

Instead, she said, 'Dawn seems to get upset when you've visited her.'

'That's not my fault; that's how she is. I can't change that.'

'Why do you think she gets upset?'

'I'm not a doctor. How should I bloody know?'

Heather paused, then said, 'Do you think it's something you talk about that upsets her?'

A cunning look, which wasn't lost on Heather Joyce, flashed across Meadows' face. He said, 'Maybe she hates living there? Maybe she hates it when I have to leave?'

'Do you think that's it?'

'I've already said, I don't bloody know. Why all the questions, anyway?'

'Dr Sanderson is concerned that Dawn is deteriorating, and he thinks part of that is to do with your visits. What do you talk about with her?'

'What I say to her is private and none of your business. You can leave now.'

'He could stop your visits, Stephen.'

She saw his mood change instantly. It frightened her. Heather Joyce was not easily spooked, but something in Stephen Meadows' eyes made the hair on the back of her neck stand up.

He curled his lip and snarled, 'That's fucking bullshit and you know it. He can't stop me visiting my own sister. She's not in a fucking prison.'

Seeing Meadows' rage up close, and feeling fearful of the outcome if she pushed any further, Heather said, 'Whatever it is you talk about is your business, and if you're saying it's private, I'll have to respect that. The fact is, it's upsetting your sister and causing her to have seizures. You don't want that, do you?'

'Of course not. I've got nothing else to say to you. Leave now.'

There was real menace in his voice. Bizarrely, she was suddenly glad she hadn't visited after dark. She took a step back and turned to walk down the drive. She stopped, turned back and said, 'Try talking about something else on your next visit.'

Meadows just stared at her. The silence was more chilling than if he had been ranting at her.

She walked back to her car, got in and immediately locked the doors.

Something about Stephen Meadows had made her blood run cold.

55

11.30 pm, 19 June 1987
Helmsley Road, Rainworth, Nottinghamshire

He had felt angry and frustrated as he walked around the streets. There seemed to be coppers everywhere. Twice he'd been forced to duck into a garden to avoid a police foot patrol as they walked by.

For three days he had wandered around the streets, during daytime, to try to find a suitable property, all to no avail. His need had felt so strong that he had decided to risk everything and venture out tonight, to try to find the perfect property to burn down.

After three hours and a couple of scares caused by the police patrols, he was almost ready to give up for the night. The full can of petrol had grown steadily heavier as the night wore on, and the plastic carrier bag handles were now biting into his fingers. He decided to make his way back to Rainworth and try again tomorrow night.

Another police car came hurtling along the B6020 from Mansfield towards Rainworth. He ducked into Helmsley Road, so he wasn't seen, and carried on walking purposefully. He wanted the officers in the car to think he was going somewhere specific and not just loitering. The police car ignored him and raced on towards Rainworth.

He stopped and looked around. Helmsley Road was noticeably quiet. On both sides of the road, it had a mixture of private dwelling houses and small blocks that contained four flats. Each of the blocks had two ground-floor flats and two on the first floor. He was standing outside one of the blocks and could see that the ground-floor flat on the left was unoccupied. There were no curtains or blinds, and it was in total darkness. Lights were on in the other ground-floor flat and in one of the upstairs flats.

Not realising he was doing it, he began to move the carrier bag back and forth, so he could hear the petrol swishing about in the green petrol can. He walked over to the empty ground-floor flat for a closer look. The gardens were all open-plan, but the street lighting was poor. There were plenty of dark shadows for him to hide in.

He crept around the back of the flat, peering into the windows as he went. None of the rooms contained any furniture. It confirmed his first thoughts: The flat was indeed unoccupied. Checking the windows, he found they were all locked and secure. He walked round to the front of the block and looked at the entrance. The front doors for each of the flats were in a sheltered alcove. After a couple of minutes, he was able to work out which door corresponded to the empty flat.

He took one last look around him to ensure he was alone on the street. He removed the petrol can from the carrier bag and unscrewed the cap. He lifted the letterbox, which squeaked loudly as he raised it. The strident noise made him hold his breath, scared that someone inside one of the other flats had heard the unusual sound. When he heard no movement, he began to carefully pour the petrol through the letterbox. He could smell the toxic vapours and hear the flammable liquid as it splashed down onto the threadbare carpet in the hallway of the empty flat.

When the last of the petrol had dripped from the can, he replaced the screw cap and put it back inside the carrier bag. He then removed a length of rag and a cheap, disposable Zippo lighter from his jacket pocket. He lit the rag, lifted the letterbox very slowly to avoid a repeat of the noise, and shoved the burning rag inside.

There was an instant whooshing sound as the petrol vapour ignited. The hallway of the downstairs flat was engulfed in a wall of flame. He picked up the carrier bag containing the green petrol can and ran down the street.

He stopped at the junction and looked around. He quickly stuffed the carrier bag under a gorse bush, then walked slowly back down Helmsley Road, towards the fire. He ducked into a shadow as the first screams started.

He could hear a woman's voice shouting for help and screaming. He ventured closer and could now see the block of flats. The downstairs flat was now burning fiercely, and he could see a young woman at one of the upstairs windows. She was inside the flat directly above the burning property. She was screaming for help and holding a small baby. He could see the orange glow of flames in the room behind her. A man emerged from the other ground floor flat, coughing and spluttering. He was wearing pyjama bottoms and a T-shirt.

He watched as the man looked up and saw the young woman holding the baby. He heard him shout, 'Throw me the baby, Jackie. I'll catch her!'

The woman opened the window, but it was only wide

enough to hold the baby outside. There was no way the woman could squeeze through the tiny gap and jump to safety herself. She was effectively trapped.

The neighbour standing below the window repeated, 'Come on, Jackie! You've got to throw the baby down to me.'

In a desperate act to try to save her child's life, the woman dropped her baby into the arms of the neighbour below. He caught the child by one leg, just preventing the baby smacking into the concrete paving slabs. The screaming baby added to the crescendo of sound as the trapped mother cried out in terror, the flames inside her flat growing in intensity.

Other people were now emerging onto the street. They had been roused from their slumbers by the cacophony of noise on the street. In the distance came the sound of sirens approaching as fire engines raced towards the unfolding drama.

The woman inside the upstairs burning flat was no longer screaming. Savage orange flames were now licking out of the window she had dropped her baby from.

He mingled with the crowds of onlookers and watched as the first fire engine skidded to a halt. Firemen, wearing breathing apparatus, leapt from the vehicle and stormed into the upstairs flat to try to rescue the woman.

After twenty minutes, the fire had almost been brought under control. An ambulance had been and gone, rushing both the small baby and the neighbour who had caught her to hospital to be treated for smoke inhalation.

He had remained on the street, watching as the drama unfolded. He had seen the same people arriving as the last fire. He saw the press arrive, taking photographs. He saw uniformed police officers, and he saw the same three men who had arrived in plain cars. He knew they were from the CID; he recognised the stern-faced one from the television appeals.

He smirked as he stole away down the street. He rejoiced in the knowledge that those detectives were no closer to catching him, even though he had struck again. He retrieved the carrier bag containing the petrol can from beneath the gorse bush and made his way home. He stayed off the main roads, keeping to the backstreets.

What he didn't stay to witness was the firemen removing the black plastic body bag that contained the burned remains of the young single mother, Jackie Hardstaff. The woman who would be hailed a heroine for saving her infant's life from the devastating fire that had killed her.

56

6.00 am, 20 June 1987
MCIU Offices, Mansfield, Nottinghamshire

The mood in the MCIU office was a dark, cheerless one. The three men, Danny, Rob and Tony Parrish, had just got in from the scene of the fire at Helmsley Road in Rainworth. The smell of smoke from that devastating fire still hung heavily on their clothes. The acrid stench made the mood in the room feel even more sombre.

Rob broke the melancholy silence. 'Bastard! That poor young woman never stood a chance.'

Danny nodded. 'I know what you mean. Thank God she had the presence of mind and courage to save her baby.'

He turned to Tony and asked, 'Definitely petrol through the letterbox again?'

'I'm afraid so. Lots of it as well, judging by the shadowing. It's almost identical to the Finningley Road fire.'

'How did the fire spread so quickly between the flats?'

'It's all to do with the construction and how the stairs were set out in the build. The fire in the hallway of the ground-floor flat was directly below the stairs that led to Jackie Hardstaff's flat. Once the fire broke through the ceiling, it meant she was trapped. The fire was so intense because of the amount of petrol used; it would have spread rapidly. There was no way she could have battled through those flames, and with the double-glazed windows being so small and having the restricted openings, she couldn't jump to safety, either.'

'Are those bloody windows even legal?'

Tony nodded. 'I'm afraid so. We try to discourage builders from fitting them, but they continue to do so.'

Rob said, 'Has anyone heard how the baby's faring?'

Danny said, 'The last I heard, she was comfortable. When I saw the baby in the ambulance, looking so small and vulnerable, it made me think of my own child. Hayley's about the same age now. I had to walk away. Just the sight of that pathetic little bundle, coughing and spluttering, made me so mad. I could feel myself getting ready to explode.'

There was a knock on the door. Danny said, 'Come in.'

Professor Sharon Whittle walked in and said, 'The officers you sent to pick me up from the guest house said there's been another fire.'

Danny said, 'There has. A young woman died, and her baby and a neighbour have been injured.'

'Is the method the same? Is it arson?'

Tony said, 'It's definitely arson, and it's identical to the other fires.'

Danny said, 'Sorry. Sharon, this is Tony Parrish, the fire investigator working on this case. Tony, this is forensic psychologist Professor Sharon Whittle. She's assisting us with this investigation and the River Trent murder investigations.'

Tony said, 'Hello, Professor, good to meet you. I'm of the opinion that the same person has set all three fires. What are your thoughts?'

'I've spent most of the last two nights in my room at the guest house, trawling through every reported fire in Nottinghamshire. The exorbitant amount of smaller grass and rubbish fires that have happened within the last six months in this area makes me think you have a developing arsonist working locally. It seems that he's now graduated from lighting small fires to setting far more devastating ones. There's no mention in the reports of anyone being detained for these smaller fires, so other than confirming what we already know, it doesn't take us any further forward.'

Rob said, 'I think last night's fire also knocks out our tentative theory about the arsonist targeting the elderly.'

Sharon said, 'I don't believe any of the victims have been deliberately targeted. I think it's far more likely that the person responsible is fixated by fire. I think it's someone who revels in the power of fire and takes something from unleashing it. The more devastating the blaze, the more catastrophic the results, the more he likes it.'

'What sort of person could do that?'

'It's usually someone insignificant. Somebody who's never amounted to anything in their life. This is their one chance to achieve notoriety. I think it's almost certainly a male, someone local to this area. I think they've demonstrated a good knowledge of all the footpaths and shortcuts.'

Danny said, 'That's all well and good as a theory. How will it help us catch the bastard?'

'Check other records. I checked the records for Nottinghamshire last night, but there's nothing to say this person doesn't live in another area entirely. You need to look for hoax calls to the fire brigade, grass fires, rubbish bin fires. Arson is always an escalatory crime; he will have started small and gradually built up to this. There's a good chance he's already been cautioned by the police for setting small fires in the past.'

She paused before continuing. 'There's one other thing that has been extremely useful to police departments in the past.'

'Go on.'

'Someone like the person I've described will have wanted to stay and watch the mayhem he caused. Have you got all the photographs of the fire scenes taken by the press?'

Rob said, 'We have. I've been working on that myself, with two other detectives. We have been endeavouring to match the faces in the crowds to known arson offenders.'

Danny said generally, 'Does anyone in this room think he'll stop?'

Sharon responded, 'The only way he's going to stop now is when he gets caught. You need to increase the foot patrols, stop everyone who is seen carrying a bag or container. Increase stops on cars in the area. He's carrying petrol to these fires; you must become more proactive to catch him. Right now, you're reacting to what he's already done. Lastly, try to locate any derelict or unoccupied dwellings that are immediately adjacent to occupied properties. These are an easy target. Find them and watch them.'

'I hear what you're saying, Sharon. But the amount of manpower that would take is simply beyond our capabilities.'

'If you want to catch this person, you'll have to find a way to do it.'

'I'll talk to Potter. There may be a way he can organise something with all the divisional commanders, to draft officers in from neighbouring divisions.'

'I'm sorry to be so negative, Danny. I just don't see any other way to catch this person. You can forget about getting a break forensically. That's never going to happen in an arson case.'

Danny nodded. 'I'll try to organise more manpower.'

10.00 am, 20 June 1987
Kelham Bridge, Newark, Nottinghamshire

Detective Sergeant Andy Wills had been disappointed when overlooked for promotion to detective inspector. Especially after he had done such a good job in the role following the death of Detective Inspector Brian Hopkirk. He had been taken to one side by DCI Flint and quietly given the bad news.

The disappointment had been tempered by the promise of a promotion soon. That conversation with Danny Flint had been almost two weeks ago, and was now consigned to the past. The entire MCIU had since been pushed to its limit by the two ongoing investigations. Andy had been given no time at all to dwell on his disappointment.

It had been no problem for him to subsequently work under the newly promoted Detective Inspector Tina Cartwright. He had worked alongside her on previous enquiries and already held her in high regard, both for her professionalism and competency as a detective.

For the last four days, he had been painstakingly visiting every property in and around the Kelham Bridge area, looking for CCTV cameras. He had started by working from the bridge and heading towards Newark. It was the more densely populated direction, so there was more likelihood of cameras being found, and he had indeed found several. The most promising one had been located two days ago, at the Newark Rugby Club. They had a security camera that covered the car park next to the clubhouse. It looked out towards the A617 road that travelled over the bridge.

Andy had spent hours going over the grainy black-and-white images until he found the time and the night in question. He had been excited to see what appeared to be a white Transit hurtle by the entrance to the rugby club. The image was blurred by the speed of the vehicle, and nothing could be done to enhance the grainy image. Several other cameras were located, but none provided any clear images of the suspect vehicle. Having exhausted the direction towards Newark, this morning he intended to start looking between Kelham Bridge and Mansfield.

As he approached the entrance to the impressive Kelham Hall, Andy noticed a set of ornate black-and-gold wrought iron gates directly opposite the entrance to the hall.

He stopped the car and looked closer at the gates. There were four magnificent detached properties beyond them, in what was a secluded, gated community. He got out of the car and approached on foot. As he suspected, the gates were operated by an intercom system. There was a camera facing out onto the road so that residents could see who was at the gates.

Andy pressed the call button on the intercom. There was

a buzzing sound, followed by a series of intermittent clicks before a voice said, 'Hello. Can I help you?'

Andy held up his warrant card to the camera and said, 'Detective Sergeant Wills. I'd like to talk to someone about this camera on your gates. Is anyone able to help me?'

The voice from the speaker said, 'I'll open the gates. Walk down to the first house on the left. I'll wait for you there.'

Andy stepped back a pace as a motor suddenly whirred into life, opening the heavy gates at a snail's pace. He waited until they were fully open before walking down the long driveway that led to the detached properties.

He could already see a middle-aged man, dressed as though he was heading for the golf course, emerging from the front door of the first house on the left. He was struggling with what looked like an extremely heavy golf bag. He opened the boot of the BMW on the drive and placed the golf bag inside. As Andy approached, he closed the boot.

Andy offered his identification for the man to inspect.

The man handed the warrant card back to Andy. 'Always happy to help, Sergeant. You said you were interested in the camera. What do you want to know?'

'I could see that the camera points out onto the road. Do you record the images at all, or is it just for people visiting the houses?'

'Let me introduce myself. My name's Bill Singleton. I'm the elected neighbourhood watch coordinator for our small community. I look after the camera system; it's my baby. We had the system installed after a series of quite devastating burglaries last year. Come inside, and I'll show you the recording equipment. You only just caught me. I was on my way to the golf course at Southwell. I've got a tee booked for eleven o'clock.'

Andy walked into the beautifully decorated home and followed Bill Singleton into what appeared to be a study.

Sitting on a sideboard was a small television screen with a video recorder. At the side of the recorder, there stood a stack of six videocassette tapes. Each cassette had a day of the week printed on the case.

Singleton said, 'Each of these tapes records images for a twenty-four hour period. It's quite an expensive, sophisticated system. The images are in colour and condensed. I can retrieve them on a specialist player if I need to. After seven days, we just record over the tapes. So, in effect, we have images stored for the last seven days. Were you interested in any particular time and day?'

Andy couldn't believe his luck. With a growing sense of excitement, he said, 'I was hoping you'd have the images for the early hours of the fourteenth. Five days ago.'

Singleton picked up a videocassette from the pile and said, 'We'll need to use the other video player.'

Andy followed him across the room to another video player sat below an even bigger television.

Singleton slipped the video into the player. He switched on the machine and the television, then picked up a remote control. The recording started at six o'clock on the night of the thirteenth. As he fast-forwarded the video, Singleton explained, 'I decided to start all the tapes at eighteen hundred hours. That way, either my wife or I would always be at home at that time to swap the tapes over.'

As the digital clock on the corner of the screen approached 0200, Singleton slowed the images.

At exactly 0237 on the digital clock, Andy saw what he had been looking for. A white-coloured Ford Transit van had been driven slowly by the gates.

Andy said, 'Could you rewind back to that van, please?'

'Of course.'

The image was wound back until the side profile of the white van was shown in full.

Andy said, 'Pause it there, please. Thanks.'

It was a side view of the van, so there was no chance of getting a view of the registration plate. However, the white Ford Transit had a very distinctive red arrow-shaped logo on the side panel.

'Is there any way I can get a still photo of this image?'

With a smile on his face, Bill Singleton pressed another button. A printer at the side of the video recorder whirred into life, and an A4 colour image of the van appeared. In one corner of the image, in red figures, was the time and date.

A beaming Singleton passed the image of the van to Andy. 'How's that, Sergeant?'

'That's bloody amazing!'

'Will you need to keep the original tape?'

'I would like to if possible?'

'I thought you might; best evidence and all that. It's not a problem. We have spare tapes for emergencies.'

Singleton took the tape from the player, placed it back into its cover and handed it to Andy.

Andy said, 'That's great. Thank you so much for all your help. You seem to know a lot about how we work, Bill. Were you ever in the job?'

He said, 'I spent thirty years as a captain in the Royal Military Police. Twenty years of that was spent on the Special Investigation Branch. So, kind of in the job, I suppose.'

'Well, thanks again, Bill. This could be a massive help to us. I know you've got a round of golf organised, but would you be able to make a quick statement now? That way, I can exhibit the image and the tape.'

'Let me make a quick phone call to the golf club; then I'll stick the kettle on. We can make the statement over a cup of tea. How does that sound?'

Andy grinned. 'That sounds perfect, thanks.'

Having rearranged his tee-off time to the afternoon,

Singleton took his time and made a detailed written statement. Andy asked him to sign the exhibit labels for both the printed image of the van and the tape before getting up to leave.

After showing Andy to the door, Bill Singleton said, 'I know you probably can't tell me, but is all this anything to do with that poor chap who was dragged from the river the other night?'

Andy gave him a knowing wink, smiled and said, 'Thanks again for all your help, Bill. Enjoy your game of golf.'

58

10.00 am, 20 June 1987
Lady Bay Bridge, Nottingham

Once again, PC Nick Kerridge prepared a diver to traverse the River Trent directly underneath a bridge. This would be the third bridge in as many days, and the divers were getting fatigued. The river was running high and fast. Hauling yourself repeatedly along a search line across the river was both exhausting and dangerous for the divers.

This time, the diver was the experienced PC Simon Morton. The bridge was the Lady Bay Bridge near to the football ground used by Nottingham Forest football club. The Underwater Search Unit van and trailer had been parked in the car park of the football ground, adjacent to the river.

Nick checked that the radio in the diver's Interspiro AGA full facemask was working. He said, 'The line's in place on the bottom, Simon. You know what to do and what to expect down there. The river's running extremely fast today, so the muddy bottom could well be a bit churned up. I think if you find anything today, it will be by touch rather than sight.'

Simon nodded and made the *okay* sign before waddling awkwardly in his fins towards the concrete steps down to the river. He stepped sideways so the fins would fit on the steps, and Nick played out more of the safety line attached to the diver's midriff.

The experienced diver took his time. He inhaled deeply through the demand valve to fully oxygenate his body before slipping into the icy-cold water. The red dry suit would keep the freezing temperatures out to a certain extent. As the diver made his way across the river, it would quickly become very cold.

The going was hard, as the current on the bottom was so strong. Simon fought with all his strength to keep on track. He gripped the guideline on the bottom of the river with his right hand. Slowly, he pulled himself forward a foot at a time. He would then reach around in front of him and as far to the sides as he could with his left hand. He heard Nick's voice on the radio: 'How's it going?'

Simon breathed in deeply and said, 'The current's so strong on the bottom. It's fucking hard work this morning.'

'Take your time, mate. You've got plenty of air.'

'Will do.'

After twenty minutes of exhausting work, Simon estimated that he was somewhere near the centre of the river. The bottom here was thick, black mud. The fast current was whipping it off the bottom, making visibility nil.

Once more, he pulled himself forward. As he did so, his head bumped into something. He reached forward with his left hand and found what his head had bumped. His searching fingers first touched a cold, hard oval of metal. Allowing his hand to slide along the object, he found another metal ring. Then his fingers touched what he knew was flesh. He pressed harder with his finger. He felt the soft flesh yield until his finger was embedded up to his first knuckle. Having been fully briefed on what they were searching for that morning, Simon realised that the metal ovals were links of heavy chain that were wrapped around a human leg.

He greedily sucked more air through the demand valve, trying to remain calm. He tentatively allowed his hand to slide above the chain. His hand rested on a kneecap. He said, 'Nick, there's another body down here. I estimate I'm about halfway across by now.'

Nick Kerridge trusted that the experienced diver knew what he was talking about. He said, 'I think you're right, Si. I reckon you're about halfway out. Have you got a marker you can attach to the line?'

'Yes, mate. I've already clipped one on. I've felt the lower leg up to the kneecap. There are chain links wrapped around the leg.'

'Okay. Take your time and make your way back to the bank.'

'Will do, Nick.'

As Simon Morton began the arduous task of turning in the strong current and making his way back to the riverbank, Nick waved one of the other divers across to come and look after the diver's lifeline. As soon as he had handed the lifeline over, Nick walked up the bank to the USU van in the car park. He sat in the passenger seat and picked up the radio handset. 'PC Kerridge, Underwater Search Unit to control. Over.'

'From control to PC Kerridge, go ahead. Over.'

'Can you contact the MCIU and let Detective Chief Inspector Flint know that the search we're carrying out at Lady Bay Bridge is positive. We've just located a body below the centre of the bridge. We'll be commencing the recovery operation shortly. Over.'

'From control, will do. Over.'

He got out of the van, locked the door and made his way back down to the bank. The other five divers in the team were all now gathered expectantly on the riverbank, waiting for PC Morton to emerge from the cold water. They would then need to formulate a plan to recover the weighted body from the soft, muddy bottom of the fast-flowing river. Nick Kerridge knew that was going to be no easy task.

59

12.30 pm, 20 June 1987
Lady Bay Bridge, Nottingham

Danny and Professor Whittle followed Tina and Rachel across the car park at the back of the football ground, towards the river and the gathering of divers on the bank.

There was the rumble of a diesel engine. Danny looked over his shoulder and saw the white scenes of crime van being driven into the car park.

Nick Kerridge approached the detectives and said, 'It's the same as the others, sir. This one's a white female, looks a bit older than the woman at Gunthorpe. Her legs have been weighted down with heavy chain links in exactly the same way.'

'Have you had problems recovering the body? It seems to have taken you a lot longer today.'

'Yes, sir. Visibility down there is nil. So we've been

working blind, and the current's incredibly strong on the bottom. It's been a difficult recovery.'

'It wasn't a criticism, Nick. You and your team have done an amazing job.'

'It was a good call to ask us to search beneath the other bridges. We've still got a few left to do. We're going to search Clifton Bridge tomorrow, weather permitting.'

Danny glanced over towards Sharon Whittle. He nodded in a gesture of acknowledgement that it had been her idea to search below the other bridges. The group then continued to walk towards the river. They paused as scenes of crime officers began erecting a white tent around the body bag to prevent any prying eyes from watching the detectives.

Danny looked at his watch. Seamus Carter would be arriving within the next ten minutes. He decided to wait until the pathologist arrived before having a look at the body.

He turned to Nick and said, 'How long's she been in the water?'

'It's hard to say. Judging by the high level of putrefaction, I'd guess at between two to three weeks. It can never be determined accurately, sir.'

A dark-coloured Volvo pulled up behind the CID cars, and Seamus Carter got out. He walked around to the boot and grabbed a small bag and a face mask. He joined Danny by the side of the white forensic tent and said, 'Same?'

Danny nodded.

Putting on his face mask, Seamus said, 'Let's go and have a look, then.'

Danny turned to Sharon Whittle and said, 'Do you want to have a look? My advice would be don't, but it's up to you.'

The psychologist shook her head and said, 'I'll take your advice. I'll wait here.'

Danny and Tina then followed Seamus Carter inside the tent. The portable floodlight inside gave off a stark, white light that almost hurt the eyes. The pathologist carefully unzipped the body bag, exposing the rotting remains of a middle-aged female. He reached inside his jacket pocket, took out his Dictaphone and began speaking.

His voice was slightly muffled by the face mask as he said, 'The body is that of a white female, fifty to sixty years. Very overweight – borderline obese – and short in stature. Probably around twelve to thirteen stones in weight and five-feet-one-to-three inches. She's completely naked, and both legs below the knee are secured with a white nylon cord that is in turn intertwined with heavy chain links. This chain is blue in colour and appears to be similar, if not identical, in appearance to the chains used to weight down the two previous bodies recovered. No obvious marks of violence can be seen at this time. I would estimate the body has been submerged for at least two weeks.'

Danny nodded and said, 'I've just spoken to the divers. They reckon between two and three weeks.'

Seamus switched off the Dictaphone. 'There's nothing more I can do here, Danny. How soon can we get her to the City Hospital for a full post-mortem examination?'

'Scenes of crime should have finished what they need to do within the next hour. It's only going to be obtaining photographs and bagging up the chains and bindings.'

'Let's say four o'clock this afternoon for the post-mortem, then. I'll call ahead and arrange it with the City Hospital. I'll stay here with Tim Donnelly and supervise the removal of the chains before we call out the undertakers for transportation. I know taking off the chains will damage the putrefied flesh on the legs. I want to see it as it happens before the post-mortem. That way, I'll know exactly what damage we have caused. I can already see a lot of damage to the arms and legs, where the dive team have completed the recovery.'

Danny nodded. He and Tina then gratefully stepped

outside, into the fresh air. The smell of the decaying body was still strong in their nostrils. Danny took deep breaths in and exhaled through his nose. He knew he would continue to smell the body for a long time. There was nothing he could do about it. It was something he could never get used to.

He and Tina walked over to where Rachel was standing with Sharon Whittle. Danny said, 'The demographic has changed again. This body is a white female, but in her mid-fifties, probably. Nothing at all like the other two victims.'

Sharon Whittle looked thoughtful. 'There has to be a link between the three victims. Have we any idea who this woman is?'

Tina said, 'Not yet; she's been stripped naked. We'll have to employ the usual painstaking ways of trying to identify her – fingerprints, dental records, missing persons files. All are labour intensive and can take a long time.'

'Identifying her has got to be your top priority. You need to examine the victimology of all three victims minutely. It's the only way you'll find the link.'

Tina said, 'Any ideas on a profile for the killer yet, Professor?'

'In general terms, the killer will be male and physically extraordinarily strong. It's no easy feat to lift the dead weight of a body, especially one weighed down by chains. He will have access to a large vehicle, possibly a van, to transport his victims around without arousing suspicion. I think he most probably lives alone in a semi-rural or rural location, in a secluded property. He obviously keeps his victims somewhere in-between abduction and deposition. The profile won't help you much. The key to identifying and catching this killer lies with the victims.'

Danny nodded. 'Any other thoughts on a reason why?'

'It's like I said before, Danny. The person doing this is making all these quite different people suffer in a similar way.

I don't think he strips them of their clothes because he's particularly forensically aware. I think it's done to degrade his victims in a way that they may have made him feel degraded or abused in the past. I see these killings as being motivated by nothing other than revenge. All these victims will, in one way or another, have done something to aggrieve our killer. That could be physical, it could be mental, or any other way. Working that out is the key. That's what you will need to discover to catch this man.'

60

8.00 pm, 20 June 1987
MCIU Offices, Mansfield, Nottinghamshire

Tina and Rachel walked into the main office. They both looked exhausted; it had been a long day. Andy Wills leaned back in his chair and said, 'How was the post-mortem?'

Rachel replied, 'It was awful. Probably the worst one I've ever been to. I've got a strong stomach, but bloody hell.'

A very pale, drawn-looking Tina said, 'Let's not talk about it, shall we? I'm feeling nauseous just thinking about it.'

Andy said, 'Well, I might have some good news for you. I think I may have found the van that Jimmy Birch saw.'

Her face creasing into a wan smile, Tina said, 'Where?'

Grabbing the image taken from the camera at Kelham, Andy walked over to Tina's desk. He said, 'I found a private housing estate that has a set of gates controlled by a camera system. The camera faces the road, so I enquired if it's just a monitor, or if there's a recording system. The guy who controls it is a retired officer from the Royal Military Police. The system is state of the art. Have a look at this image. It's in colour, and it's time- and date-stamped too. This vehicle was leaving Kelham at 0237 on the fourteenth. It's got to be the vehicle Birch saw.'

Tina took the printed image from Andy and frowned.

Andy said, 'I know it's only a side-on view, so we can't get the registration number. Look at the red logo on the side of the van, though. It's very distinctive.'

'Do you think we can trace it from that?'

'I've been working on that since I got back from Kelham, and I've narrowed it down to a few possibles. I'll be following them up with physical visits tomorrow morning.'

'That's great work, Andy. If we can locate and identify the van, we will get the driver.'

Danny came out of his office and said, 'Tina, can you come in here for a minute? Thanks.'

Tina nodded and said to Rachel, 'Start cracking on with the missing persons forms. We still need to identify our Lady Bay victim.'

'Will do.'

Tina walked into Danny's office. She was surprised to see Sharon Whittle still there. Danny said, 'How did the post-mortem go?'

'The cause of death was drowning, the same as the others. She was still alive when she was thrown in. There was a lot of damage and decay to the body because of the amount of time spent in the water. Seamus was satisfied that there were no obvious marks of violence caused by the killer.'

Sharon Whittle spoke up. 'And that's something else that's really been puzzling me.'

Danny said, 'What's that?'

'The person responsible for these deaths seems strangely averse to physical violence.'

Danny and Tina both looked incredulous. Sharon saw the looks and continued, 'I know that seems a strange thing to say about a killer. This is my point, though: Apart from the bruising caused when the victims were incapacitated, there are no marks of gratuitous violence. Our killer wants them all to suffer, of that I'm sure, but he doesn't seem capable of being able to inflict the pain to make them suffer himself. It's almost as if he's killing them in this way so the river does his work for him.'

Tina's temper snapped. She said angrily, 'And maybe you're overthinking all of this! Perhaps he's just an evil bastard attacking people at random, for the sake of it!'

Danny was shocked at the outburst. He said, 'Thanks, Tina. That will be all.'

She stood up and stalked out of the office.

Five minutes later, the door to Danny's office opened, and Sharon Whittle walked out. Danny came into the main office, sat down next to Tina and said quietly, 'What was that all about?'

'I'm sorry, boss. It's been a long day. Sitting listening to Professor bloody Whittle prattling on with her fanciful ideas about this monster just didn't sit well after watching that awful post-mortem.'

'Okay. I hear what you're saying, and I'll let your immature show of unprofessionalism pass this once. Let's get one thing straight, Professor Whittle is here to advise and offer opinions. Her sole input in this investigation is to put these theories out there. It's then up to us – up to me – whether we take any notice of them. Got it?'

Tina nodded, but remained tight-lipped.

Danny continued, 'I know that some of her ideas seem a little off-track, but she was spot on about searching beneath the other bridges, wasn't she? I've got to be honest; I wouldn't have done that. So let's cut the woman some slack and keep an open mind.'

'Will do. I'll apologise to her first thing tomorrow.'

'Thank you, Tina. I think you should.'

He stood up and addressed everyone in the office, 'Okay, everyone. It's time we all called it a day and went home. Rachel, Andy, that means you two as well. Get off home, and let's be back here at six o'clock in the morning, ready to go again after a good night's sleep.'

As Tina grabbed her coat, she knew that after what she had witnessed at the City Hospital earlier that day, sleep would not come easily.

61

11.00 am, 21 June 1987
Castle Sounds, Lister Gate, Nottingham

The mood in the Castle Sounds recording studio was sullen. Staff were keeping busy, but there was none of the usual laughter, banter or smiles.

After spending the morning speaking to the half-dozen employees at Castle Sounds, Tina and Rachel were finally speaking to Angela Thomas, the girlfriend of Rex Poyser. She was the woman who had originally reported him as a missing person.

Tina said, 'Thanks for seeing us again this morning. I know you've already spoken at length to Rachel about everything. I just wanted to be sure that we haven't missed anything before we leave.'

'That's okay. I want to help you find whoever did this to Rex. He was such a lovely, gentle guy. I still can't get my head around what's happened.'

'Thanks, Angela. I really appreciate all your help. Have you had any other thoughts about who could have done this? Did Rex have any enemies?'

Becoming tearful, the glamorous blonde said, 'That's just it – he was such a sweetheart. He didn't have a bad bone in his body. Everyone loved Rex.'

'What about the business here? I know he wasn't the owner and only managed the place, but have there been any ongoing disputes here at work?'

'I haven't been here that long, but everyone gets on really well. There's no animosity.'

'What about outside deals?'

'I don't know of any problems. Rex never mentioned anything to me.'

'How long had you and Rex been dating?'

'Off and on, for about a year. Why do you ask?'

'I know this is a tough question. Are there any previous boyfriends who may still hold a torch for you?'

'No.'

'Are you sure? No previous boyfriends who may have wanted Rex out of the way?'

Tears started to flow steadily now, and with an indignant tone, Angela replied, 'No. Definitely not. What do you take me for?'

'I'm sorry, Angela, I have to ask. If you can think of anything that could help, please don't hesitate to call us.'

Angela Thomas dabbed at her eyes with a tissue, as the heavy mascara on her lashes started to run. She said, 'I will. Sorry for blubbing. It doesn't take much to get me upset and tearful right now.'

Tina put her hand on the woman's shoulder in a comforting way. 'Don't apologise, Angela. We understand. We'll see ourselves out.'

Tina and Rachel left the studio, walking out the front door and onto a busy, bustling Lister Gate.

Rachel said, 'What did you make of Angela Thomas?'

'She seems like a nice enough girl. She's incredibly young, though.'

'She's twenty-three.'

'I wonder what she saw in Rex Poyser. He was twice her age.'

Rachel shrugged her shoulders and said, 'God knows. Do you fancy a quick coffee before we drive back?'

'That sounds a good idea. Why not?'

There was the sound of footsteps running behind them, and a woman's voice shouted, 'Just a second, Detectives!'

They turned around and saw a young woman with bleached blonde hair and very dark eye make-up. She was wearing a maroon sweatshirt with the Castle Sounds motif on the front.

Rachel said, 'You were in the studio.'

The young woman nodded. 'Can we talk privately? I didn't want to say anything up there.'

Rachel said, 'Why? What's wrong?'

'There are some things you need to know about Rex Poyser. He wasn't the bloody saint everyone's making him out to be.'

'It's Zara, right?'

'Yeah, Zara Carmichael.'

Tina said, 'Listen, Zara. We were just going for a coffee; why don't you join us? You can tell us exactly what it is you think we should know.'

The woman nodded. 'I've only got half an hour. I told my supervisor I had to nip to Boots Chemist for a prescription.'

Rachel said, 'There's a quiet coffee shop just down the road. We'll nip in there.'

Zara nodded. 'Okay.'

Five minutes later, the three women were sitting in Franco's coffee shop. They occupied a private booth, away from other customers. Rachel placed the tray of hot drinks on the table and said, 'The cappuccino's yours, Tina. The two Americanos are ours.'

As she passed one of the cups to Zara, she said, 'Okay, Zara. What can you tell us about Rex Poyser?'

Zara took a sip of her coffee and said, 'It's like I said outside. Rex was no saint.'

'In what way?'

'He could be horrible, a vicious, nasty bully.'

'Did he bully you?'

'No, not me. It was always Stephen he picked on.'

'Stephen who?'

'Stephen Meadows.'

'I don't recall speaking to Stephen just now?'

'No, you won't. He left. Rex drove him out with his constant bullying and nastiness. It was such a shame. Stephen was easily the best sound engineer we had.'

'So why did Rex bully him?'

'You were just talking to the reason.'

'Sorry?'

'Angela Thomas is a sound engineer. She's shit at the job, but she's still a sound engineer. She was also fucking Rex. You work it out.'

Tina said, 'Rex bullied Stephen, forcing him to leave, so he could give his girlfriend a job at Castle Sounds.'

Zara nodded as she drank her coffee.

Rachel said, 'When did all this happen?'

'A few months ago. It was just after both of Stephen's parents were killed. Rex was being particularly vile towards him, and Stephen just suddenly quit. The very next day, Rex moved Blondie Big Tits into Stephen's job.'

'If Stephen was so good at his job, how did Rex bully him?'

'He just did. Stephen was into the heavy metal rock scene in a big way. A lot of the bands only ever wanted Stephen to work on the sound production of their tracks, but Rex would always find the least little excuse to trash his work. He even tormented him over the way he spoke.'

'What do you mean?'

'Stephen has a really bad stutter, I mean, *really* bad. Rex would constantly laugh at him, which just made his stuttering worse.'

'Are you still in touch with Stephen?'

'No. I haven't seen him since the day he left.'

'Any idea where he went to work?'

'No. I'm sorry; I need to be getting back to work.'

Tina said, 'One last thing, Zara. You mentioned that Stephen's parents were both killed recently. How were they killed?'

'In a car accident, I think. It was such an awful time for Stephen. He was really suffering, and Rex just made things worse.'

Rachel said, 'Let me take your details so we can contact you later at home. At some stage, we'll need to get a written statement from you, and obviously we don't want to do it when you're at work.'

Zara gave her details, then said, 'I'm sorry, but I've really got to get back to work now.'

She stood up and bolted from the coffee shop.

Tina said, 'I think we need to get back to the office and have a good look at Stephen Meadows.'

62

11.00 am 21 June 1987
Mansfield Police Station, Nottinghamshire

'Good morning, sir. Are all your staff out and about this morning?'

The voice belonged to Sergeant Mick Welch. He was standing behind Danny in the canteen queue. Danny replied, 'Most of them are out on enquiries, but the office manager should still be up there. Why?'

'There's a bloke called Luke Hardy waiting at the front desk. He wants to talk to someone about Suzy Flowers. He's been working abroad, but got back a couple of days ago. He saw your latest press conference on the news and wants to speak to somebody urgently.'

'Is he still at the front counter?'

'Yeah, I told him somebody would be down to see him shortly. He was quite happy to wait.'

Danny forgot about his bacon sandwich. 'I'll go and see him.'

Sergeant Welch said, 'You can't miss him, sir. He's one of those heavy rockers, all hair and leather!'

Danny grinned and said, 'Thanks, Mick.'

He walked through the police station to the front desk. He saw a man, as described by the sergeant, waiting patiently in the foyer.

Danny approached and said, 'Luke Hardy?'

The man nodded, and Danny said, 'I'm Detective Chief Inspector Flint. I understand you wanted to speak to someone about Suzy Flowers?'

'Yeah.'

Danny opened the door wide and said, 'Come through.'

The man walked in, and Danny showed him into an interview room. He said, 'Grab a seat.'

When both men had sat down, Danny said, 'So, Luke, what do you know about Suzy Flowers?'

'I saw the press appeal a couple of nights ago, and it occurred to me that I saw her the night before she disappeared.'

'Where was that?'

'We were all standing in the queue outside Rock City in Nottingham, waiting for the Hammer of Thor concert.'

'How well did you know Suzy?'

'Not that well. She's only started hanging around with our group recently. I've only seen her a couple of times, but she's one of those women you don't forget easily, if you know what I mean. She was going out with one of the guys who regularly goes to the concerts, so she tagged onto our crowd.'

'I see. So, if you don't really know her, how come you remember her so well from this particular concert at Rock City?'

'It's like I said, she's a bit wild. The clothes she wore that night were very revealing and left little to the imagination. If I'm being honest, she looked a bit tarty, but she had a great body. If you've got it, flaunt it, I suppose. Anyway, having said that, it was really the nasty argument that stuck in my mind and made me remember.'

'Go on.'

'I reckon she was a bit tipsy. No, she was more than tipsy, she was pissed. Anyway, for no reason that I could see, she started slagging off her boyfriend. I mean really taking the piss, ridiculing him badly. Do you know what I mean?'

Danny shook his head. 'No, I don't, Luke. Explain it to me?'

'She was mocking him sexually. Saying he was crap fuck, that he had a small dick, that sort of thing. Everyone in the queue started laughing at him, the poor bastard. Then it got worse, and she started mocking his stutter, as well.'

'Then what happened?'

'He ran off.'

'What?'

'He ran away. He flew down Talbot Street like a scalded cat, which made everyone laugh even more.'

'What did Suzy do?'

'She joined in with the laughing and stayed to watch the concert.'

'Did you see either of them after the concert?'

'No. I haven't seen either of them since that night.'

'Who's the boyfriend?'

'I've been racking my brains all morning, trying to think. I know his first name's Stephen, because everyone knows him as "Stuttering Steve".'

'Stuttering Steve?'

'Yeah, man, he's got the worst stutter you've ever heard. Sometimes he can barely string a sentence together.'

'I see. Can you recall his surname?'

'No, not really. I just knew him as Stuttering Steve.'

'Do you know anything else about him?'

'Not really. He's not a close friend. I just know him through the music, that's all.'

'Thanks, Luke. Are you okay for time? I'd like to get someone to sit down and get a written statement from you, outlining what you saw at Rock City.'

'It's my day off, so I haven't got to be anywhere this morning. Will it take long?'

Danny stood up and shook his head. 'Not long at all. Sit tight, and someone will be with you shortly. Thanks for coming in, Luke.'

'No problem.'

Danny walked into his office and jotted the name 'Stuttering Steve' into his enquiry log.

His thoughts turned to something Professor Whittle had said. She had been convinced that the killer was making his victims suffer because he had suffered. From what Luke Hardy had just described to him, it sounded like Suzy Flowers had really made Steve suffer that night.

63

11.30 am, 21 June 1987
MCIU Offices, Mansfield, Nottinghamshire

Tina and Rachel walked into the MCIU office and were met by Fran Jefferies. The office manager said, 'The woman recovered by the divers at Lady Bay Bridge has been positively identified. She was retired schoolteacher Sarah Milfoyle. She was reported missing by the headmaster of the Minster School in Southwell on the twelfth of June.'

Tina said, 'Do we know the circumstances?'

'From what I can glean from the missing persons report, Milfoyle was working at the Minster School on a temporary basis. When she didn't arrive for work on the twelfth, the headmaster, Mr Guilfoyle, went to her home address that evening. Apparently, the house was secure, and her car was there, but there was no sign of her. He called the police and reported her missing. The police checked the property on the night. There were no signs of a struggle or a break-in, and everything appeared in order. She had just vanished.'

'Thanks, Fran. Can you do me a favour and run this name through all our systems, please?'

'Fire away.'

'Stephen Meadows.'

TINA WALKED across to Danny's office and knocked on the door. Danny said, 'Come in.'

Tina walked in and closed the door. Sharon Whittle was sitting opposite Danny.

Danny was still writing in his notebook as he said, 'Good morning, Tina. How did you and Rachel get on talking to the staff at Castle Sounds?'

'We found something that could be interesting. One of the younger women there told us how Rex Poyser bullied a member of staff until he quit his job as a sound engineer. Then Poyser gave his girlfriend, Angela Thomas, the man's old job. It seems from the witness's account that the bullying was sustained and brutal. Poyser even attacked the guy personally, over a speech impediment. Apparently, he kept it up until the poor sod resigned. The staff member's name was Stephen Meadows.'

Danny looked up. 'Did you say this Stephen Meadows had a speech impediment?'

'Yes, a really bad stutter. Why?'

'Because there's a bloke downstairs called Luke Hardy, who's come in this morning after seeing the most recent press appeal for information. He's just told me that Suzy Flowers was going out with a guy called Stephen, on the night she was last seen alive. Luke says everyone refers to this boyfriend as "Stuttering Steve". Ask Rachel to go downstairs and get a full statement from Luke Hardy. Tell her to ask Hardy if he recognises the surname Meadows.'

Tina said, 'Fran is already researching Meadows in our records.'

Sharon Whittle interrupted, 'You'll need to look deeper into his background than just your records. Learn his history; learn everything you can about him as a person. You might find something that connects Rex Poyser and Suzy Flowers. You may even find a motive.'

Danny said, 'I think we've already found the motive. It's something you alluded to previously. We now know that Rex Poyser made Meadows' life a misery at work. He made him suffer until he quit. Luke Hardy has described how Suzy Flowers ridiculed Meadows in front of his friends, making him suffer until the only thing he could do was run away. You're right, Sharon; we do need to start digging deeper. Tina, I want you and Fran to start researching everything you can find about Meadows. Let's find about his likes, dislikes, childhood, everything. Let's see if there's also a link between Stephen Meadows and Sarah Milfoyle as well.'

Tina nodded, then turned to Sharon Whittle and said, 'I want to apologise for my outburst yesterday. It had been a long stressful day, especially after the post-mortem. There was no excuse for my rant at you. I'm sorry.'

Sharon smiled. 'Don't worry, Tina. I understand you'd had a crap day. It's forgotten, but thank you for the apology.'

Tina walked out of Danny's office and into the main briefing room. She tasked Rachel with obtaining the written statement from Luke Hardy, then sat down with Fran to begin researching Stephen Meadows.

After half an hour, they were starting to make progress.

Fran came off the telephone and, with a real sense of excitement, announced, 'I've found a connection between Milfoyle and Meadows. He was a pupil at the Minster School when Milfoyle was teaching there. I've just been speaking to the headmaster, Mr Guilfoyle. He's given me details about a complaint made by Stephen Meadows' mother against Sarah Milfoyle.'

Tina said, 'What were the circumstances of the complaint?'

'As a child, Stephen Meadows had a terrible stutter. Apparently, Sarah Milfoyle had ridiculed Meadows in front of his classmates. She had forced him to read aloud to the class until everyone was laughing. If that isn't bad enough, it was Milfoyle who first gave Meadows the nickname "Stuttering Steve". His mother was rightly incensed and made the complaint.'

'What was the result of the complaint?'

'Milfoyle was initially suspended, but then reinstated. However, she never taught Stephen Meadows again. She refused to have him in her class.'

'What a horrible woman. I bet the other kids made Meadows' life a misery, with his stutter.'

The door to the office opened, and a beaming Andy Wills walked in. He announced loudly, 'I've cracked it!'

Everyone looked up. Fran said, 'What have you cracked, Sarge?'

'I've cracked the mystery of the white van. The van Jimmy Birch saw at Kelham Bridge is one that's owned and operated by a company who are based out at East Midlands Airport. The company's name is Red Arrow Couriers Ltd.'

He was perplexed why nobody was jumping around at his breakthrough. Tina finally said, 'That's great, Andy. Good work. Can you get back in touch with Red Arrow Couriers and establish if they now employ Stephen Meadows?'

Andy said, 'Of course, but am I missing something here?'

'I'll brief you in a minute. Make the call, and if they do employ Meadows, find out everything you can from his work records. I want his current address, routes he drives, any time off he's taken over the last few months, what hours he works and any sickness record.'

Andy scribbled down the name *Stephen Meadows* and picked up the phone.

64

2.30 pm, 21 June 1987
The Oaks Residential Care Home, West Bridgford,
Nottingham

Stephen Meadows had noticed a distinct change in the attitudes of the nurses when he had walked into the care home today. Gone were the welcoming smiles. They now eyed him warily, wondering what the result of his visit to his sister would be today.

Dr Sanderson had left a note on the reception desk that he was to be notified the moment Stephen Meadows turned up requesting to see his sister.

The nurse on reception had asked Meadows to wait, as the doctor would like to see him. Stephen now waited patiently in reception.

Dr Sanderson walked across to him and said, 'Hello, Stephen. How are you keeping? You look tired.'

Sanderson had been fully apprised by Heather Joyce

about her recent visit to Stephen's home. She had told him about the way Meadows' entire demeanour had changed, and how there was a wild look in the man's eyes, when she questioned him about his previous visits.

The neurologist knew that he would have to tread very carefully so as not to antagonise Meadows.

Meadows said quietly, 'What do you want? I need to see my sister, and I haven't got long. You've already had me sitting here for ten minutes.'

'Your sister is very tired today. Is your visit going to be a long one?'

'No. There's something I need to tell her, though.'

'Can I ask you what that is?'

'No. It's family stuff. It doesn't concern you.'

'Is it going to upset her?'

'No. I can promise you that this time, I won't upset her at all. She'll be so pleased when she hears what I've got to tell her.'

Sanderson knew he was going round in circles. It was obvious from the expression on Meadows' face that he was enjoying talking in riddles. The doctor said, 'You can go and visit your sister now, Stephen. I'll be waiting right outside the door to meet you on your way out. I need to insist that you keep the visit short today. As I said before, your sister is extremely tired.'

Meadows smiled. 'Whatever you say, Doctor.'

65

2.45 pm, 21 June 1987
The Oaks Residential Care Home, West Bridgford,
Nottingham

Stephen walked into Dawn's room and closed the door behind him, grinning at Dr Sanderson as he did so. He could see Dawn in her wheelchair near the door. He removed the brake and pushed her across the room until they were next to the bay window, as far away from the door as possible.

There was no way he wanted Sanderson or the nurses to hear what he was going to be saying to his sister. This was private family business.

He stroked his sister's long dark hair, calming her. After a few minutes, he pulled her hair back gently, so it was away from her ear. He leaned forward and whispered, 'Today's the day, Dawny. When I leave here, I'm going for the man who robbed us of our parents. I'm going to take him and cleanse him for what he did to Mum and Dad. Does that make you happy, Dawny?'

He stared into her big brown eyes and could see the recognition behind her glassy expression. She started to become agitated again, but this time it was different. There was no arching and no shouting. Instead, he could see that she was smiling broadly. Spittle dribbled down her chin as she did her best to laugh. She started making noises, and among the cacophony of sound coming from her mouth, he heard one word that he recognised.

Dawn had said, *Good*.

66

5.00 pm, 21 June 1987
Queen's Medical Centre, Nottingham

It had been another busy day for James McEllery.

The consultant orthopaedic surgeon had carried out two hip replacements that afternoon, and he was feeling exhausted, ready for a drink.

Drink was his downfall, his one big vice.

Before his wife left him two years ago, he had hardly ever touched the stuff. After Jenny had walked out on him for somebody ten years younger than his forty-five years, he had hit the bottle hard. He hadn't suspected a thing. His wife's infidelity had come as a devastating shock to him.

Throughout their fifteen-year marriage he had always concentrated on his career, often to the detriment of his personal relationship. He worked long hours. His work was very physically demanding, so much so that he was always exhausted by the time he got home. Jenny, who was five years younger than he was, had soon grown bored. The long evenings spent on her own were lonely and not what she had expected when they married.

That was back then, in his darkest days. He had strived hard to be different now. He hadn't touched a glass of whisky since the terrible accident.

Two people had died because of his drink-driving. It was only because he had employed a hotshot barrister from a London chambers that he had managed to escape a conviction for drink-driving and to escape a custodial sentence. He had also somehow managed to keep his high-profile job at the hospital.

That decision to keep him in post, made by the Health Trust, could have gone either way. Stanley Wainwright was the chairman of the Trust and a personal friend. He was a man who understood McEllery's domestic problems. He had given him the benefit of the doubt and stood by him.

The lack of other orthopaedic surgeons at the Queen's Medical Centre had also figured large in Wainwright's generous decision.

It was days like today that he really craved a glass of single malt. Both the operations he had carried out that day had been a complete nightmare. The artificial hips had been fitted in people who were grossly overweight. The actual physicality of performing the surgery was hard, demanding work.

He was so dog-tired that as he walked up to the second floor of the hospital's multistorey car park, he never noticed the long-haired man walking behind him up the stairs. He walked out onto the second level of the shadowy car park and saw his silver grey Mercedes parked on its own. As he fished in his pocket for the car keys, he heard a voice behind him say, 'Dr McEllery?'

Without a second thought, McEllery spun around and said, 'Can I help you?'

The long-haired man was now standing right in front of him.

McEllery thought he knew the man's face, but then he saw that the man was holding something in his right hand. As soon as his brain registered that the object was a heavy metal spanner, he spluttered, 'My wallet's in my jacket pocket. Just take what you want!'

Without saying a word, Stephen Meadows crashed the spanner into the head of McEllery. The blow landed flush on the portly surgeon's left ear, sending him to the floor. As darkness closed in around him, McEllery could feel his attacker snatching the car keys from his hand.

67

5.00 pm, 21 June 1987
Queen's Medical Centre, Nottingham

Once McEllery had slipped into unconsciousness, Meadows opened the boot of the Mercedes. He lifted the consultant from the floor and threw him in the boot of his own car.

He then locked the Mercedes and made his way up the internal ramps to the top floor of the car park, where he had left his own vehicle. He jumped in the white van, started the engine and drove back down the three levels before parking up directly beside McEllery's Mercedes.

He sat in the van with the lights off for five minutes, making sure there was nobody else on that floor of the car park. As soon as he was satisfied that he was alone, he got out and opened the side door of the van. He then popped the boot of the Mercedes and lifted out the still-unconscious McEllery. He threw the surgeon roughly into the van. He climbed into the back and secured the doctor's feet and wrists with nylon cord before gagging him with sticky gaffer tape.

He closed the sliding door of the van and quietly shut the boot of the Mercedes before sliding the car keys behind the front tyre of the car.

Meadows showed no emotion as he got back in the van and drove out of the car park. Dr McEllery was the man who had been responsible for the death of his parents, and Meadows would make sure that the good doctor now fully atoned for his crime.

HE HAD something very special in mind for James McEllery. He intended to make him suffer badly before he cleansed him for good. After all, this was the evil bastard who had effectively murdered his parents and then used his money and connections to escape justice.

Memories of that trial flooded through Stephen's brain as he drove through Nottingham's streets. His mind was filled with an image of McEllery's fat face. The jowls in the doctor's neck wobbling as he roared with laughter, standing outside the court with the smart-arse lawyer who had got him off the drink-driving charge on a feeble technicality.

Stephen knew that very soon McEllery wouldn't be laughing. He also knew that there would be no smart-arse lawyer to save his skin this time.

68

10.00 pm, 21 June 1987
MCIU Offices, Mansfield, Nottinghamshire

The briefing room was full. There was a low hum of noise in the room, as the gathered detectives discussed the developments in the case that had necessitated this late briefing.

Danny stood at the front of the room and said loudly, 'Quiet! Settle down; let's get started.'

Danny said, 'For those of you who have only just come into the briefing, we now have a very good suspect for the three Trent River murders. Andy, can you give us all a summary of what we now know about Stephen Meadows.'

Andy Wills said, 'Stephen Meadows is twenty nine years of age. He lives in what was his parents' house at Ridge Hill, Lowdham. Preliminary enquiries show that this property was developed as a smallholding when it was owned by his parents. They liked to see themselves as living like the characters in the television programme *The Good Life*. They kept animals and grew crops on the three-acre plot. The property itself is a large, detached bungalow with several workshops at the rear of the property. There's also a detached garage, which used to house farm machinery.

'Having resigned from his job as a sound engineer at Castle Sounds, Meadows got a job as a delivery driver for a company called Red Arrow Couriers Ltd. They specialise in county-wide deliveries and are based at East Midlands Airport. The company have confirmed that Meadows has the use of the works van full time, as he pays half of the cost of insurance and tax required to keep the vehicle on the road. The vehicle is a wide-wheelbase Ford Transit. It's white in colour, with a distinctive red arrow logo on each of the side panels.

'Meadows has no previous convictions with the police, and everyone I've spoken to refers to him in the same way. He's described as being a quiet and timid man who kept himself to himself, mainly because of his devastating stutter. He's also described by people as being extraordinarily physically strong. A genuine gentle giant. There's one other thing that could be extremely relevant – there are weapons registered to the Ridge Hill address.'

Danny said, 'Can you elaborate on that?'

'I did the usual checks with firearms licensing, and they found that two shotguns are registered to that address. The shotgun licence holder was Meadows' father. Following his death, there was every likelihood that the guns would have been removed by the firearms licensing department. Unfortunately, they can find no record of this happening.'

'So Meadows may have access to two shotguns and ammunition at Ridge Hill?'

'Yes, sir.'

'Thanks, Andy.'

'There's one other thing that's maybe relevant, boss. Stephen Meadows has a sister.'

'Does she live at the property in Lowdham?'

'No. Dawn Meadows suffered a catastrophic brain injury. From what I can gather, she is now twenty years of age. She was always cared for at home by her parents, but after their death in a car accident, she was moved to a specialist care home.'

'Do we know which one?'

'Yes, sir. It's the Oaks at West Bridgford.'

'That's good work, Andy. As soon as the briefing is over, I want you to call the Oaks and ascertain if Stephen Meadows ever visits his sister, and if so, what time of the day he goes. I know it's late, but do your best.'

'Yes, boss.'

Professor Whittle looked concerned and said, 'Has anyone researched the car accident in which Meadows' parents were killed?'

DC Jeff Williams said, 'I've been looking into that. The fatal accident occurred on the Lowdham bypass, between the villages of Epperstone and Oxton. The vehicle they were travelling in was hit head-on by a Range Rover being driven in the opposite direction. The driver was Dr James McEllery, a consultant orthopaedic surgeon.

'Meadows' parents were killed outright, but Dr McEllery only sustained minor injuries. He was breathalysed at the scene and was found to be three times over the legal limit. The accident investigation team found that the Range Rover had drifted onto the wrong side of the road, and that there was no evidence of any braking by McEllery prior to the collision. He was charged with death by dangerous driving and drink-drive offences.'

Danny said, 'And what was the outcome?'

'This is where it all gets a bit weird, boss. McEllery got off all the charges at court.'

'How did he manage that?'

'He paid for some high-flying lawyer from London to represent him. This barrister specialised in finding loopholes in the breathalyser law. His clients have included footballers, pop stars and politicians. Somehow, this barrister managed to show that the equipment used during the breathalyser process was faulty. This meant the drink-drive charges were thrown out of court. It was then like a domino effect. Because the drink-drive charge had been dropped, they could no longer prosecute the charge of death by dangerous driving. McEllery ended up pleading guilty to a lesser charge, of driving without due care and attention. He blamed the long hours he was working for his inattention when driving. The court accepted this mitigation, and he walked away with a heavy fine.'

'Was he disqualified from driving?'

'No. He only received six points for the driving without due care offence. He kept his licence.'

Sharon Whittle said quietly, 'Do you know if Stephen Meadows attended that trial?'

DC Williams nodded. 'I've spoken to the Traffic Patrol officer who investigated the accident. He told me that Meadows attended court every day and was distraught at the final verdict.'

'Thanks.'

She turned to Danny and said in a whisper, 'I need to speak with you in your office after the briefing.'

Danny said, 'Of course.'

He then turned back to the room and said, 'I've been in contact with the Special Operations Unit. They are providing two sections to raid the property at Ridge Lane and arrest Meadows early tomorrow morning. As a result of the information gathered by Andy, I'll need to go back to them now and tell them about the possibility of firearms at the address. This could put back the timing for any raid. We'll need to obtain the necessary authorisation for an armed arrest, from senior command level. I'm hoping they'll be arriving here sometime in the early hours for a full briefing. I want you all to use this time to find out everything we can about the property at Ridge Hill, ready for that briefing. We'll also need to start making contingency plans in case our target isn't at that location. Let's get busy.'

Danny walked into his office, followed by Rob, Tina and Sharon Whittle.

Danny turned to the professor and said, 'What's the problem, Sharon?'

'I didn't want to throw a spanner in the works out there, but I think you could have a serious problem.'

'Go on?'

'There's every likelihood that Dr McEllery will also be a target for Meadows. Is it possible for you to trace the doctor before the armed officers carry out the raid at Ridge Hill?'

Danny turned to the two inspectors and said, 'Rob, Tina, can you both start making enquiries into McEllery? Let's make sure he's tucked up, nice and warm in his bed at home, before we raid Ridge Hill.'

Rob and Tina left the office.

Danny turned to Sharon and said, 'Why are you so convinced that Meadows would go after this doctor?'

'I'm just trying to think like him. If I were Meadows and feeling what he feels, I would definitely want payback against the man who snatched my parents away and then cheated the justice system. Wouldn't you?'

Danny nodded. 'I suppose I would. Let's hope he hasn't got to him yet. Is Stephen Meadows at all how you envisaged our killer to be?'

'The physical disability that led to a lifetime's ridicule, the secluded property, his physical strength, his access to a large vehicle. The way he's now seeking some sort of retribution against people who have wronged him. How he's been described as a gentle giant, averse to physical violence and confrontation. It all fits the profile I had in mind. So, do I think Stephen Meadows could be your killer? Yes, I do.'

'Do you think the sister would play a part in how he's thinking?'

'It's possible. If she was always cared for at home before the accident, and he has had to place her in permanent residential care for her own well-being, he could have some guilt over that. We'll know more once DS Wills has made his enquiry with the care home.'

'What about the firearms at the house? Do you think he would use them?'

'Ordinarily, I would say no. But if he's cornered and desperate, God only knows what he'll do.'

'I was afraid you were going to say that.'

There was a knock on the door, and Andy Wills walked in. He said, 'I've just spoken to the matron at the Oaks. She told me that Meadows has been visiting his sister quite regularly lately, and those visits have caused all sorts of problems.'

Danny said, 'In what way?'

'Apparently, every time he visits, he whispers quietly to his sister, and she has an adverse reaction to what he's telling her. Whatever he's talking to her about induces an epileptic seizure.'

Sharon said, 'Did you ask how frequently he visits?'

'Yes. He hadn't visited her at all until recently, and now the visits are quite regular.'

Danny said, 'What are you thinking, Sharon?'

'I could be wrong, but I was just wondering if he's confiding in his sister. He's a man who has nobody to share what he's doing with. You'll need to speak with the sister's consultant neurologist and ascertain what cognisant level she has. Meadows could be telling his sister what he's done, and what he's planning. The distress of what she's hearing is inducing a seizure. I know that emotional distress is one of the main triggers for epilepsy. You need to talk to her doctor.'

Andy said, 'The neurologist is Dr Sanderson. He's at work tomorrow morning at eight o'clock.'

'Thanks, Andy. I want you to be at the Oaks to meet Dr Sanderson when he arrives. Did you ask what time Meadows usually visits?'

'It's usually late afternoon. He arrives in a big white van, so the staff are assuming he comes to see his sister after work.'

'Thanks. Let me know what Dr Sanderson says.'

Danny picked up the telephone and dialled the number for the Special Operations Unit. They would need time to prepare for a fully armed operation, to raid the property at Ridge Hill.

It was going to be a very long night.

69

5.00 am 22 June 1987
Ridge Hill, Lowdham, Nottinghamshire

It had taken much longer to obtain the relevant authority from the assistant chief constable for an armed raid on Ridge Hill, so Danny had briefed the Special Operations Unit officers later than planned.

The briefing couldn't be rushed. The man they would be trying to apprehend was suspected of committing four murders and was also physically powerful and strong. The officers involved in the raid were all aware of the possibility there could be loaded firearms at the property. None of them were under any illusion about the very real threat Stephen Meadows posed.

The operation to raid the property and arrest Meadows had become significantly more complicated when it was discovered that Dr James McEllery was not at his home address. Enquiries at the Queen's Medical Centre had quickly determined that McEllery had left work at five o'clock. Officers searching the multistorey car park had located the doctor's Mercedes still at the hospital. A search around the vehicle had found the car keys stuffed behind the front wheel. Officers checking the CCTV at the entrance to the car park had seen the white Transit van with the red stripes on the side panels leaving the car park just after five o'clock. No registration plate on the vehicle could be seen.

The doctor's whereabouts were still unknown, but having viewed the CCTV footage, Danny was satisfied that the vehicle on the tape was probably the transit van Meadows had access to. He had to assume that McEllery had already been abducted by Meadows.

The armed officers tasked with raiding Meadows' home had planned for the hostage situation and were now waiting in their unmarked vans outside the Ridge Hill smallholding.

Sergeant Graham Turner would be leading the raid.

He gave his final instructions to the eight men conducting the raid. He said, 'You all know what you've got to do. Move carefully, but move fast. The quicker and quieter we can make entry, the more chance we have of taking down Meadows before any hostage becomes an issue. As planned, entry will be made at the side of the property where the main door is located. It's a uPVC frame, so we'll use the hydraulic door opener to force the door. That will give us a silent entry into the bungalow. I'll lead the search through the property, backed by PC Matt Jarvis as my Raid Two. The search will be methodical and silent until we locate the offender. We have officers on containment on all sides of the bungalow. Are there any questions?'

There were no questions.

Sergeant Turner said, 'Remember your training, and good luck.'

The black-clad officers, armed with Heckler and Koch

MP5 submachine guns, made their way in single file down the driveway. It was a dirt track, so the men didn't have to worry about noise from their footfalls. Less than a minute later, they had reached the designated point of entry. Two officers carrying the hydraulic door opener moved forward. They placed the device near the lock of the uPVC frame. The opener was pumped twice, and the door opened with a barely audible popping sound.

Sergeant Turner was first through the door, followed by PC Jarvis. Once inside, the two officers squatted and paused, listening intently for any noise from inside the remainder of the property.

The bungalow was silent.

Turner signalled for the other officers to enter. Once inside, they regrouped before Graham Turner and Matt Jarvis moved forward, systematically searching each room in turn. As each room was searched and cleared, the tension within the two men rose. The rooms where Meadows could be hiding were beginning to run out. With every door they opened, they expected to be confronted by a shotgun-wielding Meadows.

Graham paused outside what was obviously the last bedroom to be searched. He had a limited view into the room, as the door was slightly ajar. He could see what appeared to be a figure lying in the bed, beneath a duvet, with his back towards the door. The only thing he could make out in the dim light was the bulk under the bedclothes.

He called forward Matt Jarvis and said, in a voice barely a whisper, 'Contact. The target's in bed and appears to be asleep. I want you to cover him from here while I move forward into the room. Be ready to move forward on my command.'

Matt nodded and raised the Heckler and Koch into his shoulder, aiming at the figure still asleep in the bed.

Graham Turner slowly opened the bedroom door and crept inside the room until he was standing at the side of the bed. He motioned for Matt to move forward into the room. As he did so, other officers filled in behind him and remained in the doorway, with their weapons also trained on the prone figure.

Suddenly, Graham flicked on the torch attached to his weapon and shone it directly at the bulge beneath the duvet. At the same time, he shouted, 'Armed police! Remain still!'

There was no movement.

Graham said, 'Cover me, Matt.'

Matt Jarvis pressed the torch on his own weapon and illuminated the bed as Graham gripped the edge of the duvet.

Matt took up first pressure on the trigger as Graham yanked the duvet from the bed.

There was no sleeping figure beneath the duvet cover. It was just a stack of crumpled-up bedding. The experienced sergeant placed the palm of his hand on the bedding. It was cold. The bed had been empty for a while.

There was no sign of Stephen Meadows.

Graham hissed, 'Stay switched on. We've still got to clear the outbuildings yet. He could be in any one of them.'

The two men moved forward once again. There was one final door to go through. It led from the rear of the bungalow directly into the first of the outhouses.

Graham slowly eased open the door. The room had a small night light on in the corner. Through the small gap, between the door and the frame, Graham could see a naked man, who appeared to be unconscious. He was tied to a chair in the centre of the room and had slumped forward.

He turned to Matt and said, 'Contact. Possible hostage. No sign of Meadows, but I haven't got a full view into the room. Be ready to check the corners on entry. Are you ready?'

Matt Jarvis nodded. Graham Turner counted down *three,*

two, one on his fingers before both men moved swiftly into the room, scanning their weapons into the corners. Apart from the bound man in the centre of the room, it was empty.

Sergeant Turner spoke into his radio. 'We've completed the search of the bungalow. There's no sign of Meadows, but we've located an unconscious male in the first outhouse, behind the bungalow. He's naked and tied to a chair. He has multiple injuries. It looks like someone's given him a real beating. There's a particularly bad wound to the side of his head that looks serious. He's in a bad way. Send the paramedics forward now.'

Danny snatched up the radio and said, 'DCI Flint. Is it the doctor?'

Graham Turner replied, 'It could be. He's unconscious and has been stripped of his clothes.'

'The paramedics are on their way; I'm coming forward with DI Cartwright as well.'

'Okay. No problem. We've cleared the bungalow, so it's safe to approach. We still have the smaller outbuildings and the large garage to clear, at the rear of the property, so don't come forward any further than the first outbuilding. As soon as we've cleared the other buildings, I'll come back and find you.'

Danny and Tina walked along the driveway, followed by the paramedics, and into the property. The bungalow was still in darkness, but they could still make out the dilapidated state of the property.

When they reached the first outhouse, the two paramedics immediately began treating the man in the chair. One of them turned to Danny and said, 'We need to get him to a hospital quick as we can. His vitals are extremely low.'

'You can take him out whenever you're ready. Just retrace your steps. There are other officers outside who will escort you back to the ambulance.'

Sergeant Turner came into the room. 'All the outhouses and the garage have now been cleared. There's no sign of Meadows, and no sign of the white Transit van, either. I think the injured man is Dr McEllery. One of the lads has found a brazier behind one of the outbuildings that's stuffed with clothes ready for burning. The jacket sitting on the top had a wallet in it that contained a driving licence for James McEllery.'

Danny growled, 'The driving licence he shouldn't still have.'

Sergeant Turner said, 'Yeah, you've got a point, boss.'

The outhouse they were standing in was rigged out like a sound studio. The paramedics were still treating McEllery, who had been untied from the chair and was now lying on the floor.

Tina said, 'Is he going to be okay?'

The paramedic nearest to her turned and said, 'He's lost a fair bit of blood. Most of these facial injuries are superficial, but there could be an underlying fracture to his skull. We need to get him to a hospital to make sure there's no intercranial bleed.'

Danny said to Graham Turner, 'Where's the brazier you mentioned?'

Turner said, 'It's outside; follow me. I reckon he was planning to burn the clothes at some stage, but just hadn't got around to it yet.'

Twenty yards from the rear of the property stood a dilapidated outbuilding. Immediately behind it was an old-fashioned iron brazier. It was crammed full of clothes. Danny could see a mixture of men's and women's items.

Tina said, 'It's a fair bet these are from our victims?'

'I expect so. Let's get Tim Donnelly and his scenes of crime teams in here sharpish. This place needs going over with a fine-tooth comb. There's evidence everywhere. As soon as the paramedics are out of that room, I want the whole place sealed off. Nobody in or out until scenes of crime have finished.'

Tina said, 'I'm on it.'

Danny turned to Graham Turner and said, 'Great job, Graham. It's never easy doing a search like that, expecting the offender to be lurking behind every door.'

Turner wiped imaginary sweat from his brow and said, 'Best diet known to man, boss!'

Danny laughed and said, 'Have any of your men found any farm machinery in the other outbuildings?'

'Give me a minute.'

Sergeant Turner spoke into his radio. The reply came quickly.

He turned to Danny and said, 'In the double garage at the side of the property, there's an old tractor and lots of various attachments for it.'

The two men made their way around the outside of the property to the garage. The door was wide open, and the light was on. Danny could see the tractor and the various implements that could be attached to it. In the corner of the garage stood a pile of blue-coloured chains, which were obviously used to attach the implements to the rear of the tractor.

Danny had seen enough.

He walked with Turner to the front of the property and found Tina talking to Tim Donnelly, the scenes of crime supervisor.

He said, 'Have you got enough staff here, Tim? It's an evidential gold mine inside. I don't think Meadows is at all forensically aware. There's a brazier full of clothes out the back, and chain links identical to the ones found on our victims in the garage. Then there's the room where Dr McEllery was found. God only knows what you'll find in there.'

Tim said, 'Tina's just told me about the brazier and the sound studio. I've just this second requested another full team to be called out. It's going to be a long job, and we don't want to miss anything.'

Danny said, 'Tim, I want you to stay here and supervise the forensic search. I know you're well appraised of the enquiry, and you'll know what's relevant.'

Tim nodded, confident in his knowledge of the case and his own ability.

Danny then turned to Graham Turner. 'Can you and your men remain on standby until we locate Meadows? I think he must have already left for work. A quick telephone call into the courier service where he works will soon confirm that.'

Turner nodded and said, 'I'll get my blokes together and tell them what's happening. If you're contemplating an armed stop on the van, you're going to need the armed Traffic cars, sir. We haven't found any shotguns or ammunition here, but that could mean Meadows has them with him right now.'

Danny nodded and got into the passenger seat of the CID car. He grabbed the radio and said, 'DCI Flint to DS Wills.'

The radio crackled with static before Danny heard, 'DS Wills, go ahead.'

'Andy, I want you to contact the Red Arrows Courier Service and find out if Meadows is at work today. If he is, I want to know if he's still at the airport, or if he's already started his deliveries. If he's already picked up, I want to know the exact locations of all his deliveries today. Quick as you can, please.'

'I'll get straight back to you, sir. Stand by.'

Five minutes passed before the radio burst into life again: 'DS Wills to DCI Flint. Over.'

'Go ahead, Andy.'

'Meadows is at work and has already picked up his deliveries for the day. The company are going to fax over the list of addresses he's delivering to today. The problem we're going to have is that there's no set route. He doesn't have to deliver them in any order.'

'Okay. I'll be back at Mansfield with Tina in twenty minutes. Over.'

He turned to Tina and said, 'Quick as you can.'

Tina gunned the engine and drove quickly away from Ridge Hill.

70

10.35 am, 22 June 1987
Moorcroft Farm, Bingham, Nottinghamshire

After studying the list of addresses provided by the Red Arrows Courier Service, outlining exactly what addresses Meadows was scheduled to deliver packages to on that day, Danny had looked for the one that was closest geographically to the suspect's own address. He had discussed his thought process with Rob, Tina and Sharon Whittle. He had then gambled that one of the last deliveries Meadows would make that day would be at Moorcroft Farm, just outside the village of Bingham.

A quick telephone call into the farm had confirmed that they hadn't yet received any packages from Red Arrow Couriers.

Moorcroft Farm was accessed by a single dirt track that led down to the remote, red-brick farmhouse. The farmer and his family had been shocked when Danny and Tina had gone to the farmhouse and told them they would need to leave the property for the next few hours.

Danny's plan was to wait for Meadows to deliver the parcel expected at the farmhouse. He would then intercept him at gunpoint while he was out of the vehicle. If Meadows could be detained while he was away from the vehicle, it was the safest option for everyone, as there was still the possibility that Meadows could have a loaded shotgun in the van. The deserted farmyard was the perfect location for the arrest, since there were no passers-by who could inadvertently get in the way of the armed operation.

With everything now in place, it was a waiting game.

Danny and Tina were upstairs, in the main bedroom of the farmhouse. From behind the net curtains of the window, they had a perfect view along the dirt track that led to the main road.

Sergeant Turner and other armed officers from the Special Operations Unit were hidden in various locations around the farmyard. It would be the responsibility of Graham Turner to call the strike and make the arrest of Meadows at gunpoint.

Danny could hear the Special Ops team regularly checking their radio signals, ensuring that all communications were clear.

Tina said quietly, 'He's here.'

Through binoculars borrowed from the Special Operations Unit officers, Tina could clearly see the registration number of the vehicle. Red Arrow Couriers had supplied the registration number of the vehicle being used by Meadows. That number matched the number on the van now approaching Moorcroft Farm.

Danny looked out of the window and could see the white Ford Transit trundling down the long driveway. He grabbed his radio and said, 'DCI Flint to Sergeant Turner. Be advised, suspect vehicle is now on the track and approaching the farmhouse. Over.'

'Received. To DCI Flint, maintain radio silence from this moment. Wait for my signal. Over.'

Danny clicked his radio twice, acknowledging the last instruction.

He then heard Graham Turner organising his men. Going quickly over the last-minute instructions for the arrest.

71

10.35 am, 22 June 1987
Moorcroft Farm, Bingham, Nottinghamshire

Stephen Meadows had the cassette player on in the van as he drove down the uneven farm track. He was shaking his head back and forth to the growling rhythm of the new Candlemass release, his long hair moving to the same beat as the loud music.

This was the last delivery. He had worked fast today, as he desperately wanted to visit Dawn and let her know that he had the doctor. He looked at the vivid purple bruises on his knuckles and smiled a malevolent smile.

He hated physical violence, but it had felt so good beating the fat face of McEllery last night. The late night and all the physical exertion had caused him to oversleep a little. He couldn't afford to be late for work, so he hadn't had time to cleanse the doctor on his way to work as he had planned. He wasn't overly concerned. There was no way McEllery could escape, so he would have the pleasure of the final cleansing later tonight, after dark. He had already chosen the bridge at Dunham to be McEllery's final resting place.

He brought the van to a stop in the farmyard of Moorcroft Farm. He knew the last box he had to deliver wasn't a big one.

He jumped out of the van, leaving the engine running and the heavy metal music blaring. He opened the side door of the van and retrieved the last cardboard box. Now that the van was empty, he could clearly see bloodstains in the back. He made a mental note to wash out the van as he closed the door.

Carrying the box under one arm, Meadows walked towards the front door of the farmhouse.

Still holding the box under one arm, he knocked loudly on the wooden door. He winced slightly at the impact on his bruised knuckles.

There was no answer.

He was just about to knock again, when he was shocked to see a black-clad figure emerge from around the side of his delivery van. The man was aiming a gun at his chest.

He heard the man in black shout, 'Armed police! Stand still!'

Shocked by what was happening, Meadows dropped the cardboard box and turned away from the armed man. He was immediately confronted by a second armed man emerging from the other side of the van. He was holding the same kind of gun as the first, and it too was aimed directly at his chest.

He then heard the first police officer shout, 'I said stand still, Meadows!'

He froze, unsure of what to do next. As his brain was weighing up his options, the loud, aggressive voice of the police officer polarised his thoughts.

Still pointing the weapon directly at his chest, the officer shouted at him, 'Get on your knees! Do it now!'

He knew he had no choice.

He dropped onto his knees.

His head was now flooded with thoughts of his sister, Dawn. He had let her down again. He knew the police would visit his house; he knew they would find McEllery. He had failed. The doctor would walk away again.

His thoughts were interrupted as he heard the armed officer shout, 'On the floor, face down! Do it now and keep your hands out to the sides, where I can see them!'

Once again, he complied meekly with the command and lay on the cold ground, with his arms out to his sides.

He felt detached from what was happening to him. Inwardly, he cursed that he had overslept. He should have cleansed McEllery on his way to work, as he had planned.

He felt strong hands grabbing him and felt the cold steel of the handcuffs as they were snapped onto his wrists.

He thought of Dawn, and a tear trickled down his face.

72

10.40 am, 22 June 1987
Moorcroft Farm, Bingham, Nottinghamshire

With the arrest of Meadows completed safely, Danny and Tina made their way downstairs and walked outside. Other police vehicles were arriving in the farmyard as they walked out.

Danny said, 'Good work, Graham. Get onto the control room and stand down the ambulance waiting on the main road.'

'Will do, sir.'

He turned to Tina. 'Make sure nobody goes in the back of that van. I want a full lift arranged, and a full forensic search back at headquarters, in their examination bay.'

Tina nodded and said, 'I'll get the full lift arranged straight away.'

Danny nodded and stepped over to Meadows, who was

now in a sitting position with his hands cuffed behind his back.

Danny said, 'Stephen Meadows, I'm arresting you on suspicion of the murder of Suzy Flowers.'

Danny cautioned Meadows, who sat cross-legged and stared straight ahead.

Danny hauled him to his feet and said, 'Did you hear what I said? Do you have anything to say?'

Meadows remained tight-lipped and stared straight through Danny.

DC Simon Paine drove a CID car alongside the two men. Danny opened the back door and sat Meadows in the back of the car. He turned to DC Jeff Williams in the passenger seat and said, 'Jeff, get in the back with Meadows, and watch him like a hawk. He's been arrested and searched. I don't want him questioned at all between now and Mansfield, understood?'

Jeff Williams immediately got out of the front seat and sat in the back of the vehicle next to Meadows. Danny said, 'If he volunteers a comment, just make a note of it. As soon as DI Cartwright has organised things here, we'll follow you in convoy back to Mansfield, so Meadows can be booked into custody.'

DC Paine nodded. 'Right you are, boss.'

73

1.45 pm, 22 June 1987
MCIU Offices, Mansfield, Nottinghamshire

Danny and Sharon Whittle were waiting for Tina and Rachel to return from their first taped interview with Stephen Meadows.

There was a knock on the office door, and Rob Buxton walked in. 'Have you got a minute?'

Danny said, 'Of course. What is it?'

'I just wanted to let you know that vehicle sighting is a non-starter.'

'This is the vehicle that came to light from the house-to-house enquiries on the Bellamy Estate?'

'That's the one. The dark blue Vauxhall Cavalier that was seen being driven away from the estate after the fire. I've had a team working on intelligence reports involving blue Cavaliers, but without even a partial registration plate, we're stuffed. You wouldn't believe how many Vauxhall Cavaliers there are in this area.'

Sharon said, 'Did you get anywhere with the photographs of people watching at the fire scenes?'

Rob shook his head. 'We've had all the photographs taken by the press. I've gone over and over every one of them with a magnifying glass. There are no faces in the crowd that match anyone of interest from our photographic records.'

Danny said, 'How's the enquiry progressing generally?'

'I'll be honest, boss. It's stalling badly. We're getting nowhere fast. The grim reality is that our only hope of catching this bastard is if he starts another fire, and nobody wants that.'

'No, we bloody don't. Keep at it. Organise another press appeal. Let's try to jog the public's memory a little. It might turn something up.'

A crestfallen Rob said, 'Will do.'

There was another knock on the door, and Tina and Rachel walked in. Rob said, 'I know you're busy. I'll let you crack on.'

Danny nodded as Rob left the office. He then asked, 'How did the first interview go?'

Tina said, 'Well, Rachel asked a lot of questions. Meadows stared at the wall and said nothing. That was it, really.'

Danny said, 'So he went "no comment"?'

'He didn't even go "no comment". He just totally ignored us, never said a word.'

Rachel said, 'It's like he's in a different place. I don't even know if he's hearing what I'm asking him. I always give a long pause in between questions, but there isn't even a glimmer of recognition on his face.'

Danny said, 'Did you concentrate on his knowledge of the victims?'

'I tried to stick to the interview plan, but it was difficult without getting any feedback. It was like, 'Do you know Rex Poyser?' Nothing. 'Do you know Sarah Milfoyle?' Nothing. When it's a one-way street like that, it's bloody difficult.'

Sharon looked over her glasses and said, 'You could try changing tack a little.'

Tina said, 'How?'

'You could try being extremely sympathetic towards him. Tell him you understand how he's suffered. Let him know that you can see how these people you're asking him about have all made his life a misery. Tell him you know what's been going on; elaborate if you must. If he thinks you understand the reasons for his behaviour, he may feel more inclined to engage with you. He may even start to respond to your questions. I think you should also refer to his sister. Tell him that you understand she is part of that suffering. Let's see if we can hit a nerve that way. From what Andy found out, after talking to Dr Sanderson and that social worker Heather Joyce, it seems to me that the bond between brother and sister is still extremely strong.'

'It's got to be worth a try, I suppose.'

'Did Rachel lead the first interview?'

'Yes, she did.'

'Then swap roles. You lead this time, Tina. Impress on Meadows that you're the only other person in the room who understands him and what he and his sister have been through. Tell him to ignore everyone else in the room if you must. Try to get him to think he's having a one-to-one conversation with you.'

Tina nodded. 'What do you think, Danny?'

Danny nodded. 'Try it. Anything that might get him talking is worth having a go at. Having seen everything at Ridge Hill, I'm convinced that when scenes of crime have finished, we'll have more than enough evidence to charge him anyway, but it would be nice to get his version of events. Give it an hour. Get yourselves organised, have a coffee, then go and speak to him again.'

74

3.00 pm, 22 June 1987
Custody Suite, Mansfield Police Station

The cramped interview room was spartan, containing a single table and four chairs. On one side of the table sat Tina and Rachel; on the other side, Stephen Meadows was flanked by his solicitor, Margaret Truman.

All his clothes had been seized for forensic examination, and Meadows now cut a sinister figure, sitting hunched over wearing a bright white forensic suit. His long hair framed the malevolent face, and his piercing, unblinking brown eyes stared out from below heavy brows.

Rachel put in the tapes and switched the recorder on.

Meadows was expecting Rachel to start speaking again. He was a little startled when the first voice he heard was Tina.

She said quietly, in little more than a whisper, 'I understand why you're here, Stephen.'

Tina noticed the small flicker of emotion and said, 'I know what's been going on, Stephen.' She deliberately paused before saying his name.

He remained silent, but his eyes were now locked firmly on Tina's, meeting her gaze.

She said, 'I know all about Rex Poyser, Sarah Milfoyle, Suzy Flowers and James McEllery. I know exactly what they've all done to you and your little sister, Dawn. I can feel your pain.'

He said nothing, but allowed the slightest shake of his head.

Tina noticed the brief, non-verbal communication and pressed on. She nodded and said, 'Yes I do, Stephen. I understand how each one of those awful people have hurt you, and how one in particular has caused you and Dawn so much pain. I know why you despised them all so much. I understand the reason why you took them and why you killed them.'

When he spoke, it surprised everyone in the room, especially his own solicitor.

Through clenched teeth, he uttered the single word: 'Cleansed.'

Tina echoed his comment and said, 'Cleansed?'

It was a standard interview technique that she used, to encourage people to elaborate on what they had just said.

It worked.

After thirty seconds of silence, Meadows leaned back in his chair and said in a loud, far more confident voice, 'Cleansed, not killed. I didn't kill anybody; the river cleansed them. The river made them different.'

There was no sign of the stutter Tina had been expecting. Everyone she had spoken to about Meadows had described the severe stutter he suffered when trying to communicate.

'Why don't you tell me about the cleansing, Stephen? Who was first?'

'That bitch of a girlfriend. She made everyone laugh at me. The river changed her, made her stop.'

'Suzy Flowers?'

He nodded. 'Yes. Suzy fucking Flowers. She thought I was the joke, then suddenly, at the bridge, she stopped laughing.'

A sly, hateful grin formed across his face, and he said, 'My teacher was next.'

'Sarah Milfoyle?'

'She had to learn the harshest lesson, and the river is the best teacher.'

'Did you put Suzy Flowers and Sarah Milfoyle in the river to drown?'

'Yes, I did. It's where they needed to be.'

'I understand that, Stephen. What about the others?'

She deliberately left the question open, to see if there were any other victims they didn't yet know about. It was a clever move, but one that was instantly spotted by Margaret Truman.

The solicitor interrupted, saying, 'Stephen, you're my client, and my advice to you is the same as before. You really shouldn't be answering any questions at this time.'

Meadows ignored his solicitor, brushing off her advice. Maintaining eye contact with Tina, he curled his top lip into a wicked sneer and said, 'The other one needed to be cleansed, as well.'

'Rex Poyser?'

'Rex Poyser. The big man. He thought he was clever. He made my life a misery for months just so he could give his woman my job. Well, it doesn't matter now, does it, Rex? You don't have your blonde bimbo anymore, and the river made sure you'll never have another woman. So, all in all, you're not very clever really, are you, Rex?'

'Stephen, when we went to your house, we found somebody else. Why was he there?'

Meadows shook his head. 'I'm disgusted that the good doctor escaped cleansing. I should have taken him straight to the river last night. He's the worst of them all. I was going to cleanse him on my way to work today.'

He sighed loudly and said, 'The river should have been changing him right now.'

'So it was your intention to drown McEllery as well?'

'Detective, Dr McEllery killed my parents. He would definitely have been cleansed; the river would have seen to it.'

'Where did you intend to do that?'

'Dunham. Because I never had time this morning, I was going to take him to the river tonight.'

Tina paused, then said, 'Have you killed anyone else, Stephen?'

'No. I was going to cleanse more; there are many others who deserve it for what they've done over the years.'

'Why didn't you?'

'Dawny.'

'Your sister?'

'She told me to stop. She didn't mind if I cleansed McEllery, but she wanted me to stop. I've failed her.'

'What do you mean you've failed her, Stephen?'

'I haven't cleansed the man who caused all our pain, and now I'll never see her again.'

He leaned forward until his forehead made contact with the desk and let out a loud, pain-filled moan.

He remained in that position, with his head resting on the table.

Tina glanced at Meadows' solicitor, who shrugged her shoulders.

Tina said, 'Are you sorry you killed all these people?'

With Meadows' head still down, the muffled reply was, 'Should I be?'

'Is there anything else you want to tell me?'

Meadows sat up straight, leaned forward, resting his elbows on the table.

With cold eyes, he stared at Tina and said, 'Cleansed, not killed.'

Tina nodded to Rachel, who switched off the tapes.

75

4.00 pm, 22 June 1987
Hardwick Avenue, Rainworth, Nottinghamshire

He felt excited. He'd waited a long time to get the photographs developed. He had picked up them up earlier from Boots Chemists in Mansfield and desperately wanted to open the envelope and look at them straight away. He had resisted the temptation. Now that he was alone in the house, he could enjoy looking at them properly.

He sat down at the kitchen table, removed the envelope from the Boots carrier bag, and took the photographs out. He spread them out across the table, ending up with all twenty images facing him.

He stared down at all the images of the blackened remains of the houses he had destroyed. The semi-detached property in Blidworth, the bungalow in Mansfield, and the block of flats in Rainworth.

As he looked at each photograph in turn, it allowed vivid memories of the nights when he had unleashed the beast in all its fury to come flooding back. The Nikon camera provided needle-sharp detail. Staring at the photographs, he felt that if he touched them, he would be able to feel the texture of the charred brick, or smell the sooty, charred timbers.

After carefully studying each image, he gathered them up and took them upstairs. He retrieved the album that contained the newspaper clippings reporting on all three fires. As well as the grainy newspaper images of the properties burning, he would now have the aftermath of the destruction.

He took out the Pritt Stick and began pasting the photographs into the album.

It had been worth the effort to revisit all the different locations. He had been very careful, surreptitiously using the camera to snatch a photograph only when he was sure nobody was watching. They would now be his for ever. He could stare at them whenever he felt the urge.

After sticking the last photograph in the scrapbook, he carefully went through every page. He read every newspaper report and studied every photograph. He saw all the blank pages at the back of the album. He made a silent promise to find another property soon.

Perhaps next time, it would be in one of the neighbouring villages of Mansfield Woodhouse or Forest Town.

76

5.30 pm, 22 June 1987
MCIU Offices, Mansfield, Nottinghamshire

Danny walked into the main briefing room and said, 'Listen up, everyone, I've just finished speaking with Tim Donnelly. Scenes of crime have finally completed the forensic examination of the main parts of the bungalow at Ridge Hill. There are several other rooms still to be examined. Tim tells me that these rooms look as though Meadows never used them. He's not expecting to get a lot of forensic evidence from them.'

Tina said, 'Have they found much?'

'I'll recap what Tim has just told me. That way, you'll all know what we now have evidentially. The iron brazier found behind the bungalow has now been emptied. It contained items of clothing that match the descriptions of what all our victims were wearing when they were last seen. We have an old tweed twin set that was worn by Sarah Milfoyle, a camel-coloured Crombie coat owned by Rex Poyser and a leather jacket belonging to Suzy Flowers. Obviously, there are other garments as well, but the ones I've mentioned are the most easily identifiable. Inside the recording studio, they've recovered a piece of notepaper that contained a list of the victims written in longhand. This note will be compared to Meadows' handwriting later. A set of heavily bloodstained headphones have also been recovered from the recording studio. These have been fast-tracked for analysis. It could explain the damage caused to the ears of Rex Poyser. I wouldn't be surprised if the blood analysis shows an exact match for Poyser. Heavy chain links, in the distinctive blue colour, have been recovered from the garage. These look identical to the chains found on our victims and will also be fast-tracked for forensic comparison. The Red Arrow Couriers van seized at the farm this morning has now been lifted to headquarters. It will be forensically examined tomorrow morning. There are lots of other smaller details. The bottom line is, we now have physical evidence that supports the confessions obtained during the interview with Meadows.'

Tina said, 'Meadows talking to us was down to Professor Whittle. The tactics she suggested worked a treat. They were perfect. Once he started talking, he didn't want to stop. Even when his solicitor tried to close him down, he was having none of it. He was desperate to finally share his reasons for killing all those people.'

Tina turned to Sharon Whittle and said, 'There was one thing that was strange, during the interview. When he was answering my questions, Meadows never stuttered once. That terrible stammer every witness has told us about just wasn't there. Why was that?'

The professor said, 'It's all to do with control. Stephen Meadows now feels like he's the one controlling events. A bad stutter is always more of a psychological problem than a physical one. Meadows finally feels in charge of his life now. In his mind, he's grown in confidence and self-worth. So there's no need for him to stutter. The human brain is an extraordinarily complex machine.'

Tina turned to Danny. 'So, do we have enough to charge Meadows with all three murders and the abduction of Dr McEllery?'

'More than enough. Well done, everyone.'

With the impromptu briefing over, everyone got back on with their work. Tina walked across to Rachel's desk and said, 'Once we've got all the charges prepared, do you fancy going for a celebratory drink?'

'Any other time, and I would have jumped at the chance. I'm sorry, Tina, I've already got plans for this evening. As soon as we've finished up here, I'm meeting my boyfriend, Jack, at the Hutt in Ravenshead. He's there with some of his friends from the school where he's a teacher. We're just going for a few drinks; why don't you come, too? There'll be a crowd of us. If you come along, it will save me from being surrounded by boring teachers and their equally boring partners all night.'

Tina laughed and said, 'As tempting an offer as that undoubtably is, I'm going to pass on the boring teachers and their boring partners. I think I'll just go home, open a bottle of red wine, have a nice meal and quietly celebrate the result of this case.'

Rachel said, 'I can't say I blame you. We still need to get these charges organised and typed up before either of us can think about going anywhere.'

Both women smiled and began typing out the charge sheets for Stephen Meadows.

77

9.30 pm, 22 June 1987
The Hutt Public House, Ravenshead, Nottinghamshire

Rachel felt exhausted. It had been a long busy day, and now that she had drank a couple of large red wines, she was starting to feel the energy drain from her.

Tina had given her a ride to the busy pub in Ravenshead. She had left her own car at work so she could have a drink and get a lift home with her boyfriend, Jack Mellors. Rachel had been dating the handsome physical education teacher for six months, and she felt their relationship was progressing at just the right pace.

Jack was never demanding. He understood the long hours she had to work in her job. He was supportive, and that was something Rachel cherished.

Jack took a sip of his cola and said, 'You're very quiet tonight, sweetheart. Is everything okay?'

She half smiled. 'I'm shattered; it's been a long week. I haven't eaten a thing all day, and this Malbec has gone straight to my head.'

He winked at her and said, 'I thought you murder detectives were all hard-drinking, no-nonsense, burn-the-candle-at-both-ends kind of people.'

Rachel laughed out loud. 'I think you're getting me mixed up with Regan and Carter from *The Sweeney*!'

Overhearing their conversation, a young, dark-haired woman, standing next to Rachel, said, 'You must be Jack's girlfriend, the detective.'

Jack winced at the intrusion, but said politely, 'Rachel, this is Tammy. She teaches Spanish to the year elevens at the Joseph Whittaker school in Rainworth. Tammy, this is Rachel.'

Before Rachel could say anything, Tammy blustered, 'I love all the detective shows on the TV. What's it like in real life, though? Have you ever caught a murderer?'

'Funnily enough ...'

Tammy interrupted again, gushing: 'Are you working on these dreadful fires?'

Rachel said in a firmer voice, that warned against another interruption, 'Partly. Just lately though, I've been working on a different case.'

Tammy's eyes widened. She was in full flow now, standing directly in between Rachel and Jack. He grimaced and shrugged his shoulders behind the annoying Spanish teacher.

Tammy said, 'In the staff room at the Jo Whit school, we've got our own theory on who the mad arsonist is.'

Rachel said in a disinterested fashion, 'Really?'

'Oh yeah! We all think it's one of our pupils, Smoky Simpson.'

Rachel tried to stifle a laugh. 'Who the hell is Smoky Simpson?'

'He's a typical spotty fourteen-year-old. He's got no mates, a proper loner. The main reason for our theory is this, the kid constantly smells of smoke. When he walks by you in the corridor, it's as though you're standing right next to a smoky bonfire. His clothes constantly reek of smoke.'

'Does he really smell that bad?'

'Yeah, he does. His form tutor sent a note home to his parents about it. Well, they're his foster parents, I think. Either way, it didn't change anything. He still pongs to high heaven.'

She tutted dramatically and rolled her eyes before saying, 'I don't suppose for one minute he's got anything to do with those dreadful fires, though. I mean, he's only fourteen. Somebody that young couldn't possibly have killed all those people. Right?'

'Right. Of course not, Tammy. What's Smoky Simpson's real name?'

'Billy Simpson.'

'And he goes to your school, Joseph Whittaker?'

'Yeah. Your glass is empty; can I get you another drink, Racquel?'

'It's Rachel, and I'm alright for a drink. Me and Jack are just leaving, but thanks anyway.'

Rachel spun around, searching for Jack, who was by now chatting to a man at the bar. She made her way over and said, 'Can we go home now, sweetheart? I'm dead on my feet here.'

Jack's friend grinned and said, 'Yeah, Tammy tends to have that effect on most people.'

Rachel said, 'It's not Tammy; she was just being friendly. I am literally shattered, Jack.'

Jack finished the last of his cola and said, 'Come on then,

shweethart, I'll drive you home. I've only had a couple of shmall beersh, offisher.'

Rachel knew that Jack never drank alcohol, but she still grinned at his poor joke.

She said loudly, 'I bloody hope not! The traffic cops are waiting outside, with their breathalysers.'

Jack zipped up his leather jacket and said, 'Come on, let's go before the landlord bars us.'

Twenty minutes later, they were sitting in Jack's sports car outside Rachel's house. She turned to him and said, 'Would you mind if I didn't make you a coffee tonight, sweetheart? I'm dead on my feet. I just want to get into bed.'

With a jokey lecherous grin, he said, 'I'm glad we're both thinking along the same lines here.'

She playfully punched his arm and said, 'I just want to get into bed to sleep, you idiot.'

He laughed and said, 'Of course I don't mind, honey. I'll call you tomorrow.'

She leaned over and kissed him hard on the mouth. 'Thanks, Jack. See you tomorrow.'

Rachel got out of the car. As soon as she was at the front gate, Jack wound the window down and shouted, 'Sweet dreams, gorgeous,' before he drove off.

Rachel walked into the dark house. She switched on the hall light and glanced at her watch. It wasn't just tiredness that had prevented her inviting Jack in for a nightcap. Her brain was working overtime after listening to the puerile comments made by Tammy the Spanish teacher. Could there possibly be anything in this juvenile who constantly reeked of smoke?

It was now almost ten thirty. Was it too late to call Danny?

She grabbed the telephone. After the third ring, she heard Danny's voice. 'Hello.'

Rachel said, 'Hello, boss. I hope it's not too late, and I didn't wake you or the baby.'

'What's up?'

'I didn't know whether to bother you or not. It's probably nothing, and I do feel a bit stupid now.'

'Rachel, what is it?'

'I've just been talking to a teacher who works at the Joseph Whittaker school in Rainworth. She's been telling me about a fourteen-year-old pupil at the school, whom the teachers all refer to as Smoky Simpson because his clothes constantly reek of smoke. I know it's probably nothing.'

'And it might be something. Look, I'll be in the office early tomorrow morning. See me there at seven o'clock, and we'll do some research into this Smoky Simpson. What's the kid's real name?'

'Billy Simpson.'

'Goodnight, Rachel. I'll see you in the morning.'

78

9.00 am, 23 June 1987
MCIU Offices, Mansfield, Nottinghamshire

Danny, Rachel and Rob had spent the morning researching the schoolboy Billy Simpson. They now knew that he lived with foster parents, Mike and Sheila Grant, at Hardwick Avenue in Rainworth.

The boy had no criminal record, but the research done by Rachel with the Social Services had raised several interesting factors. His biological parents were both serving long custodial sentences in prison. They had been found guilty at Nottingham Crown Court for offences of neglect against the boy, based on an incident that had happened six years ago. Billy Simpson, then aged eight years, had been left alone at the family home in Carlton, Nottingham. There had been a devastating fire at the property, and Simpson was rescued from the blazing house by the fire brigade. The extensive injuries he suffered in the fire were so severe that he had almost died.

The parents' only defence at court was that it had been the boy himself who had started the fire. They maintained that they had only left him alone briefly, for an emergency. The police had quickly proved that both parents had been out drinking in a public house over a mile from the house for at least three hours prior to the fire starting. There had been no emergency. The court disregarded their assertion that it had been the child who started the fire, as he should never have been left alone in the first place.

Professor Whittle was also in the office early. She busied herself looking over the results of the three detectives' research. She said to Rachel, 'For Billy Simpson to have been involved in such a traumatic event at such a young age would have a profound effect on his behaviour. In my experience, this behaviour usually manifests itself in one of two ways. Simpson would either have a morbid fear of fire, or an uncontrollable fascination for it. Until you talk to him face-to-face, you'll have no way of knowing which it is.'

Danny was weighing things up in his mind. He knew there was only scant evidence connecting the boy to the offences. Should he take a risk and arrest him? An arrest would mean he could search his home address and interview him under caution at the police station. The alternative was to wait until there was more evidence and risk yet another fatal house fire.

He knew he would be held accountable if he made the decision to arrest the boy, and he subsequently couldn't be connected to the fires. Danny felt he would rather face that possibility than wait and watch another house fire in which people lost their lives.

Danny said, 'Do we have a contact number for the foster parents?'

Rachel said, 'Yes, boss.'

'Right, I'll call them and see if the lad's at home. If he's there, we'll pick him up and bring the foster parents with us, to act as appropriate adults. If he isn't at home, we'll arrest him at school and ask the foster parents to come into the station. As soon as we've got him at the police station, we can get an authority under the Police and Criminal Evidence Act to search the home address.'

An eager Rob nodded. 'Sounds like a plan to me, boss.'

Danny picked up the telephone and dialled the number Rachel had given him. After two rings, the telephone was answered.

A man's voice said, 'Hello, Mike Grant.'

Danny said, 'Mr Grant, my name's Chief Inspector Flint from the CID at Mansfield. Is Billy still at home?'

'No. He left for school twenty minutes ago. He'll already be in registration by now. Is there a problem?'

'I want to ask him a few questions about the house fires that have been happening recently. If we picked him up from the school, would you and Mrs Grant be able to come to the police station, to look after Billy's welfare?'

'I'm not sure I like the idea of a load of coppers going to the school and dragging young Billy out of the classroom.'

'Don't worry, Mr Grant. It wouldn't be like that at all. We'll see Billy in the headmaster's office, away from all the other kids. Can you and your wife come to the police station to look after his welfare while we question him?'

'There's no way I can get to the police station. I'm laid up in bed with a heavy cold. I've just dragged myself out of bed to answer the phone. I can't stop shivering now. I feel bloody awful.'

'What about Mrs Grant?'

'Sheila's out at work.'

'Where does she work?

'At the Mansfield Shoe Company, in town.'

'Okay, don't worry. I'll contact your wife at the factory and arrange for her to come to the police station. I hope you're feeling better soon, Mr Grant.'

Danny put the phone down and said, 'Billy Simpson's already at school. We need to pick him up there.'

Having made his decision, Danny picked up the telephone again. This time, he spoke to the schools liaison officer, PC Trudy Armitage.

'Good morning, PC Armitage. I know we should avoid detaining pupils on school premises, but I need to get Billy Simpson in for questioning, sooner rather than later. He's a pupil at Joseph Whittaker school. I want to arrest him there and then search his home address. Obviously, I'd like the arrest to be carried out as discreetly as possible.'

'Okay, sir. I'm surprised you need to speak to Billy Simpson. I know him, and he's an incredibly quiet individual. He's one of the few kids at that school who's never in any bother. You do know he's in foster care, boss?'

'Yes, I do. I've just been speaking to one of his foster parents on the telephone. Mr Grant's nursing a heavy cold. He says he's too ill to come to the station. I'm going to contact Mrs Grant at her workplace now and arrange for her to act as appropriate adult when we question him.'

'Okay, sir. Let me make a call to the headmaster at Joseph Whittaker school. I'll make all the arrangements so the arrest can be done discreetly. Give me five minutes.'

'I'll wait for your call.'

Danny put the telephone down. 'Right. Rob, I want you and Glen to travel to Simpson's home address at Hardwick Avenue and wait outside for further instructions. As soon as the boy's been detained at the school, I'll get an authority signed up by the duty inspector. I'll then contact you and give you the okay to get inside and search the house.'

He turned to Rachel and said, 'Rachel, I want you to go to the school with PC Armitage. Detain Simpson on suspicion of the first arson, at Blidworth. Do it as discreetly as you can; I don't want any dramas. I'm acutely aware that this could all blow up in my face if we're not careful. If it stops other innocents dying in a fire, I'm prepared to take that risk. I'll drive to Mansfield Shoe Company myself and pick up Mrs Grant.'

The telephone began to ring. Danny snatched it up and said, 'Chief Inspector Flint.'

PC Armitage said, 'It's all arranged, sir. I've spoken with the headmaster, and at nine forty-five, he's going to fetch Billy from the classroom and take him to his office. The headmaster has requested that I be the officer who talks to Billy initially, as he already knows me. It will be less stressful for him if he sees a face he knows.'

'That's fine. I've got no problem with that. I want DC Rachel Moore to go with you and do the formal arrest, in the car. I take it you won't be in full uniform?'

'No, sir. I'll wear a civvie jacket over my uniform. The kids are used to seeing me around the school, so there'll be no problems. It will all be done very quietly. Have you sorted out an appropriate adult?'

'I'm going to arrange that myself. By the time you get back from the school, there'll be someone here to look out for Billy. DC Moore will be ready to go at nine thirty.'

Danny put the telephone down and said, 'Right, let's get things organised. There's only a few of us at work today, so we need to be on the ball. Make sure you've all got a radio. Rachel, I'll do the interviews with you. Rob, as soon as you can, I want to know what you've recovered from the search of Simpson's home address. I don't care if you're forced to interrupt the interview. This whole strategy will stand or fall on whether we find any incriminating evidence at the house. No evidence and Billy Simpson will be leaving as quickly as he got here. Everyone know what they're doing?'

Everyone nodded.

Danny said, 'Sharon, have you got a minute?'

He closed the door and said, 'Are you okay to hang around the office? I'd like your input as this develops. You may be able to help us with the interviews. You know, maybe give us an insight into how this young lad's mind works.'

'No problem. I know it's possible for a fourteen-year-old to have committed these terrible offences, but I just don't see these fatal fires as being the work of a juvenile offender; they seem a bit too well organised. There's a structure and a level of cunning involved that I wouldn't usually associate with someone so young. Although, with Simpson's troubled upbringing, I could well be wrong.'

'We'll soon find out, Sharon.'

79

10.00 am, 23 June 1987
Hardwick Avenue, Rainworth, Nottinghamshire

The house on Hardwick Avenue was unremarkable. It was an ordinary three-bedroom, semi-detached property with a small front garden and a larger, more expansive garden at the rear. Immediately behind the house was an alleyway, and beyond that, open fields and farmland.

Rob Buxton and Glen Lorimar sat outside the property, waiting patiently in an unmarked CID vehicle. The radio crackled into life: 'DCI Flint to DI Buxton.'

Rob grabbed his radio. 'DI Buxton, go ahead.'

'Rob, Billy Simpson has been arrested at the school and is now at Mansfield Police Station. The duty inspector has signed an authority for you to carry out a Section 18 search at the Hardwick Avenue address. Mrs Grant is with her foster son while the custody sergeant sets out his rights and books him into custody. I don't want this boy in custody any longer than he needs to be. I don't want to delay the interview, so get inside the house and crack on with the search. Make sure you knock loudly, as Mr Grant could well be in bed. If you find anything significant, contact me on the radio straightaway.'

'Will do, boss.'

Rob turned to Glen. 'Come on, mate, let's go.'

The two detectives walked down the short path, and Glen banged loudly on the door with the fleshy part of his fist. Almost instantly, the door was opened by a short, stocky man with a full head of steel grey hair and a goatee beard that was the same colour. He was wearing scruffy jeans and an equally worn, red-and-black check shirt.

Rob held out his identification and said, 'Mr Grant? We're from Mansfield CID. We have an authority to enter and search your property.'

Mike Grant looked carefully at the warrant card that he had been shown, and blocked the doorway, saying, 'You'd better tell me what this is all about, or you're not getting in anywhere.'

Rob could see there was a wild look in Grant's eyes, so he said calmly, 'Mr Grant, your foster son has been detained at his school this morning on suspicion of arson. We've been granted an authority to enter and search his home address, following his arrest. This is under a search power contained in the Police and Criminal Evidence Act. Everything's above board, Mike. Why don't you calm down, start cooperating, and let us in?'

Hearing his Christian name seemed to calm the angry foster parent down. He stood to one side, allowing the two detectives access to his house.

He closed the front door behind them and chuntered, 'Bloody foster kids. This one's been nothing but trouble ever since he got here.'

Glen asked, 'In what way?'

'He's a surly, scruffy shit. He's out until all hours and thinks he can do just as he likes. He's a pain in the arse.'

The two detectives exchanged glances. Rob said, 'Can you show us his bedroom? We might as well make a start in there.'

As Mike Grant showed them up the stairs, Rob said, 'Have we met before, Mike?'

Grant said, 'I don't think so.'

'You look really familiar, that's all.'

'I doubt it. It's been years since I was in any bother with the law. Back then, it was just young lads scrapping, and nothing ever came of it. I've got a clean record.'

Rob said nothing. He thought, *That was a lot of information I hadn't asked for.*

Grant stood on the landing, pointed at a door, and said, 'This is Billy's room.'

The two detectives walked in while Grant remained at the doorway.

ROB OPENED the door of the wardrobe. The smell of smoke was immediately evident as the door wafted open. He took out a duffel coat that absolutely reeked of smoke.

He said, 'Is this coat Billy's?'

Grant nodded.

There was a pile of clothes stuffed at the bottom of the wardrobe. Rob shifted them to one side and saw a black plastic bin liner.

He took out the bin liner and carefully undid the knot.

The smell of petrol was evident immediately. Inside the bag was a green petrol can. Rob moved the can from side to side. It still contained petrol.

Rob turned to Grant. 'Have you seen this before?'

Grant shook his head. 'No, but I never come in here. My wife, Sheila, does all the cleaning.'

THE TWO DETECTIVES made a thorough search of the boy's bedroom and then a more cursory search of the rest of the house.

Rob turned to Glen and said, 'Wait here, I'm going to let the boss know what we've found, and see what he wants us to bring back.'

Glen nodded.

Rob walked outside to the car. He sat in the passenger seat and grabbed his radio. 'DI Buxton to DCI Flint. Over.'

'From DCI Flint, go ahead.'

'Boss, we've recovered a half-full petrol can from the wardrobe in this kid's bedroom. His clothes all reek of smoke as well. Over.'

A despondent-sounding Danny said, 'What does his foster parent have to say about the petrol can?'

'Mr Grant seems a little shocked, but that's all. He says he never goes in the lad's room.'

'Okay. Don't bring all the clothes back. Just pick the worst one. The one that smells the smokiest. We can pick the rest up later. You and Glen get back here as soon as you can. I want to put the clothes and the petrol can you've recovered to Simpson during the interview. How long will it take you to complete the search and get back here?'

'Another ten minutes and we'll be good to go.'

'That's great. Well done, Rob.'

80

11.45 am, 23 June 1987
Custody Suite, Mansfield Police Station

There had been a delay before the first interview could start, after Sheila Grant had requested that legal advice be provided for her foster son.

The duty solicitor, Graeme Poole, had now been given disclosure by Danny and Rachel, and had been afforded the time to advise Billy Simpson.

Danny and Rachel sat on one side of the desk, with the exhibits recovered from Hardwick Avenue in bags on the floor between them. Billy sat next to his solicitor on the other side of the desk. His foster mother sat immediately behind them.

Rachel placed the tapes in the recorder. She switched it on and began the interview by introducing the people present in the room. Finally, she explained the role of the appropriate adult to Sheila Grant.

With the interview tapes recording, Danny said, 'Billy, do you understand why you've been brought here today?'

The boy looked at Rachel and said, 'She says it's about the fires.'

'Do you know what fires she means?'

'The fires that have been on the news. The ones where those people died.'

'That's right. What do you know about those fires, Billy?'

'Only what I've heard the other kids at school saying about them. I've seen little bits about them on the news. I try not to watch it when it comes on the telly.'

'Why is that, Billy?'

'I don't like hearing about fires. It scares me too much.'

'Is there a particular reason why the news reports scare you?'

'Because I'm terrified of fire.'

'And what is it about fire that scares you so much?'

The boy suddenly stood up. He raised his shirt and jumper and turned around, exposing his torso.

Danny could see the extensive keloid scarring all over the boy's back.

He said gently, 'Thanks for showing me that, Billy. Cover yourself up and sit back down, please.'

Danny waited for the boy to tuck his clothes back in and sit down. Then he said, 'Was all that scarring caused in a fire?'

'Yeah, that's why I'm so scared of it. Every time I see a fire, I think about the pain from my scarring.'

Danny took the duffel coat from the exhibit bag. Instantly, the room was filled with the smell of smoke.

Danny said, 'Is this your coat, Billy?'

The boy nodded.

'Can you answer, please, Billy? The tape recorder can't record you nodding.'

'Yes. It's my coat.'

'Thanks. Can you smell the smoke on the coat?'

'Yes.'

'If you're so afraid of fire, how did your coat get to smell of smoke so badly?'

'Because he makes me burn stuff.'

'Who does?'

He pointed over his shoulder, towards Sheila Grant and said, 'Her twat of a husband!'

Sheila said indignantly, 'That's rubbish. I've never seen you burning anything.'

Billy said, 'That's because he only starts the fires when you've gone out. He knows I'm shit scared, but he still makes me burn stuff on bonfires, in the back garden. He says it will cure my fear of fire. He makes me stand really close to the flames. I'm only allowed to move away when it gets too hot and I can't stand it anymore.'

Danny said, 'How many fires has he made you light, Billy?'

'Loads. Then he makes me put my smoky clothes back in the wardrobe. All my clothes stink.'

'When the detectives searched your room, they found something else that I want to talk to you about now. Is that okay?'

'Okay.'

Danny took the green petrol can from the exhibit bag and said, 'Have you seen this before, Billy?'

'No. Never.'

'It was found in your bedroom, under clothes at the bottom of your wardrobe.'

'That's mad. I wouldn't have a petrol can in my room. I can smell it from here. It stinks.'

'So, you're telling me that you've never seen this petrol can before?'

'I haven't.'

'How did it come to be found in your wardrobe then, Billy?'

The boy was becoming frustrated and almost tearful. 'I don't know. I didn't put it there.'

'Okay, Billy. How do you spend your evenings?'

'What?'

'What do you do when you go out at night?'

'I don't.'

'Don't what?'

'I don't go out at night. I don't know anyone around here, so I stay in my room.'

Sheila Grant said, 'That's true. He never goes out at night. I've tried to get him to join the Boy Scouts, but he's not bothered.'

Danny was troubled. There was something about the boy's responses that had him worried.

He was thoughtful for a moment; then he turned to Rachel and said, 'We're going to stop the interview and take a short break.'

Rachel stated the time and the date, then switched off the tape recorder. Danny said, 'Mrs Grant, can I talk to you alone for a second while DC Moore signs up the tapes with Billy and Mr Poole?'

'Of course.'

Danny stepped outside, followed by Sheila Grant, he said, 'What do you make of all that? Do you think he's telling us the truth?'

'He's only been with us for about six months, so it's hard to tell.'

'What about these bonfires with your husband?'

'I've never seen them lighting bonfires. But I do go out to bingo three nights a week and leave them on their own.'

'Surely you must have smelled the smoke on his clothes?'

'I can't smell anything, Detective. I've worked with strong glue at the shoe company for so many years, I've got no sense of smell anymore.'

'I know what teenagers are like for not keeping their rooms tidy, Mrs Grant. Who cleans Billy's room?'

'I do, of course. If the cleaning were left to Billy, the place would be little better than a swamp.'

'When you've cleaned his room, have you ever seen the petrol can?'

She shook her head. 'Of course I haven't. I wouldn't allow him to keep petrol in his bedroom.'

'When did you last clean his room?'

'I gave it a good fettling two days ago.'

'And you didn't see the petrol can in his wardrobe then?'

'No, I didn't.'

'Have you seen it anywhere else in your house?'

'No.'

'Okay, Mrs Grant. We will need to interview Billy again, but for now he'll have to wait in a detention room. I've no objection to you sitting with him while you're waiting.'

'Thanks, I'll do that. He's only a young kid, and I can see that he's scared.'

Danny began to walk away. Then he paused and said, 'I'm sorry I had to get you out of work to come and do this, but your husband told me he couldn't come. How long has he been suffering with this bad cold?'

She laughed. 'Mike hasn't got a cold. He's just bone idle and doesn't want to bother with all this.'

Rachel joined Danny, and they left the cell block. As they walked upstairs to the MCIU offices, Danny said, 'This doesn't feel right to me, Rachel. I think the boy's telling the truth.'

81

12.30 pm, 23 June 1987
MCIU Offices, Mansfield, Nottinghamshire

Rob and Glen were already waiting in the office, with Professor Sharon Whittle, when Danny and Rachel walked back in.

Rob said, 'How did it go?'

Rachel said, 'Full and frank denials all the way. He's adamant that he's never seen the petrol can that you and Glen recovered from the house, and says he knows nothing about the fires whatsoever. He's also given us a very plausible explanation why his clothes are so smoky.'

Danny was a bit more thoughtful.

He said, 'How was Mike Grant when you saw him this morning, Rob?'

'What do you mean?'

'Well, when I spoke to him this morning on the phone, he

pretended to be at death's door with the worst case of man flu ever.'

'No, he was fine. There was no sign that he had a cold.'

'Was he still in bed when you got there?'

'No, he was up and dressed. He's a moody, belligerent bastard, though. He wasn't going to let us in the house at first.'

'Did he seem surprised when you found the petrol can in the boy's room?'

'A little bit, I suppose, but he didn't say much.'

Sharon Whittle said quietly, 'Maybe he was expecting you to search the house after your phone call this morning, Danny?'

Danny said, 'You're suggesting he put the petrol can in the boy's room?'

'It's one explanation how it got there, if you believe the boy isn't lying.'

Rob said, 'There was something else about Grant. I thought it was strange at the time. He went to great lengths to convince me that he had a clean criminal record, after I'd told him that I thought I recognised him. I remember thinking, "you've given me way too much information for the question I asked you". The funny thing is, I still think I know his face from somewhere.'

Danny said, 'With that legendary photographic memory of yours, it's not like you to forget a face.'

Rob jumped up. 'Photographs!'

He raced over to his desk and grabbed the folder with all the press photographs inside. He tipped them out onto his desk and started flicking through them.

He shouted, 'Here it is!'

He held up the photograph to Glen and said, 'That's him, isn't it?'

'Bloody hell! That's him alright.'

Rob turned to Danny and showed him the photograph. 'This is a photograph taken by the press at the Finningley Road fire. Mike Grant was there. Look at the photo, he's standing at the back, but he's watching alright.'

Glen was now searching through the other photographs. 'Christ almighty! He's in this one, too.'

He held up another photo and said, 'This photo was taken at the Helmsley Road fire.'

Danny snatched up the telephone and called the custody suite. 'It's Danny Flint. I want you to go to the detention room and ask Mrs Grant if her husband drives a car. If the answer is yes, I want to know what make and colour it is. Thanks. I'll hold while you go and ask the question.'

A minute later, Danny spoke again into the telephone. 'Go on. Her husband drives a dark blue Vauxhall Cavalier SRi. Thanks.'

Danny said, 'Rob, Glen, grab your coats. We need to fetch Mike Grant in, now. Rachel, I want you to stay here and start researching Grant. I want you to find out everything you can about him by the time we get back.'

The three detectives raced out of the room and down the stairs, to the car park.

82

1.15 pm, 23 June 1987
Hardwick Avenue, Rainworth, Nottinghamshire

Danny said, 'Stop the car. I'll jump out here and cover the alleyway that runs behind the houses. You two go and knock on the front door. Tell Grant you've come to collect some more of Simpson's clothes.'

As Danny got out, Rob said, 'Be careful, boss. There's something not quite right about this bloke. He's got a bit of crazy going on inside his head.'

'Will do, Rob.'

The CID car sped off. Danny ran around the corner and into the wide alleyway. Halfway up the alley, he could see a dark blue Vauxhall Cavalier Sri parked, unattended.

He started to jog up the hill, towards the car.

Around the front of the house on Hardwick Avenue, Glen parked the car, and the two detectives got out. They walked into the small front garden of Mike Grant's house, and Rob knocked loudly on the front door.

Mike Grant shouted from inside, 'Who is it?'

Rob shouted, 'It's Detective Inspector Buxton again. We've come to pick up the rest of Billy's clothes.'

'Can't it wait? I was just going out.'

'No, it can't. Open the door, Mr Grant!'

There was silence.

Rob shouted again, 'Open the door!'

Glen said, 'He's doing a runner!'

Rob began to shoulder barge the door around the lock. On the fourth attempt, the flimsy Yale lock gave, and the wooden door flew open. Glen ran into the house just in time to see Mike Grant run into the kitchen.

Grant was running towards the back door.

As he ran through the kitchen, he snatched a black-handled kitchen knife from the draining board, then ran out the back door. He closed the door behind him and locked it just as the two detectives entered the kitchen.

He slipped the knife with the six-inch blade into his leather bomber jacket pocket and sprinted down the back garden. His car was parked in the alley. If the kitchen door held long enough, he would still be able to get away.

Inside the kitchen, Glen and Rob were trying desperately to kick open the back door. It was a heavy mortice lock in a hardwood frame. It wouldn't budge.

Rob carried on kicking at the door and said to Glen, 'Get back outside and fetch the car. You need to back the boss up, in the alley.'

Glen immediately sprinted out the front door of the house and back to the car.

Danny was waiting at the side of the blue Cavalier. He could hear loud banging coming from the rear of the house. Suddenly, he saw Grant burst out the back gate. As Grant approached the blue Cavalier, Danny shouted, 'Mike Grant! I'm DCI Flint. That's far enough.'

Grant felt inside his leather jacket for the knife. He gripped the handle and said, 'I'm warning you, copper, don't try to stop me!'

'It's over, Grant. Other officers are on their way. Don't do anything stupid.'

Grant took the knife from his pocket. Holding it in a downward grip in his left hand, he growled, 'Get out of my way! Don't think I won't use this!'

Danny slipped off his jacket, wrapped it around his right arm and said, 'Don't be an idiot, Grant. Put the knife down!'

Grant rushed towards Danny and brought the knife down in a wide arc. Danny blocked the knife attack with his right arm. He felt the knife slice through the material of his jacket and shirt before penetrating his skin. The blade of the knife felt like a hot razor as it sliced deep into his forearm. As Grant tried to retrieve the knife, Danny could feel the blade twisting in his flesh as the handle snagged on the material of his jacket. Ignoring the pain in his right arm, Danny stepped in closer to Grant. He punched him hard in the face with the clenched fist of his left hand.

Grant didn't go down; he continued to try to wrestle the blade from Danny's jacket. Every time Grant wrenched at the knife handle, the pain in Danny's arm was excruciating. As the pain increased, so did Danny's determination to stop Grant. He continued punching the man in the face as hard as he could. Eventually, Grant loosened his grip on the handle of the knife, then let go completely, trying to block the continual punches from Danny.

By now, the only thing Danny could see was the baby from the fire on Helmsley Road, lying helpless and soot-blackened in the back of the ambulance. It was this image that fuelled his rage and allowed him to ignore the pain in his arm.

Grant was now on his knees. His hands were down by his sides, unable to protect himself from the flurry of vicious punches. Still Danny kept punching. The rage inside him had overtaken all the pain in his arm. All he wanted to do now was hurt this monster kneeling in front of him as much as he could.

Suddenly, Danny could hear footsteps running up the alley behind him. Glen Lorimar pulled Grant away from Danny's punches, shouting, 'That's enough, boss. He's out cold!'

Danny stepped back. A wave of exhaustion crashed over him as the pain in his arm suddenly screamed again. As Glen Lorimar handcuffed Grant and sat him against the wall, Danny unwrapped his suit jacket from around his damaged arm. As he did so, the six-inch kitchen knife finally came away and clattered to the floor.

Rob Buxton, having finally kicked his way through the back door, ran out into the alleyway. The first thing he saw was Danny's bloodied arm and the knife on the floor. He shouted, 'Bastard!'

Danny said, 'It's not that bad. I can still wiggle my fingers, but it's bleeding a lot and hurts like fuck.'

Rob spoke on his radio. 'DI Buxton to control. We need an ambulance to the rear of Hardwick Avenue. Make it quick. We've got an officer down with a stab wound.'

Feeling suddenly light-headed from the blood loss, Danny felt his legs go. Rob grabbed him and sat him down against a wall, on the opposite side of the alley to the still unconscious, but now handcuffed, Mike Grant. Rob began to tear the sleeves off Danny's bloodied jacket.

He tied one sleeve around his upper arm and used it as a makeshift tourniquet to staunch the bleeding. He said to

Danny, 'The good news is he hasn't hit an artery. The bad news is it's a deep wound. The blade's gone right through your forearm, but it's nothing that can't be fixed.'

Danny growled, 'Have you nicked the bastard yet?'

Rob grinned. 'After the battering you've just given him, we'll be nicking him later. After they've patched him up at the hospital, and he regains consciousness.'

As the sound of approaching sirens grew louder, Danny said, 'Good. I must admit I lost it for a minute, Rob. It had nothing to do with the knife or the stab wound. All I could see in my mind was that baby from Helmsley Road. She was so like my Hayley. It made me so mad that this monster could harm such an innocent.'

'Don't worry about Grant. Nobody's going to give a rat's arse about his injuries. He stabbed you, for Christ's sake! You were defending yourself.'

Danny nodded as the ambulance pulled up. 'Can you go and see Sue? Let her know what's happened, and that I'm fine.'

Rob nodded. 'Will do, Danny. Now stop fretting and let these ambulance guys get you sorted out properly.'

83

8.00 pm, 23 June 1987
Custody Suite, Mansfield Police Station

Rob Buxton sat next to Glen Lorimar in the interview room. Sitting opposite them was Mike Grant and his solicitor.

Grant's face was swollen and bruised. He had two black eyes and a couple of stitches in a cut above his right eye. His nose was badly broken, and his lips were swollen. He had been patched up at King's Mill Hospital, the same hospital Danny Flint was still in. Danny had needed emergency surgery to repair the damage to his forearm.

After treating Grant, the doctors at the hospital had informed the detectives that he had no concussion. That although his injuries looked bad, they were superficial, and he was fit to be detained and interviewed. That had been two hours ago.

Grant had been arrested at the hospital and then taken to Mansfield Police Station. He had elected to have a solicitor present during his interview. The detectives had given disclosure to the solicitor and allowed time for the solicitor to advise his client.

It was now time for the interview to start.

Glen Lorimar switched on the tape recorder. He made the introductions of people present, cautioned Grant and said, 'First things first. The doctors at the hospital, who treated you for your injuries, are of the opinion that you are now fit to be interviewed.'

Through bruised and swollen lips, Grant said, 'I want to make a complaint.'

'About what?'

'My injuries, for fuck's sake. That crazy fucking copper beat me up!'

'Is that the same officer who's currently undergoing surgery on the stab wound that you inflicted on him when you resisted arrest?'

'I didn't mean to stab him.'

'But whether you meant to or not, you did stab him. He was protecting himself, as he is entitled to do. At the end of this interview, if you still want to make a complaint, I'll arrange for a senior officer to take the details of that complaint, and it will be investigated.'

Grant nodded. 'Don't you worry; I will.'

Rob said, 'Tell me what you know about the house fires. Were they all your work, or did you have help?'

It was an opening question that had been devised by Professor Whittle. She had spoken at length to Rob about the personality of Grant. She believed the best way to get him speaking about the fires was to try to make him brag about his exploits. She was sure that the thought of someone else being able to claim any credit for what had happened would appal him. She felt he would desperately want to correct that wrong assertion.

Grant smirked, then twisted his face as the pain of his swollen lips registered. He said, 'Of course it was all my work. I didn't need any help.'

'Really? I can't believe you managed to start all those fires by yourself.'

'Why not? Don't you think I'm capable of controlling the beast?'

'The beast?'

'Fire. It's a beast that can only be tamed and mastered by a chosen few.'

'And you've been chosen?'

'A long time ago. I've always enjoyed fire. I've set hundreds of fires over the years.'

'Where?'

'Who do you think starts all the grass fires in the summer? The bin fires in the winter? I do.'

Rob smiled and said, 'Grass and bin fires are one thing; houses are another.'

'That was the boy's influence.'

'Do you mean Billy Simpson?'

'Yeah, Billy. When he came to live with us and told us his story, how the beast had almost claimed him, it made me want to do the same.'

'What do you mean?'

'I wanted to offer the beast victims.'

Rob took a minute to process the coldness of Grant's statement; then he said, 'Tell me about the fire at Blidworth?'

Grant smiled. 'That was such a beautiful accident. I only intended to burn down the empty house. I was amazed how the fire spread so quickly into the house that was occupied. I could hear the man screaming as the beast devoured him. It was the most delicious sound I've ever heard.'

'If you knew someone was inside, why didn't you call the fire brigade?'

'Because I didn't want to, Detective. Is that so hard for you to understand?'

'How did you start that fire? It couldn't have been easy.'

It was another question, devised by Professor Whittle, loaded to bring out his ego.

'It wasn't easy at all, Detective. But I possessed all the skill needed to get it alight.'

'How?'

'I knew from a previous visit that the empty house was cold and very damp. So I took petrol in the green can to kick-start the beast into life. I poured it all over the stairs and lit it; then I stood outside on the street and watched all the fun.'

'We have a photograph of you standing in the crowd, watching as the firemen tried to put out the fire. Why did you stay?'

'I wanted to watch the so-called hero firemen. I tried four times to be a fireman, and each time I was turned down. They couldn't see that I understood the beast better than any of them. They disregarded me and treated me like rubbish. Big mistake.'

'Tell me about the second fire on Finningley Road?'

'That was the best one. I stood watching the old people inside for a couple of hours. I watched them pottering around in their little bungalow, oblivious to their fate.'

'How did you start that fire?'

'The petrol had worked so well at Blidworth, I used it again. I just poured it through the letterbox and let it soak into the carpet for a few minutes. Then I set light to a rag and chucked that through the letterbox as well. It went up like a bomb. The flames got so hot, so quickly. It was a spectacular, amazing inferno. The heat was staggering. I stayed to watch until the fire was out, then walked through the estate to where I'd left my car. I drove that night because I'd heard on the television about the extra foot patrols everywhere.'

'So you started that fire even though you knew that two people were inside the bungalow?'

'No, I started that fire *because* the two people were inside. That's why it was the best.'

'What did you think would happen to those people?'

'I knew they'd die. There was no way they could escape the beast once I'd unleashed him.'

'What about the fire at the Helmsley Road flats?'

'That was the copper's fault.'

'What?'

'I had given up on finding a place to burn that night. I was walking home, along the A617, when I saw a cop car. To dodge the police, I ducked onto Helmsley Road, and that's when I saw the empty flat. Don't you see, if the copper hadn't driven the cop car past at that exact moment, I wouldn't have found the right property to burn.'

'Having seen the empty flat, what did you do next?'

'I knew it was a block of four flats. I could see lights on in two of the others, so I had to be careful to make sure I got the right door. Once I'd sussed out which door belonged to which flat, I poured the petrol in through the letterbox and lit it.'

'You saw the lights on. So, once again, you knew the other flats were occupied. You knew that people were at home, but you still lit the fire. Knowing that those people in the other flats could be hurt or killed?'

'Yes, of course. I couldn't see them in their flats, though. That's why it wasn't as good as Finningley Road.'

'Did you stay to watch?'

'I ran off at first so I could hide the empty petrol can under a bush. Then I walked back slowly and watched the drama unfold. I could hear the woman in the upstairs flat screaming. I saw her drop her baby from the window. I thought the neighbour was going to drop that baby for sure, but he managed to grab one leg. The woman stopped screaming soon after that, and I knew the beast had her.'

'Why did you light these fires, Mike?'

'To show everyone that I could control the beast.'

'But you couldn't control the fires. You just started them, using petrol. All you did was allow the flames and the smoke to kill people.'

'You're so wrong, Detective. I guided the fire to those people. I chose them. I decided how the flames would consume them. Just me.'

'Why did you try to set up your foster son, Billy Simpson?'

'After the telephone call, I knew at some stage you would come and search the house. I didn't want that obnoxious kid in my house anymore; he was such a disrespectful, ungrateful wretch. I tried to help him conquer his fear of the beast, but he threw all that help back in my face and verbally abused me. So, I thought I'd set him up for the fires. That would get him out of my house and leave me free to set more fires in a year or so, after things had settled down again.'

'Did you put the petrol can we found in his bedroom?'

'Yes. I knew you'd fall for it. I could see from all the television appeals you made that the police were desperate to blame someone for the fires. I knew you would jump at the chance to charge young Billy. With Billy locked up, I would have remained free to continue to hunt other people with the beast.'

Rob shook his head. 'Do you want to ask anything, Glen?'

Glen Lorimar said, 'I've got no questions.'

Rob said, 'In that case, the time is now eight twenty-five, and I'll terminate the interview.'

Glen switched off the tapes.

Grant said, 'Can I make my complaint now? That copper shouldn't have punched me like that. I'll have his fucking job!'

84

10.30 pm, 23 June 1987
King's Mill Hospital, Sutton in Ashfield, Nottinghamshire

Rob walked into the side room, just off Ward 9, at the hospital. He wasn't surprised to see Sue sitting by Danny's bedside. His friend was sitting up, propped up by pillows. His right arm was elevated and heavily bandaged. His eyes were closed, and the room was dimly lit.

He smiled at Sue and said quietly, 'Hello, Sue. How's the patient?'

Before she could answer, a very groggy-sounding Danny said, 'The patient's trying to bloody sleep!'

Rob mouthed the word *sorry* to Sue and sat down.

Sue said, 'He's in a bad mood because the doctor won't let him come home until later tomorrow. They want him to rest, and to check the repair job before they sign him off.'

'Who's looking after little Hayley?'

'My best friend. As soon as you called, I took Hayley around to her house so I could get down here. I know she'll be fine with Mandy.'

'How's his arm?'

'Mr Sawyers, the consultant surgeon, is incredibly happy with the outcome of the surgery. He thinks Danny will make a full recovery and will regain full use of all his fingers. Before the operation, he was worried about deep-seated tendon damage. Luckily for Danny, that nutter's blade missed everything important.'

'That's great news. We've all been worried.'

Danny opened his eyes. 'Okay, I give up. If you're going to sit there gossiping, you might as well tell me how the interviews with Grant went.'

Rob said quietly, 'No. You need to rest, boss. I'll go now, and we can talk tomorrow.'

Danny grimaced against the pain and said, 'Detective Inspector Buxton, I just gave you a lawful order.'

Sue said, 'You might as well tell him, Rob. He won't settle properly until he knows what's happened.'

Rob said, 'He's coughed everything, Danny. It was hands down one of the most chilling interviews I've ever had with a suspect. The way he spoke, so matter-of-factly, about killing all those people. He's one dangerous individual. We went back and did another search of the house. We recovered several items from the loft that tie Grant to the fires, on top of his admissions.'

'Like what?'

'A scrapbook containing newspaper clippings and photographs of all the burned-out houses after the fires had been put out. The camera those photographs were taken on was also recovered. We've also got a video tape of all the police press conferences, starring yours truly, we made after each fire. I'm sure we'll subsequently find Grant's fingerprints all over them.'

'Have you charged him?'

'I charged him just before I came here.'

'What are the charges?'

'I've charged him with four counts of murder, one section 20 wounding, four counts of arson with intent to endanger life and attempting to pervert the course of justice. There will be numerous other offences of arson, grass fires, bins and such, that will probably all lie on the file as detected no further action.'

'Nice work, Rob.'

'I reckon this will end up being one for the psychiatrists to argue over at trial. Personally, I think Grant's as mad as a box of frogs.'

'Talking about psychiatrists, has Professor Whittle gone home yet?'

'She's going back to Newcastle first thing in the morning.'

'That's a shame. I would have liked to thank her before she left. I've got to say I was very sceptical at first, but some of her ideas were right on the money.'

'She was switched on all right. Who would have thought Potter could come up with a good idea for a change?'

Both men laughed, until Danny started coughing. Sue said, 'That's enough, you two. Right, Danny. It's time for you to get some sleep.'

Danny grinned. 'Yes, Doc. Whatever you say.'

Rob said, 'Do as the doctor orders and get some rest. I'll pop in and see you again tomorrow.'

Danny gave a thumbs-up sign with his good hand as Rob walked out the door.

As he walked down the corridor, he heard the door close behind him. He turned around and saw Sue walking quickly to catch him up.

She said, 'Hold on, Rob. I'm going home now as well. Danny needs to rest, and I need to pick Hayley up and get her settled.'

As they walked, she said, 'I don't know. Your job's so bloody dangerous; you never know what's going to happen next. When I think about what happened to Brian, and then all this today, it makes me shudder.'

Rob was thoughtful, then said, 'You mustn't dwell on what might happen, Sue. It would drive you mad. We all know the risks, and we act accordingly to protect ourselves and each other. What happened to Brian was a sheer fluke, and what happened today was also extraordinary. I don't want you to think that every time Danny goes out to work, he's going to be facing down some knife-wielding nutjob. It's just not like that.'

He gave her a reassuring smile and continued. 'I've been doing this job for almost twenty-five years now. In all that time, the only knife I've ever seen on duty was the one alongside my fork just before I tucked into a full English. I know it's hard right now, but you must keep everything in perspective.'

Sue stood on tiptoe, pecked Rob on the cheek and said, 'Thanks, Rob. That's exactly what I wanted to hear tonight. See you tomorrow.'

Rob watched Sue to her car, then waved as she drove out of the car park. He chuckled and said aloud to himself, 'It's a good job I didn't tell you about the three times I've had a gun pointed at me, then, isn't it, lass?'

EPILOGUE

2.00 pm 21 July 1987
Nottinghamshire Police Headquarters

After being off work for a full month, today was Danny's first day back at work. His arm was fine. He had a three-inch scar on the front of his right forearm, and a smaller inch-long one on the back.

He had full use of his arm and no longer experienced the numbness and tingling that had been a concern initially. The only problem that remained an issue was that after writing for any length of time, his forearm started to ache. The consultant had assured him that this would eventually reduce, then stop, as time went by.

He hadn't been surprised to be called in to headquarters to see Adrian Potter. It was expected that an officer injured on duty was always welcomed back to work by his supervisor.

Most bosses would take the time to go and see the officer.

Potter wasn't most bosses and had instead instructed Danny to drive to headquarters and see him in his office.

He stood outside Potter's office and knocked politely.

'Enter!'

Danny smiled at the now-expected curt instruction.

He walked in. Potter said, 'Danny, take a seat. How's the arm?'

Now Danny was taken aback. Potter had never referred to him by his Christian name before.

He answered, 'It's fine, sir. No problem at all.'

'I'm glad to hear it. That must have been a very frightening experience. I can't imagine what it must have been like, to be confronted with something like that.'

Danny thought, *No, I bet you can't.*

He simply said, 'It all happened very quickly, sir. I didn't really have time to think about it.'

'I'm afraid the Complaints and Discipline department will want to interview you about the assault allegations made by Mike Grant.'

'Seriously? He tried to kill me; I was defending myself.'

'And I'm sure I don't agree with those who say that his injuries portray a different picture. That you continued the assault on him way after you had stopped him from attacking you.'

'That's nonsense.'

'I'm sure it is. But just be ready when they come to see you.'

Danny nodded. 'Don't worry, sir. I'll be ready for their nonsense.'

Potter changed the subject. 'How did Detective Inspector Cartwright do on her first case?'

'Tina did extremely well. She's an asset to the MCIU. She worked long, hard hours without complaint and brought the case against Stephen Meadows to a successful conclusion. I doubt she'll have many other cases as difficult as that one throughout the rest of her career.'

'Are we ready for Crown Court with the Meadows case?'

Danny smiled inwardly at the use of the word 'we' by Potter.

He said, 'The court file has been prepared; we're ready. The evidence is overwhelming.'

'That's gratifying to hear. I'm glad I selected the right individual to fill the void after the untimely death of Detective Inspector Hopkirk.'

Danny said, 'Quite.'

Potter continued, 'I'm also extremely interested to hear what you thought about working alongside Professor Whittle?'

'I've got to be honest, sir. As you know, I was very sceptical at first, but having worked closely with her on both the Meadows enquiry and the Grant enquiry, I found her input extremely valuable. She was an asset to the enquiry team. If, God forbid, the need ever arose, I would gladly work with her again.'

'That's fantastic. I'll pass on your comments to the chief constable.'

With just the faintest hint of sarcasm, Danny said, 'I'm sure the chief will be pleased to hear how your brilliant idea helped us to crack two extremely difficult murder enquiries, sir.'

Potter looked over his spectacles at Danny, trying to find any underlying hidden meaning to Danny's comment. Perhaps not unsurprisingly, he couldn't detect any.

He said, 'Well, that will be all, Chief Inspector. Make sure you're ready for the complaints department. We don't want an otherwise excellent job tainted, do we?'

'No, sir. We don't. I'll be ready for them.'

As he stood up to leave, there was a knock on the door. Potter shouted in his reedy voice, 'Enter!'

Glad it's not just me, thought Danny.

The door opened, and Potter's secretary came in.

She turned to Danny and said, 'There's an urgent message for you, Chief Inspector Flint. A woman's body has been found hidden in undergrowth in Woodthorpe Park, Sherwood. Detective Inspector Cartwright's travelling to the scene, and she's asked if you could join her there.'

WE HOPE YOU ENJOYED THIS BOOK

If you could spend a moment to write an honest review on Amazon, no matter how short, we would be extremely grateful. They really do help readers discover new authors.

ALSO BY TREVOR NEGUS

EVIL IN MIND
(Book 1 in the DCI Flint series)
DEAD AND GONE
(Book 2 in the DCI Flint series)
A COLD GRAVE
(Book 3 in the DCI Flint series)
TAKEN TO DIE
(Book 4 in the DCI Flint series)
KILL FOR YOU
(Book 5 in the DCI Flint series)

Published by Inkubator Books
www.inkubatorbooks.com

Copyright © 2021 by Trevor Negus

Trevor Negus has asserted his right to be identified as the author of this work.

KILL FOR YOU is a work of fiction. People, places, events, and situations are the product of the author's imagination. Any resemblance to actual persons, living or dead is entirely coincidental.

No part of this book may be reproduced, stored in any retrieval system, or transmitted by any means without the prior written permission of the publisher.

Printed in Great Britain
by Amazon